Fly A\

Nits'it'ah Golika Xah

Canadian Historical Brides

Northwest Territories & Nunvavut, Book 8

By Juliet Waldron and John Wisdomkeeper

LSI Print 978-1-77362-971-1

BWL Publishing
A quality publisher of genre fiction.
Airdrie Alberta

Copyright 2017 Juliet Waldron and John Wisdomkeeper
Series Copyright 2017 BWL Publishing Inc.
Cover art by Michelle Lee

Library and Archives Canada Cataloguing in Publication

Waldron, Juliet, author
Fly away snow goose = Nits'it'ah golika xah / by Juliet Waldron and John Wisdomkeeper.

(Canadian historical brides ; book 8)
Issued in print and electronic formats.
ISBN 978-1-77299-458-2 (softcover).—ISBN 978-1-77299-455-1 (EPUB).—ISBN 978-1-77299-456-8 (Kindle).—ISBN 978-1-77299-457-5 (PDF)

I. Wisdomkeeper, John, author II. Title. III. Series: Canadian historical brides ; bk. 8

PS3623.A38F57   2017
813'.6   C2017-906964-0

C2017-906965-9

Dedication

BWL Publishing Inc. ("**Books We Love**") dedicates the Canadian Historical Brides series to the immigrants, male and female who left their homes and families, crossed oceans and endured unimaginable hardships in order to settle the Canadian wilderness and build new lives in a rough and untamed country.

Books We Love acknowledges the Government of Canada and the Canada Book Fund for its financial support in creating the Canadian Historical Brides series.

Funded by the Government of Canada | Canada

Glossary

Tłįchǫ Yahtįį Multimedia Dictionary

http://Tłįchǫ.ling.uvic.ca/users/mainview.aspx

babàcho - grandfather

bebì – baby

behchà - riverbank

chekaa – teachers

dahba – wild roses

dèè – land

Dene - Tłįchǫ tribes

dehcho – big river

detsįkǫ̀ – log house, cabin

dìga – wolf

dìgatsoa - coyote

Tłįchǫ got'įį – Dogrib people

ekìıka - wilderness

Ekw'ahtı - RCMP

ewòhʔeh – hide jacket

Ehtsèe – grandfather spirit

Fly away - nıts'ìt'ah

Gam`e`t`i – Village in NWT where children are from

gochı – younger brother

goʔeh - uncle

gòet'įį – cousins

goʔǫhdaà - elders

gòichı – chosen one

gocho– ancestors

gots'èke – wife

gots'įį – human spirit
gahkwǫ̀ – rabbit meat
ink'on – spirit power
įk'ǫǫ̀ – medicine power
Ka'owae – Trading Chief
k'i – birch
kinnickkinnick – grouse berry
kw'ahtıı – government agent – indian agent
kwet'įį - white persons
łık'àdèè k'è – fish camp
Lac la Martre River Nàįlįı
mamàcho grandmother
Métis - a person of mixed American Indian
and Euro-American ancestry,
Nààka – Northern Lights
Nàįlįı - Lac la Martre River
N'asi – Feast (Christmas)
Nıts'it'ah Golika Xah (Fly Away Snow
Goose)
Nǫhtsı̨- Creator
Sahti – Great Bear Lake
snow - golika or zhah
Tłıchǫ dèè – Dogrib land
Tındeè – Great Slave Lake
ts'et'ıı tł'ehwò – tobacco pouch
ts'įįta – spirit world
whagweè – sandy places for camping
Wha't'i – Dogrib camp
xah – goose or geese
Yahbahti - Shaman
yatı – prayer

Ethnography

The Dog Rib Rae Band which is located on the west side of the Mackenzie River Delta (Peel Channel), about 110 km upstream from the Arctic coast

The Tłıchǫ (IPA: [tɬʰĩtʃʰõ], English pronunciation: /təˈlɪtʃoʊ/) people, sometimes spelled Tłıchǫ and also known as the Dogrib, are a Dene First Nations people of the Athabaskan-speaking ethnolinguistic group living in the Northwest Territories, Canada. The name Dogrib is an English adaptation of their own name, Tłıchǫ Done (or Thlingchadinne) - "Dog-Flank People"

Tlicho, also known as Dogrib, fall within the broader designation of Dene, Aboriginal people of the widespread Athapaskan language family. Their name for themselves is *Doné*, meaning "the People." To distinguish themselves from their Dene neighbours - Denesuline, Slavey, Sahtu Got'ine and K'asho Got'ine - they have come to identify themselves as Tlicho, meaning "dog's rib," although the epithet is derived from a Cree term. Tlicho lands lie east of the Mackenzie River between Great Slave Lake and Great Bear Lake in the NWT.

The Canadian Encyclopedia, article by June Helm, Thomas G. Andrews

http://www.thecanadianencyclopedia.ca/en/article/tlicho-dogrib/

"It's the land that keeps things for us. Being our home it's important for us to take good care of the dwelling, the land, for wherever you go is home". (Rosalie Tailbones PHP-98/08/05)

Prologue

Yaot'l and Sascho splashed along the shores of the behchà, spears hefted, watching for the flash of fin to rise to the surface and sparkle in the sunlight. Tender feelings flushed their faces, so they laughed and teased one another with sprays of icy water. In the distance, the warning about the kw'ahtıı sounded, but went unheard.

Chapter One

Yaot'l grew tired of scraping moose hide. She and her aunts had, off and on, been at it for a day and a half. Her thin arms ached, upward from the wrist and somehow, from there, straight into the back of her neck. It took a long time to scrape such a vast expanse of hide clear of bits of flesh and fine silver skin. Mamàcho Josette had set her to work as soon as she and her aunts, assisted by two cousins, had the hide stretched onto a frame. Building the frame, too, had been a project, but one completed yesterday.

With spring thaw underway, the Snow Goose band travelled to summer łık'àdèè k'è (fish camp,) a long traverse through bush. They hauled their few possessions, the precious metal kettles and iron spikes, on their backs and on dog skids.

The young moose had been an unexpected bonus; he had jammed a back leg in a tangle of wood in the shallow water near the island. In his struggles to get free the leg had broken. Fortunately the band came upon him before the wolves did. His quick dispatch by the men had been mercy, and they'd made an offering of tobacco to thank the animal for giving up his spirit.

The strips of flesh now smoked in an enclosure of peat and sticks prepared for the purpose. They'd made camp, near the little island of willows, taking time to prepare and preserve their bounty. The thaw had come, as it always did, with days bringing an ever longer sun, with creeks and ponds spilling over, full of water and silver fish. There was work to do at every season, but especially now in the fishing time.

Spring melt meant water everywhere, trickling through the bogs and rushing in the fullness of the streams, pooling in the pothole lakes. On the willow-covered islands where the moose had wintered, water locked inside snow and ice turned liquid again. It was still cold enough, Yaot'l thought, to shatter her bones when her hands were in it. Today, though, the sun burned hot on her back and it seemed she'd been scraping hide forever.

Pausing to stretch her arms over her head, she shook her hands to remove the sticky silver skin from her fingers. Knowing the older women would tease, she glanced around, in her head she heard their voices—*Ah Yaot'l! How will you ever get a good husband if you can't prepare a fine big hide? You're almost grown now, and no hunter wants a weak woman.*

Ah, but the sun beat down on her head and the water all around her sang. It would be such a welcome relief to take her spear and go take a stand in one of the creeks at a place where it tumbled from one level to the next, a place where the fish would jump. She could hear the sound of voices—her cousins, all down fishing already. Some kids playing, she guessed, and not working at all.

She liked being older, but at the same time she didn't. Not enough fun and a lot more work...not that she didn't like having a full belly during winter. It was up to the women, she knew, to make sure that food was carefully stored.

Mamàcho Josette and Aunt Katie were nearby, busy preparing fish. With favorite knives in hand, they gutted and sliced the Uldai, heading them first then splitting length-wise, the inner flesh scored to assist the drying process. The skin and tail remained so that the fish could be easily hung. During the long winters, dry whitefish was an invaluable staple.

Katie sent a glance her way. "Ah, Yaot'l, that's not finished, you know. There are lots more scraping needed and it must be washed again before we start curing."

Yaot'l knew the weight of the wet hide, when they pulled it from the creek again, would be great. It would take several women and children to get it back on the hanger. Then the curing would start. The brains they'd use were already rendered, the pot set aside where it wouldn't be accidentally tipped over.

"I know, Auntie." Yaot'l cleaned her blade against a flat topped rock, and returned to the task at hand. It was said that there'd been a big river here and a bad flood, very long ago in dreamtime...Round the evening campfire, Babàcho Gregorie had told them all about it in one of his "Gawoo-long ago" stories.

Mamàcho looked up from her task and smiled. "I've about got this basket emptied. I'll scrape for a while. You go down to the creek and see what you can catch. There's plenty of time before dark."

Flashing her mamàcho a smile of gratitude, Yaot'l laid her scraper on the ground beside the frame.

"You bring back some fish, you hear? No playing." Aunt Katie said, but when Yaot'l looked anxiously up at her, she caught a wink from one merry brown eye.

At the lean-to where her family sheltered, Yaot'l grabbed her fish spear. She glanced at a woven willow basket attached to a pole, but she decided not to take it. It was clumsy, and snagged on rocks and branches in the shallows.

She'd need to hurry if she wanted to enjoy the fishing. The band would keep moving until they reached the confluence of two rivers. Where they emptied into a clear, deep lake was their traditional łık'àdèè k'è, Gam`e`t`i.

Other bands—more relatives—were also on the move, into canoes and then out again, making a portage through the networks of water.

The discovery of the moose had caused a small but productive delay in the band's journey, but they would not stay long. Most of the men had already gone ahead with canoes and dogs, in order to prepare camp at the place where the fish, after a long journey, returned to spawn. The Snow Goose band would return to the home that had been theirs from time immemorial.

Since the white men had come, bringing their new and deadly sicknesses, taking land away for their diggings and towns, there had come many changes. Fewer made the trek to the fishing grounds. Some no longer looked to the land for their living, but to the white man's jobs. Even the furred and finned brothers and sisters of the people had changed their habits. Caribou no longer came so far south; mink and otter moved away from their old grounds. Every year the tribe had to travel farther into the open lands to find food and fur.

Yaot'l headed into the brush with spear in hand and a length of line for her catch looped into her belt. At the bend in the creek, water briefly slowed and sloughed. Small children played there, but the play had a purpose—to learn to fish. Already three small ones were laid out along the bank. Now, however, the children kicked water and laughed. A pair of barking puppies ran alongside.

Yaot'l waved. They waved back, but these small cousins were too involved in their play to break off. She went on a little further, looking for quiet. Here, she washed the stickiness of the silver skin from her hands and forearms before she walked into the bush.

The sun high and bright warmed her black hair. The ache in her shoulders diminished. A little breeze blew as she walked along, lifting tendrils that had escaped from her braids. The creek sparkled and danced nearby, whispering over a bottom of rock. Carried on the breeze were bird calls — the bright sounds of courtship. The birds were singing to set territories, calling from scrub and bush that marked their home range.

Yaot'l held her arms above her head, allowing the warmth from Father Sun to seep into her hands and down her arms. It was one of those blessing moments, when the light flowed through her body and joined with her spirit making all one.

* * *

The bank grew steeper. She followed a deer path as it looped higher, moving, briefly, out of sight of the water. Soon, though, the path would come down again, to a low, level sandy area where animals came to drink. Clear round about because of the intrusive rock, it was a vantage point where even a creature with its head down could see a hunter—of whatever kind—and still have a chance of escape.

Finally she spotted the small cataract she'd been seeking. Here, the fish had to jump in order to continue their journey home. It was an excellent fishing place. As she emerged slowly from the last bit of spruce shade, Yaot'l heard a noisy rattle.

She froze. Gripping her spear, she waited for her eyes to adjust to the light. Cautiously she sniffed the air. This time of year, you might come upon a bear, a very hungry one just awakened from a long winter of sleep, hungry enough to eat even a skinny human.

No. No rank smell of bear.

The rattling came again, and this time she got a fix on it. It emanated from among the rocks. Slowly, carefully, Yaot'l crept closer to the sound. It came again, and this time, she recognized it as a snore.

It was all she could do not to laugh when she spotted the boy lying there, fast asleep, propped into a stony groove. She recognized him. Sascho, they called him, from a band that often spent time in company with hers. Yaot'l knew him from other łk'àdèè k'è summers, but oh, over the winter, he'd lengthened out considerable. She knew those strong cheekbones and his rough, bushy black hair. He had, it seemed, found this bowl of rocks to be a perfect fit for a nap.

Smiling to herself, she crept away from the boy, down towards the water. If she could collect some in the palm of her hand, she'd give him a surprise.

He really was sleeping much too soundly! She had to tease him! With an ice cold handful, barely breathing, she edged back to where he lay.

Quick! Before it all leaked away she emptied her hand over his head.

"Yah!" He shouted, leaping to his feet and reaching for his belt knife,

Laughing, Yaot'l jumped backwards. "Time to wake up, Grizzly Bear, or I'll have your claws."

* * *

Sascho sheathed his knife. *Yaot'l! That tall clever girl from the Snow Goose band with her merry dark eyes...*

Warriors did NOT get caught sleeping! He hoped no one else would ever hear about this. He'd been tired, and the afternoon so warm, but that was no excuse.

Uncle John had told him not to return until he'd caught something—"not fish"—to put in the pot. He'd followed a small herd of deer since before dawn, but that had come to nothing when he'd missed his shot. He'd even tried snagging ducks. On the way here, he'd set a snare for rabbits. He'd dug after ground squirrel, but catching that sort of prey was something any woman or old man could do.

And now this humiliation, knowing he had been found sleeping! Sascho was a tall boy and people took him for older than he was, so he felt as if he was always catching up with what he should have learned yesterday. He'd gone as a helper to the winter trap lines with his uncles for the last few years, but his uncles never seemed to be quite satisfied with him.

Anxiously, Sascho's gaze moved to where he'd stashed the precious item—

The rifle was still there, tucked among the rocks just where he'd placed it. He was lucky that it was Yaot'l instead of someone else who'd come along and caught him sleeping— Although, he thought back in the days his grandparents talked about, he probably wouldn't have woken up at all. Cree or Yellowknife or kwet'įį—someone would have killed him for the rifle.

"Don't be mad, Sascho." Yaot'l crouched a little distance away. She stroked a braid, squinting against the sun.

He frowned and didn't reply. Sascho had liked her a lot last summer! He had a sudden notion that the same feeling would return this summer.

"I won't tell anyone." Now there was concern in her merry eyes.

He nodded, hoping the gesture was enough.

"Are your people already south of here?"

"Yes—ah, half day's walk, at the pond with the drowned pines. I followed deer back up this way."

"No luck?" She nodded toward the rifle. She *had* noticed his rifle, after all.

He nodded, feeling even more embarrassed than before.

"I—ah—was going to fish here," she said. "Looks like a pretty good spot."

"Go on." He bent to collect the rifle. "I've got to get back." Before she could say anything else, he'd shouldered his gun and started back the way he'd come.

"See you in a few days!" He called the words back over his shoulder, hoping she'd think these were just an afterthought.

Chapter Two

Sascho descended the rocks and moved into the scrub, determined to put the girl and the place as far behind him as possible. He tried to stay calm and make his way through the low bushes with care and quiet, even though he felt like shouting and stamping and kicking things like an angry white man. After all, the sun was beginning to wester and he still had nothing to bring back.

And that girl—she'd grown since last year. Now she was just as tall as he was, although she still had no shape. Sascho had begun to notice the softening and rounding that overtook the active little girl cousins he played with in childhood. Although he knew that was what happened next in growing up, and that boys continued packing on muscle as they grew, her new height was dispiriting. He wondered if her aim was as good as it had been, or if it was even better. Last summer at the lake camp, she'd sometimes played knife throwing games with him and his friends. They'd soon learned that she could throw hard and accurately, far better, in fact, than a lot of his cousins.

Of course, on that occasion, she'd soon been called away by one of her Auntie's, back to her woman's work, but not before Sascho and the others had also been impressed by her skill with that small bow someone had given her.

One evening last summer, he'd seen her stun a duck with a well-thrown stone. While it was dazed, flopping in the shallows, she'd splashed in, seized it, and wrung its neck in an instant. It was not her only hunting skill, either, for he'd seen her spear fish, too, as expert as anyone.

She was exactly the kind of girl a man should get for a wife. Just thinking of her bright white smile and warm brown cheeks made his pulse run a little faster. He was, all in all, happy that her family would be camping with his again this summer. It had been good to see her again, even if he had been shamed that she'd caught him sleeping.

After a trek through some scrub, a place where he'd hoped to spot more deer, he found himself facing a steeply rising slope of jumbled rocks and grass. The landform lay like a huge snake blocking his path. At the base, he paused to orient himself by the sun. He'd have to move along if he hoped to make the Blackwater camp by dark. He leaned forward, carbine over his shoulder and began to climb. It would be easier to travel along the flattened crest. Where it terminated—in a mound of gravel—was the place where he'd turn his back on the sun and head east, in the direction of the small lake beside which his band camped.

Atop the esker, he paused to catch his breath. A few low clouds traveled briskly overhead, borne upon a crisp, sharp wind which made him shiver. He was glad it was in his face, for this meant his scent was going upwind. Distantly he heard ravens calling, probably in the spruce he'd just left behind. His gaze scanned the open land below in search of movement.

It was mostly flat, with patches of gray stone and greenish brush, occasionally brightened by the golden blush of lichen. Nothing stirred. Heaving a sigh he set off again, this time at a fast trot. It was clear and easy this way, but it was also a place where he could easily be seen.

It was not a road the old timers would have traveled, back in the days when First Nation people warred with one another, but now he would cover territory between here and camp faster by walking along the flattened crest. When he reached the final mound, he would descend easily into the soggy, brushy flatland. There still might be a final chance to flush another deer. He could also check the little trap line he'd made early this morning, too, the one along the rabbit path, to see if that had yielded anything he could carry back.

As he reached the terminus, the old grave appeared. Four stones arranged to sit at the four sacred directions, with a single rock set carefully at the heart, marked the place. He'd passed below it this morning through the scrub on the trail of those elusive deer. On a visit a few years back, his uncle had taken him and his cousins to the place. Uncle John had told them the names of those who were buried here, people from his grandparents' generation, a family—two women, three children, and their husband, all of whom had died of one of the white man's terrible plagues.

The earth, when their bones were found, was still frozen and impossible to dig. So, those family members had gathered the remains and placed them within the loose stones and gravel of the esker, where digging was always possible.

The night he and John had come here, they'd gathered brush, built a small fire, sung some prayer songs, and his uncle had told a story from the old days, when the white men had just begun to change everything. It was important, Uncle John said, for them to remember the elders, for they were still here, lying in the land that had borne them. Afterwards, they had sat in the fire light and kept the spirits company for a time.

Evening had come down. Overhead, just as the sun set, they'd seen the lights of nààka streaking across the sky. The billowing sheets of color shimmered and danced like tent curtains. "The elders are showing their thanks, maybe not just the family who lie at this place, but all the others, back to the deep time, the time of *Yamǫǫzha and his dark brother."*

Sascho remembered from Uncle John that the stones had been brought up from somewhere else, for they sported little caps of rock tripe, which didn't ordinarily grow on the stones at the top of eskers. For a moment, he remembered what he knew of this grave, and of how the people had died, sheltering in the scrub at the foot of this place. Perhaps they'd come to hunt snow foxes, who often used the eskers for their dens, when the terrible new sickness had taken them.

Standing here now, alone, Sascho knew the presence of the ts'ı̨ı̨ta. He felt their voices calling to him, and forgot all about his rush to return home. There was something he needed to do before he left here.

I must build a campfire and honor the gots'ı̨ı̨.

He gathered twigs, dried branches, and pieces of bark and stacked them into the same indent in the ground where Uncle John had built his fire. Satisfied, Sascho took two matches from his ts'et'ıı tł'ehwò and crouched in front of the twigs, holding the match and blowing gently until the flames caught and smoke rose.

Satisfied, Sascho raised his hands and offered prayers to the ts'ı̨ı̨ta, thanking them for welcoming him and entreating them to share their wisdom. Next, he reached into his ts'et'ıı tł'ehwò took out a small handful of his mixture which he held loosely in his hands, letting it

24

spill from his fingers as he turned in a circle scattering tobacco to the four sacred directions.

Completing the circle and standing in the West towards the setting sun, Sascho let out a grunt of surprise. Seated on a log beside his fire was a very old man with long gray hair and piercing black eyes that searched the young man's face and then nodded, as if in silent approval.

"Beware the kwet'ji," the old man said in a low, whispery voice. "They will cross your pathway and take you to a place where your spirit will be forbidden."

Sascho, stunned by the old man's words, rose as if to come nearer, but the old man put out his hand and indicated that Sascho should stay where he was.

"Be wise my son," the old man said. "Bide your time. Be brave and wait for a messenger from ts'ḭta. Do not be tricked or fooled by kwet'ji lies for he is like dìgatsoa, full of trickery and lies. Trust Nǫhtsḭ, and wait until you are called."

While Sascho stood there trying to understand, the old man rose, walked towards a growth of bushes and disappeared into the twilight.

Sascho, mindful of the darkening skies and confused by all he had seen, reached for his ts'et'ìi tł'ehwò, placed it inside his ewòhʔeh and started to leave. A strange sensation set the hair on the back of his neck to tingling and Sascho turned to stare at the log where the old man had

25

sat when he gave his warnings. There stood a large grey wolf. His fur, bathed in the last of the twilight, shone silver and his eyes glittered like those of det'otsį.

"Thank you Ehtsèe," Sascho acknowledged grandfather spirit, "I will keep your words close."

The vision gave Sascho much to ponder. The wolf in spirit form shook his core, and even the place where he stood held a chill, a warning—clearly about the kwet'įį, who, more and more, intruded into their lives.

What would life be at the łık'àdèè k'è this summer? Would there be more kwet'įį about than there had been the year before? Kwet'įį were scornful of Tłįchǫ and not respectful to the creatures they took from the land.

Sascho had seen the northern mines when he'd gone with his Uncles two winters ago on a journey to Sahtì, The Great Bear Lake, which lay at the border of Tłįchǫ land. His elders had shown him disturbed and ruined earth from which the spirits had fled. They'd explained how the water too, and the fish in these places, had been poisoned by kwet'įį diggings. The creatures that had once made Sahtì a rich hunting ground had grown few and wary. Even the caribou had changed their ancient paths in order to avoid these places.

Would his people succumb to kwet'įį ways? Some already had. These men disrespected and ignored their elders, abused their wives and neglected their children, drank and stole, and brought shame—and the Ekw'ahtı (*Royal Canadian Mounted Police (RCMP)*)—into their camps. Others, like his family, had tried to stay as far away from the kwet'ıı̀ as possible. They, like the caribou, sought new paths. They learned to avoid the fouled ponds where the poor beaver lost his hair and the fish were filled with horrible ulcers.

But where could we go, if we are forced to leave?

His Uncles sometimes spoke of this. Now, Sascho tried to push this unhappy future away. To leave the Tłı̨chǫ Dèè was unimaginable.

We are part of this place, woven into the land like quills ornamenting a pair of moccasins. We are like the moose, the lynx, the beaver, the muskrat, the wolf and the raven, and all our brothers and sisters who live here.

Linked to the earth through the soles of his feet, Sascho's spirit rose up and poured out into the blue immensity of heaven..

* * *

"A whole day with my rifle, and you bring me two less bullets and only a squirrel and two skinny rabbits." His uncle sat beside a small fire, one of many now burning because of supper time. He was thin, and apparently ageless, strong and spry. Thoughtfully, he reached into a pouch for his pipe. Once it was between his teeth, his brown hands began to busy themselves, preparing for a smoke.

Sascho knew it was the plain truth, his day of hunting summed. Uncle John's calm never wavered. He rarely displayed anger, which made his criticism easier to hear. Sascho wanted nothing more than to do better when he went out hunting tomorrow.

Sascho nodded, "Yes, my Uncle."

"Well, well. Go clean 'em up." A nod let him know they were done talking.

Sascho double checked the safety and then leaned the rifle against a tree. He got down, and once on his knees, reached for the knife at his belt. The two rabbits, his catch for the day, lay before him. Nearby younger cousins were fooling around—partly work and partly play—that was what you did at their age. They were making a game of tossing fish skin and heads and other bits of offal to the dogs straining at the end of their ropes. Two big wolfish looking ones snapped the first bits, while the losers growled and whined and nipped at one another.

Sascho put his head down and began. Cleaning rabbits was like peeling off a glove; the ground squirrel would take a little more time and care. There was plenty of food to eat tonight despite his failure, plenty of fish, and the like. Still, he'd been sent for a deer and he hadn't brought one home. It hadn't been the day he'd hoped for.

"You and I will go out together tomorrow," Uncle John spoke, as he leaned into the fire to pull a stick from the edge of the pit to light his pipe. He drew gently and smoke rose, the first puff clouding the sharp angles of his face, obscuring his black almond eyes.

Uncle John—his mother's brother—had been teaching Sascho how to understand the world around him for as long as he could remember. He knew he was fortunate to have such a fine hunter show him how things were on the Tłįchǫ dèè, how to track, and how to watch and listen, how to avoid being detected by the prey.

This morning he'd caught up with those deer, but had, plain and simple, missed the shot. By the time he'd reloaded again, they had run too far. Sascho had sprinted after; he'd tracked—of course he had—but the deer had lost him near some spruce. Afterward, he had circled, hoping to happen upon other game. He'd sighted a beaver, busy pushing sticks into his dam, but he'd half-way known that would be another wasted shot, so he hadn't bothered. The beaver, after a warning smack of his tail, had vanished.

While he worked, Sascho's thoughts turned back to something pleasanter—Yaot'ı.

She was still almost like a boy, so lean and her face thin, just like his, after the long winter. How bright her dark sloe eyes had been, and how much fun she'd had at his expense! He couldn't really be angry, because she was right. He'd been a fool to fall asleep, and lucky it had been her, a friend, and not a bad spirit or— maybe even worse than something supernatural—Dedìi, his older cousin who would have had no end of fun at his expense.

Sascho sighed and picked up the second rabbit. His mother passed by, smiling a greeting. She lugged a pot of water, one so large he wondered why she didn't topple over. Tiny as she was, his little mother, she was astonishingly strong. He made as if to get up to help her, but she shook her head.

"No, no, finish the gahkwǫ. I can do it."

She went on by, both hands on the kettle, a few splashes left behind here and there. Mother and his Aunt Elise would prepare bannock tonight, a treat. Two tins, one of flour and the other of lard had been found in the final autumn-stocked cache they'd passed. It would be a treat to have bread, for they had run out of the makings a long time ago.

Despite the expected annual hardships, the Lynx family had returned from the northlands with a good supply of furs. These, it was hoped, would be sufficient to bring in enough supplies to start confidently into another winter.

The last season had been hard, with more snow than usual and wild winds. It had made the trap lines hard to reach. There had been a time, near the thaw, when Sascho felt his belly shrink toward his backbone, but, in the worst of it, his uncles had found a young denning bear and dragged the carcass back through a wind storm to their camp. Here, in a few dug-in turf shelters, floored with spruce and covered with branches and hides, the Lynx clan, husbands, wives, children, and grandparents, had survived another winter.

* * *

Yaot'l watched Sascho disappear into the scrub. He was taller than he'd been last year, but, her own growth spurt had kept her ahead of him. The thought brought a smile to her lips. She probably shouldn't have teased him, but it really had been irresistible, finding him snoring, so sound asleep.

In another week or so, all the families would probably arrive at Rabbit-Net Lake. Like last year, they'd pitch tents there beside those of the Tailbones, the Lafferty's, the Crooked Hands, the Gons and the Lynxes, and work the summer harvest of fish, waterfowl, and berries.

Yaot'l was happy, thinking of the coming good weather, the time of plenty, where there would be play as well as work, and where there would also be celebrations and dancing. There would be at least one visit to the trading post where they would see the kwet'ıı̀, see their stone buildings and their ceremonies, and hear of their god. These things happened every summer.

The kwet'ıı̀ would want to see any new children and to perform one of their naming rites over the new little ones. In these, they marked the child's brow with water and gave it a kwet'ıı̀ name—always the name of one of their holy men or women, of whom they seemed to have countless numbers. Yaot'l, however, like the children of other close kin, had not received this naming.

Her band came to the church and the people were polite to the black robes and their gray clad women. They listened to the Métis men who spoke to them in their language, telling them every time they came, the story of their wise dying god, the one person who had ever returned from death. Uncle John Lynx always said, "We will join in their ceremonies and make a pledge of peace. It cannot hurt to learn other tribe's stories. Those help us to understand their ways. But we will not do everything like them. If we did, we wouldn't be Tłıchǫ anymore... Our stories, the paths we travel, our way of seeing, would be lost. We would forget how to hunt. Therefore, when we go, we visit their church building, and then go on our way as we have always done. It is the Tłıchǫ way to get along with all the kinds of people they may meet, even kwet'ıı̀."

Yaot'l kicked off her moccasins and entered the stream. She was glad of the warm sun on her back, especially when she waded deeper into the freezing water. She'd seen a rock which would make a good perch right in the middle of the stream, a perfect place to hunt her silver-sided quarry. From there, she could spy the larger fish ascending the rapids. Now she'd try her skill at spearing the biggest, the best for drying.

As soon as she'd settled, there was flurry of activity, a school pushing upstream. There was no more time for reflection, only for action.

To secure her catch, she had to plunge deep into the water, hoping to keep the big fish, bleeding and fighting to their last, on the spear. The icy cold bit into her flesh and soon made her arms, feet and hands ache. Finally, Yaot'l could no longer will herself to continue. Instead, she waded back and sat down, her back against a large boulder

Then—although the breeze was growing cold—she strung her catch. She already had plenty.

The water splashed cheerfully on, the sound capturing all her senses. Reflections rose around her, patterning the scrub and causing the rocky shore to quiver with light.

Heat radiated from the rocks. Next—*even better*—the breeze dropped. Over her head was nothing but blue. In her ears, water sang. She allowed her thoughts to drift.

I will close my eyes. Just for a moment...

* * *

The harsh call of a raven awoke her. Yaot'l started. The sun was lower now, blazing into her eyes, casting long shadows. Quickly, she got up. When she did, a fox, a flash of red, went bounding across the rocks. Though it was early for him to be out, he'd apparently come from the scrub and snatched one of her fish. The tail jiggled and flopped as he disappeared. She shouted, grabbed her fish spear and threw, but it landed short with a harmless clatter. The fox and his prize were gone.

Grumbling, angry with herself, she went to check the rest of her catch. Two ravens, sitting up in the bones of a dead spruce, made noisy commentary. If she hadn't been so anxious about her fish—she had no idea how long she'd been sleeping—she would have thrown something at them too, for they seemed to be laughing.

A stringer she'd left in the water still drifted in a back eddy, safely carrying its load. The largest ones – all except for the one the fox had stolen—lay rolled up on the shore. As she counted her catch, she noticed a mess of fishy bits and scales.

"Oh," she called to the ravens. "Did you steal my fish too?"

"Ha-ha-ha-ha! Steal? Steal? Steal?" At least that's what their cries seemed to say. The two bobbed back and forth upon the ghostly branch and fixed her with their shiny eyes.

Yaot'l shivered and cast a furtive look about her. There was something odd in the way they just sat and watched. Perhaps they were not ordinary ravens? Ravens had power; their form was sometimes used by bad Shaman. After all, had the raven not greedily hidden food from the wolf in a time of famine and then been condemned by *Yamǫ̀zha* never again to eat fresh meat, only garbage and rotten flesh, from that day forth?

She wondered why she had fallen asleep in this place, exactly as Sascho had.

Was there some kind of magic here? The lengthening shadows had changed things. It had been so bright and welcoming at noon, but now long low shadows and low sun-glare could hide danger, like the dreadful Nakan.

She made sure to leave a pair of fish behind. After all, nothing had happened to either her or Sascho, although they'd both, carelessly, fallen asleep here. She shot one last glance toward the tree, where the ravens still gurgled and chuffed and lifted their feathers, as if in confirmation. As fast as her feet would carry her, bent under the dripping load, Yaot'l hurried away.

Heading back to camp, she threaded her way along a deer track, winding among boulders, around pools of dark water and stands of scrub. At one place, she first smelled and then saw a thin trail of smoke from a fire. She knew she was passing her mother's camp, where she, and whichever of her female relatives—in this case, Aunt Susie and Aunt Grace—who were also in the menarche stayed. It was not permitted for women to be around men during that time, and so they were sent out of camp to live by themselves. This was not a great hardship in summer, but in spring and winter it could be tough—and dangerous, too—for in the spring, hungry bears, and in the winter, wolves—could smell blood and take advantage of their isolation.

Still, this was the way it always had been. Yaot'l knew women's bodies carried a potent magic that men must, at times, avoid. Her mother had told her that this exile was not all bad, especially if you went with other women, which was mostly the case. They took their embroidery projects, or worked beading or quill decorations. At this time, they actually had the opportunity to sit, drink tea, and talk, or fall asleep whenever they felt like it, without the constant demands of either children or men folk.

Yaot'l knew as well as anyone how to make a shelter, how to cut and bend the young spruce or willow boughs, how to make use of a boulder or depression for a windbreak. She knew how to set snares, and she was better than some of the boys with a rock or with the little bow made by her babàcho.

She knew her mamàcho and old Mrs. Tailbone went to visit the exiles daily, bringing treats, like fresh cooked bannock, or old time herb mixtures to soothe. Yaot'l stopped moving, and, for a moment, gazed up into the bright sky, only a little marred by the faint line of smoke.

She found herself hoping Aunt Katie might have gone out there as well while she had been off fishing. Aunt Katie had been so set on her finishing that hide by herself…

* * *

Yaot'l hoped to enter camp quietly because she really didn't want to return to scraping. She'd already seen the hide as she walked in, still stretched out between the willows.

The dogs, however, scotched a secret entrance. As soon as they saw her, they began barking and spinning around their tether pegs. One black dog she particularly liked, leaned against his rope, stood up on his back legs and yapped a cheery greeting.

"Hello, Happy!" That's what everyone called him because he was so good tempered, always smiling, his pink tongue lolling. He was safe for children to pet, unlike some of the other dogs, who were wilder and less trustworthy. He got along well with the others of his kind, too, which made him popular for use in a team.

Tłįchǫ hitched dogs in a long line. Happy could be hitched between two who were inclined to fight, and there wouldn't be any trouble at all. It was as if Happy's presence calmed the others.

Yaot'l set down the string. After a head down minute of seeking, her hand searching among the sticky bodies, she found one of the smaller ones. Showing it to Happy first so he could see his treat coming, she tossed it. He easily caught it midair. Another dog that was tied nearby growled and strained at his rope, but he couldn't reach his neighbor's prize.

"Never mind, Spot. I'll find you one, too." She'd just bent down to look for another when a shadow fell over her.

"You weren't supposed to be away all afternoon." Aunt Katie already had her hands on her hips. She didn't look any more pleased than she had this morning.

"Look at these shadows—why so late? And what have you been doing? It's easy enough to catch fish at this time of year and there's still plenty more scraping to be done, you know."

"But shouldn't I prepare these, Auntie?"

"Never mind the fish—Mamàcho and I will tend to those. You get back to work on that hide. It'll be dark soon. When you finish up, we'll put it into the stream overnight for a good soak."

As Yaot'l passed where Mamàcho Josette was seated, the old lady reached out a hand to catch hers. "Nice lot of fish, my girl. We'll have a tasty supper tonight, and those big ones should dry perfect."

Mamàcho always made her feel better, and, sure enough, when Yaot'l returned to the hide, she was pleased to see there was not really so much more that needed to be done. She suddenly felt a lot more confident about finishing.

Later, when Auntie Kate was busy somewhere else, she'd tell mamàcho about the fishing place, about meeting Sascho Lynx, and about the fox and the two ravens. The more she thought about it, the more it seemed she'd done right to leave the fish. For all she knew, those birds had changed into people as soon as she'd left them behind.

* * *

The lake at Gam`e`t`i was nowhere near as enormous as Tındeè, the great lake to the south. The country still had plenty of fish, moose and birds. Beaver built their ponds in the network of creeks, seeps, and pools. Their Lake provided an abundance of food for summer and more to store for winter.

The People reached the usual camping place within a few days of one another, by water, or coming with their dog teams pulling sleds filled with pots and pans, furs, hides and the canvas tents they'd purchased at the trading post.

Yaot'l, her cousins and her aunts, too, like the dog teams, traveled with burdens. It was always a tough slog through the swampy winding paths to blue Gam`e`t`i.

As they walked, the ground beneath their feet changed. There was more soil, enough to dig down into before you'd hit rock or ropey roots. The trees grew taller, changed to aspen and birch. There was less brush. Near the lake itself, there was the fine shady, sandy Whagweè, so good to pitch camp upon. In the open spaces, some families would dig up a little of the still icy ground and eventually plant small gardens.

Her father had been ill all winter. Last year, he'd gone with two cousins into the bush to trap as was usual, but then he had come home, long

39

before ice break. He'd complained he was sick, tired and weary as never before. He'd slept for many days and nights after he'd returned to the winter camp. Mother had worried. She'd nursed him with broths and special medicines brewed by the Grandmothers.

After the first good thaw, however, he'd declared himself better and had gone, just as usual, back to the mine up north where he worked during the summer. This had been his pattern for some years. Yaot'l had grown used to his coming and going.

Her father was a quiet hard working man, never loud, even at a cheerful tea dance or hand game. Before he'd left this spring, however, he'd worried them, saying that he felt stiff and hard "like a piece of dried fish." Usually, he recovered his health once he was in the bush again. Although trapping in the deep snow was difficult, and hunters sometimes went hungry for days, he'd usually look better in the spring. This year, however, it had not been so. Her mother had appeared deeply troubled as she'd watched him walk away.

Chapter Three

Life was always busy at łk'àdèè k'è even after all the families had pitched tents or built shelters upon the rocky shelf by the water. Yaot'l and the other women were busy for a time flooring their new homes with spruce bows and then bringing in bedding and belongings. As the families came in one by one, there were big get-togethers with shared food, while kin greeted one another and talked over the winter.

There was still ice on the lake, but none of it was hard enough to cross on foot. Snow lay piled down wind of stands of spruce and willow. Standing in their shade, Yaot'l shivered, feeling how cold the wind was after crossing those snow-packed places. Still, every day the sun rose higher and higher and stayed ever longer. Water gushed forth from the boggy ground while she walked.

The women had many tasks. It was time to gather fresh willow for baskets. The spruce trees, where their boughs had been cut, dripped gum. This was collected to use in repairing holes in k'ıelà—the birch canoes—and preserved to chew and to flavor winter tisanes. In spring, all the kids ran about with their jaws hard at work on the fresh strong gum.

Now, when Yaot'l slept, she dreamed of her hands, moving, always moving, for the days were full of weaving baskets from the willow they'd pulled from the beds by the still frigid lake, or splitting spruce roots for rope or binding, or with the finer business of beading leather bracelets or gloves, the sort of small items that would go to the trading post and bring a return of goods or cash. In camp, there was a fat baby boy to show off—Jeanne, who'd married Etienne Gon, had given birth, a proud first for a young woman who'd been married just two years ago.

The Lynx family had joined them. Yaot'l noticed Sascho noticing her. Such a warm feeling, when she'd glance up from task and meet his black almond eyes! Of course, as soon as this happened, they'd look both away, and quickly get busy with something else.

They often met, however, as they went on errands about the camp and sometimes they'd speak, something about the weather, or the task in hand. At night, when the Lynxes and the Crooked Hands shared fire with the Snow Goose, she and Sascho would covertly watch one another during the time when people told stories.

Eyes, Yaot'l was learning, could say so much!

During the days, the men cut wood and worked at repairing and setting their fish nets. They sat and smoked and talked about winter trap lines and trails, about fighting their way through snowstorms, and tall tales of the doings of their smartest sled dogs—or of troubles with the bad ones. There were piles of furs, too, that had to be safely stored before the trip to the store by the Ka'owae—the trading chief—the man among them who knew how to drive the best bargains.

One clear bright evening, Yaot'l was perfectly content, sitting beside her mother near the crackling campfire. She could see Sascho sitting with his uncles nearby. Spruce boughs sputtered and shot bright red sparks that swiftly blew upward into the star-filled sky.

A little distance away, a group of men, some young, some venerable, stood together. They were sampling a pot of brew that one of the early arrivals at the lake had already made. There was just enough for everyone in the group to have a sip, so it was enjoyable, a start to the season of plenty. When they were camped here, near the traders' post, there was easy access to the makings of this white man pleasure. Sugar, raisins, plus yeast and a little time, was sufficient to make alcohol.

Among the young men in the group was one who kept trying to catch her eye—far more boldly than Sascho ever did. It was the manly Jimmy Tailbone, who already sported a fine mustache. She knew that there had been some talk over the winter about Mamàcho Tailbone's grandson working with her uncles over the winter. This could be to learn from good hunters of another family, but it could also be to earn a Snow Goose bride.

Yaot'l was strong and her hands were clever. All her older female relatives often said she would find a husband early. She shrugged it off every time. She knew other girls had their eyes—ever so covertly, as was correct—on Jimmy Tailbone. Perhaps, she hoped, if she ignored Jimmy all summer, he and his family would settle on some other girl.

So now, when he looked at her, Yaot'l pretended she hadn't seen. She lowered her eyes, hoping to suggest that she'd only been watching the dancing fire. She couldn't imagine being married to Jimmy. Even though she could get through all the work of a wife—and another full year of working with her aunts would make her even more capable than she now was—well, she thought: I already know the boy who will— someday—be my husband.

Beside her, Mother rapidly ate a fish, holding it by the stick upon which it had been impaled for grilling. She pulled away the skin then sucked the tender flesh from the delicate bones. As she laid the skeleton down beside her—it would go to the dogs—she gently nudged Yaot'l.

"I think Jimmy wants you to look at him."

"I don't want to look at him, Mother."

Her mother smiled very slightly. She reached for another piece of fish and didn't say any more.

In the meantime, Yaot'l threaded a bead and continued work on a bracelet.

"Pretty, that one."

Yaot'l nodded, happy for the change of topic.

"Last year the Ka'owae said the man who bought them liked the blue best. When I helped Aunt Susie the other day, unpacking, I found these." The beads had been stored away in the cache the family had left behind last autumn. Small items, like beads, were often carried along to the north—sufficiently light, they provided an activity for the snow-bound women—something they could make for summer trade.

"The lake sometimes looks that same color, right at the end of our stay."

The falling leaf time, when the men left to hunt the caribou...

That was when, ordinarily, her father would leave his mining job and come home for a time. The money he brought back, he shared out with the band, because he was a good man who, in his open-handedness, followed the old ways. There were always a few special things for her mother and for her and Little Brother. Mother liked to get bright beads, colored embroidery thread and new needles for her trade bracelets. For themselves, they still used sinew, the traditional method, which required no other tools.

Last autumn, before he'd gone to Hottah Lake, her brother Charlie had brought Yaot'l a beautiful—and very sharp—knife. He'd purchased a high-quality blade, but had carved the design of flying geese upon the fine bone handle himself.

Tonight as the families caught up on news, they'd learned that two members of the Gon family had died. Everyone knew the place where their gocho (ancestors) were laid to rest, along one of the trails their people walked each year. At summer's end, on the way to find the caribou, the band passed the place and would honor their old friends with offerings of food, song, and fire.

"Where is Ehtsèe tonight?" Babàcho was a traditionalist, but he was not totally averse to an occasional swallow of brew. Besides, on a night like this when so many families were reunited, there would be storytelling, tales of the winter passed, of hunting, trapping, of births and deaths, and of snow. Her babàcho was a respected story-teller, one who knew all the old songs.

"Oh, he and Uncle Bill are still trying to put the putt-putt back together."

Yaot'l made a face. That old greasy engine, stinky oily device that it was, made it a lot easier to cover distance on the lakes, and so the men now used them to drive their canvas boats.

Uncle Bill was good at getting engines to run after a long winter's storage.

As far back as she could remember, there had never been a spring in which the putt-putt had started right away—but sooner or later, after a time of tinkering, it would reward their effort and sputter to life. Small parts would come from the trading post, along with the gasoline and oil. Mamàcho didn't like a lot of these white man new things, but the putt-putt was an exception.

One of the Gon men began to tell a story about hunting forest caribou. His tale was full of observation, about wind direction, snow depth, and then a part about how his favorite dog had gotten loose, run off to fight with a wolverine and died of wounds. Like all such stories Yaot'l heard, there were digressions, like the unfortunate loss of such a good pack dog. At the last he told of his eventual success, and of the young bull he'd taken, and about the food discovered in his mouth and belly. Those signs had told him of where more caribou could later be found and about the condition of the herd.

The White Tails who had wintered with the Gons joined in, telling of the lean time of the last winter, and what they thought had caused it.

"It is because of too many kwet'įį—how they disrespect the animals. They take more than they need; they kill for the head and horns and leave the meat wasting on the ground. The caribou know these things. Where the kwet'įį come, they learn to stay away."

"It is because of the mines—their noise and dirt—those great diggings they make when they take away our land—right in the middle of the paths the caribou have always walked."

"Five seasons ago the caribou went east and south of Tındeè. Many of our hunters had to go to Lutselk'e to hunt beside the Cree. It was a hard year, for when some are hungry, no one, not Tłįchǫ, Yellowknife, Cree or Slavey gets enough to eat."

"Yes. It is like the story of that Franklin, who came and took all the fish out of the lake and then refused to share with the people whose place it was, so that they had to move again, with the cold already in."

"Ah, but when Franklin and his men disrespected the bears they had killed by hanging their heads in trees and putting silly grins on their faces, the bears took their revenge."

"Yes, in winter they ate all the food Franklin had cached and tore up his tents, so they were all starving and had to live as we do."

"I wish Franklin and all his men had starved to death." Babàcho Crooked Hand muttered. He huddled close to the fire to warm his old bones. He was a very old man now, near ninety-five some said, and he always had the darkest view of the kwet'įį.

He had cause. Everyone knew the story of how long ago, his lovely daughter, Little Marten, had been lured away by kwet'įį with promises of a fine life. She became addicted to spirits, and, in a few years, after she'd lost her looks, she'd simply disappeared. As kwet'įį often boasted of how they "got rid of" Indian women they'd cast off, what had happened to her was easy to guess.

"But it is sometimes our own people nowadays, who take more than they need," said Uncle John. "They want too much from the trading post and so they take more animals than they should; they take food out of the mouths of the rest of us to trade for white man toys."

Yaot'l, sitting among the women, was silent. It was not for them to speak when the men were talking, but she knew how to listen, which was the first lesson every child learned. She could see, as the fire flickered across the gathered faces, that some of the young men did not agree with John Lynx, even some members of his own family.

"Well, motors are not toys, and gasoline to make them run is necessary. Guns are good, too. Those things make life much easier for all of us to feed our families. How would we be able to take only what we need with all these kwet'įį everywhere? There are plenty of kwet'įį things that are good for our people to have, so that we have the same advantages they do."

"Yes, John. Even you have a motor."

"I have a motor, yes." John turned to gaze severely at the objectors. "You know when I speak of toys; I do not speak of motors. We need to see in two ways. We need to know their way, but we also should teach our own knowledge, handed down to us by our gocho, to our children."

Across the fire, Yaot'l watched as Sascho, sitting beside his uncle, nodded. She thought that she liked the way Sascho honored and followed his Uncle. Sometimes, when she looked for him, he would not be around the camp, but in the bush with John Lynx, Robert Gon, or some other elder who kept traditional ways.

My father works in the mines, yes, but when he hunts, it is with such wise old men he goes.

John Lynx was well respected as a hunter. He was a man who had learned much from his elders. He could make a birch bark canoe; he could even make stone blades and arrowheads, skills that had been lost to most of the tribe eighty years ago when the white man arrived with his metal. While some admired and honored the old crafts that he'd learned, many of the younger ones, attracted to kwet'įį ways, thought all John's traditional knowledge was not worth the trouble and said so.

There was a silence, which the crackling fire strove to fill. Then, Babàcho Crooked Hand cleared his throat in a way which indicated he was about to tell a story. The youngest children settled in next to their mothers and aunts, happy that the tension of just a moment ago would be resolved.

"This is a true story." Babàcho Crooked Hand began in the traditional way. "Soon after the beginning there came caribou, and from between the hooves? of the caribou came the twins, *Yamǫǫ̀zha* who goes to the rising sun and *Yamǫǫ̀gaa* who goes to the setting sun. As I have said, an old man, passing by, found them weeping all alone and raised them. He told them stories and taught them all about the land, and beings, and the animals. It is of Yamǫǫ̀zha, The Great Traveler, The Walker Across All Lands, that I will speak tonight, of how Yamǫǫ̀zha named all things, and how he stopped the animals from fighting all the time and eating one another. He taught the eagles to eat fish and not to eat men. He taught caribou to eat lichen in winter and leaves and grass in summer; he taught men the rules of this world, of how to show respect for the land and for the animals, but even Yamǫǫ̀zha sometimes forgot his own rules. No matter how great a Yahbahti he was, when the time came that he broke his word, he could not stop bad things from happening.

Now in those days long ago, Yamǫǫ̀zha wanted to have Beaver for a wife; he loved her industrious ways. But Beaver was wise, and objected, saying 'I am from the water, you know. It is my true place and where I belong.'

Yamǫǫ̀zha still wanted Beaver to be his wife, even though she was from the water, so Beaver said, if I am to be your wife, you must always lay down logs over the water, whenever we must go to the other side, so that I do not get my feet wet. And so Yamǫǫ̀zha agreed to that, and he did it too, and they lived together very happily for a time. They even had a baby, which

51

Beaver carried on her back. One day though, when they were going north to follow the caribou, Yamǫǫ̀zha got into a hurry. The sun was going down; he wanted to reach a place where they could make camp and rest in a dry place. There were many little creeks and streams to cross along the way, and he grew tired of finding wood in the muskeg where sometimes there is not so much wood to find and then the work of laying it down. At the end of the day, he crossed one last stream, one with plenty of rocks to walk upon. He looked around and could not see any logs. He was tired; he did not want to stop and look to find a strong log so that his wife and baby could cross. He thought that she could certainly go from stone to stone, just as he had, and follow him to the camping ground—the good Whagweè with soft sandy soil, the fine place to make camp which he knew lay ahead.

So Yamǫǫ̀zha did not put down a log for his wife, but crossed over by himself. When she, carrying many bundles, as women must, as well as her baby, came to the bank what did she see but that bright water, flowing, sparkling all around those rocks—and there was no log. She tried to cross anyway, but the edge of the sole of her moccasin touched the sweet cold water. Sure enough, the water took her back again, and before you could blink, she turned back into a beaver and so did her baby. They both went swimming away, down the creek and into the big pond below. Yamǫǫ̀zha called for her to come back to him, but it was too late; she was lost forever."

Sascho sat near the storyteller. Beside him was a young cousin who'd been listening with all his might. Little Brother said, "Babàcho, did Beaver not wish to stay with her good husband?"

"She did wish to stay, but she could not. She belonged to the water and when she touched it, the water took her back."

"Yamǫ̀ǫzha broke his own rules," Sascho said into the pause. "He promised to place logs for his wife always, but he did not."

Yaot'l admired the way the old man spoke. She'd heard this story a hundred times before, but it was a good story, and she loved the sound of Old Crooked Hand's whispery voice.

She also thought Sascho looked quite handsome with the firelight glinting on his face, respectfully listening, sitting in the circle, so near both Babàcho Crooked Hand and her own small brother.

"There are consequences when we break the rules laid down by Yamǫ̀ǫzha, the first walker over the land." So, the story teller ended.

* * *

Her father had returned to Gam`e`t`i instead of spending all summer at the mine. He'd tried to follow his usual schedule, going to work, but in the end, he'd caught a ride on one of the kwet'ı̀ı̀ wagons in order to get home. He'd been

53

lucky to get it, as it was officially forbidden for those transport vehicles to take riders—although, of course, they often did—but these favors were generally for white workers. Someone in authority, it seemed, had spoken on her father's behalf.

Yaot'l was used to him being away much of the time, so, in her mind, her father was like the caribou, the way he came and went. It was odd to have him here in summer. It was not always a happy time for the family, either, because he was so sick.

Rene Snow Goose was thin, weak, irritable, and night wakeful, although he complained too of being tired throughout the day. His chest, he said, felt heavy, as if a stone had lodged in it. Lately, he'd begun to have a constant pain in one shoulder. His cough was raspy and thick and what he spat was tinged with red.

Sascho's Uncle John was often consulted for medicine. They'd set up a small shelter of branches outside the main camp for Rene to receive his treatments. Yaot'l and Sascho too, were often asked to walk with John in order to help him carry back healing herbs. This was no hardship for Yaot'l, because she loved learning about the plants. Most of what she knew had come from grandmothers and elder aunties, but much of that was women's knowledge—curing ills peculiar to women and babies, sickness in the stomach and bowels, as well as how to clean and sew wounds. John had a wider-ranging knowledge, some in medicine, but he had also learned how to perform the ceremonies.

Sascho, if he wasn't doing other work, walked with him. His Uncle was an honored medicine man, one with much to teach those willing to learn. From his earliest days, Sascho had been interested in just about anything his Uncle John was doing. He'd begun to travel with his Uncle as soon as he could carry his own pack.

"I have treated your father with wild cherries and bark, with red cedar tips and with cleansing sweet grass smoke." Uncle John said to Yaot'l, "and we have prayed together. These things are what our people have always done, and your father and I will do these things again. But I might soon go into Behchok`o for other healing plants, one's that grow where kwet'ı̨ì is."

"Kwet'ı̨ì have healing plants?" Sascho was the one who spoke, for this idea was strange and new.

"Yes, they do. When our men go down to trade in a few days, I will go too and bring back some."

Yaot'l remembered smelling the scent of the smudge seeping from between the bent branches of the hut where her father sat. Wisps of healing smoke had gone curling away into the long twilight. Her unseen father had coughed and coughed, the sound setting aquiver the dry leaves over his head, but, later, he'd fallen asleep. He'd stayed asleep, too, quite peacefully, until the next morning.

This was one of the last times when the family had hopes he might recover. For several weeks, her father's appetite had returned and he'd been more like his old self. However, whatever strength the treatment brought had not lasted and all the while, the terrible pains grew stronger.

* * *

They noticed yellow birch leaves while they traveled to the trading post at Behchok'o, a village on the arm of Tındeè. Yaot'l's father made the journey as he'd often done before, although back then, he'd gone with his head held high and script in his pocket. John had tried the kwet'ı̀ı̀ plant medicine, but just as with everything else, it had not helped Rene for long.

Perhaps the kwet'ı̀ı̀ doctors could do something about Rene's pain. As Rene had always been strong and hearty, rarely sick in his life, the parade of illnesses he'd had in the last two years presaged what surely was on its unwelcome way.

Days shortened. Some relatives had already gone north to watch for the caribou that would soon return to the forests to over-winter. Young families, these days, might linger at the łık'àdèè k'è a little longer, but in the old days now was the time when the whole band began to travel. It was a resumption of the seasonal

56

round, as the Tłįchǫ followed the wandering footsteps of Yamǫǫ̀zha's animals.

This trip south would be the final time before winter to purchase flour, lard, molasses, dried fruit, yeast and sugar and those new necessities, gasoline and oil. Yaot'l and her parents and Little Brother, her Aunt June and Uncle Frank Lafferty and their children would go, too, along to the trading post.

They traveled by water and on foot. At the last minute, Yaot'l learned that a few Lynxes would also be coming to the post. She was delighted when Sascho said he was among them.

There was a church and a government building at nearby Fort below Rae. These were used by the Royal Canadian Mounted Police and Department of Natural Resources. There was also the big hospital, built some years ago and staffed by nuns. There were year-round houses here, some made of wood, some of stone, all with masonry chimneys. There were cars, trucks and horses. Behchok'o was just a boat ride away from Yellowknife.

Métis families met here, too, as everyone prepared for winter. Such a gathering of far-flung people, many of them kin of one kind or another, led to celebration. There was certain to be tea dances as well as several well-attended-many-days-long hand games, where the men would gamble. There would be church festivals, too, but Yaot'l and the young ones of her band had been warned to stay away from both the trading post and any gathering sponsored by the church in order to avoid being seen by the authorities.

It was tradition, this autumn voyage, by water and foot. In times past, their canoes had been of birch bark, a craft requiring skill and days and days of intensive labor to build. Now most canoes were store-bought, many of canvas. Their family had several twenty-two footers which carried trade goods like furs, dried fish, and all the baskets and trinkets the women had crafted during the summer. There were still small canoes bobbing along beside the big ones, the kind in which two people could travel. The water rushed them along on the way down to Fort Rae, on the banks of Tındeè, called by kwet'ı̨ı̨, Great Slave Lake.

They made a convoy, walking during portages, the women and dogs carrying burdens—things to trade, drums for the hand game and bright store bought shawls and hair ribbons to look pretty at the dance. Sascho, his mother and some cousins were with them, as were the Tailbones, and the Gon Family. Among them was the lovely Sharon, who was only a few years older than Yaot'l. Sharon had been married for two years but her husband died. The child she'd had had not survived the next winter, so Sharon was now an unencumbered widow. A pretty girl, the Gons hoped she would soon attract a new husband. Sharon trudged along with her share of the burdens and then paddled. She walked for hours too, Yaot'l saw, and somehow through it all, she managed to look entirely collected and pretty.

Yaot'l felt dusty and grimy. She'd acquired a big smudge of mud on one cheek this morning because she'd slapped it on, hoping to take the pain and swelling out of a deer fly bite. The sting felt like a jab with a red-hot stick and always left a swollen itching red lump behind.

Just, she thought, what I want to have on my face at the Behchok'o tea dance! She continued to watch as Sharon marched on ahead, hopping across hummocky sedge, and still looking utterly ladylike.

Yaot'l herself was straight up and down and flat-chested too, and she'd probably remain that way for another year. Women didn't bloom all that early in her family. Sharon, unreservedly female in all ways, was an eye-catcher.

While they marched through the heat, pulling canoes and carrying bundles, everyone looked forward to the next portage. Shining under the August sun, a little lake would appear like a bright oasis, and then they'd be on water again. These days, some also packed outboard engines—the putt-putts—and a can of gas, too, so there was quite a bit of weight to carry. They didn't need to use the engines much on the way down as the current flowed south, making paddling easy.

This was a young party of travelers, with a few married couples along to keep an eye on the unmarried. There were babies and a gaggle of kids, who followed their mothers and played around the adults like puppies. There was sleep under the stars, wrapped in hides and blankets, and then packing and moving on the next morning. Along the way, they hunted in the bush. At night there were always rabbits, ptarmigans, or fish to share, even after a full day of traveling.

Sometimes, when they were in the midst of a portage, they needed to pause to get clean water to drink, or make a detour among the spruce to gather gum for chewing—and for treating the cuts and scrapes that were part of any portage. All these resting spots were well known. When they took a break, somewhere near the middle of the day, they'd sit in a breezy place where the flies weren't too bad and chew on dried white fish from their packs. Mothers would nurse babies; men would gather and sit, mostly silent.

"You need to stop looking at Sascho with those dreamy eyes, little warrior." Aunt June, at her side, reached out to prod her.

Up ahead, beside his family, Sascho was at work with the others, sliding their big canoe and its cargo over a rocky patch. His shiny black hair blew in the breeze.

"Yes, Jimmy will get cross; maybe he won't ask your father about you at the tea dance."

"Let Jimmy talk with someone else's father." Annoyed, Yaot'l shook her dark head.

"Yaot'l!" Aunt June scolded. "That's not how you speak to your elders. But," she said, giving in to a smile, "talking back is a sure sign you're ready to marry. You know, Ellie Mouse and Sharon Gon both think Jimmy would make a good husband. That's why they've spent the summer making all those shoes and bracelets to trade. They both want to show him what good-earning woman they are."

"I think Sharon's hoping Armand Chocolate will be there. He's supposed to meet them at Behchok'o." Yaot'l's mother entered the conversation. Armand was good looking and also in his twenties. He had been working on the new road that went between Yellowknife and Fort Providence.

"Well, Sharon will have to make a lot of things to trade if she marries either one. They're always gambling or drinking brew."

"All men gamble and most drink— sometimes. You will have to look far to find one that does not."

Her mother seemed to agree, because she pursued the argument.

"Jimmy's had a job all summer. He's working with Uncle Frank for that American, guiding sportsmen at Yeta Lake. I heard Frank say just last night that Jimmy's a smart boy who learns fast. As for the carrying-on, he's not any worse than any of the others."

Yaot'l didn't reply. She knew that Uncle Frank, June's husband, also had a taste for brew, and that sometimes it was best to stay away from their place while Frank was off work and the couple were on a binge. Her parents would very occasionally drink a little, but they didn't make it a habit, like some others.

Mamàcho generally disapproved of alcohol, though she might sip a little whiskey if she had a bad cold in the chest. Mamàcho declared whiskey to be a medicine. The white men called it *spirits* and she said this was a case where they were wiser than they knew, for whiskey clearly contained a spirit. Therefore, it resembled medicine plants, and was a substance you should not use casually.

Mamàcho had said this so many times that Yaot'l could practically hear her.

"All these kwet'ıı̀ things are not for us. We are Tłı̨chǫ. We never had these things before they came, and we were well enough—better, in fact, with fewer sicknesses. That's what my Grandmother Marten said and she was always right. She lived to be one hundred six, you know..."

Of course, plenty of young people disagreed. Lots of them had been sent to the residential schools, and when they returned— sometimes after years—they were like strangers. Mamàcho said they'd forgotten how to be Tłı̨chǫ. They were cold and distant with their relatives and friends. Many had bad dreams, or were subject to unpredictable rages, all born of secret sorrows which nothing seemed to cure.

Some of the saddest school Indians went south, into the towns, and came back with all sorts of tools, engines—and "toys." Many, though, came back with sicknesses, in the lungs, the throat, or the drinking sickness—whatever the white's might call it, that's what Mamàcho said it was. Sooner or later, some folly, done under the influence of malevolent spirits, or just the diseases which seemed to come in company with the bottle—and from living among whites – either sent them to jail or got them killed. That was one reason her band stayed so far out—to keep distance from all the new things and incomers. The bush had provided for their gocho and it still could provide all of what anyone really needed—food and shelter.

* * *

Just as they neared the water, Yaot'l's mother turned back, scanning the area. Little Brother had been running beside his friends and two favorite puppies, throwing sticks and laughing. He too carried a pack, and his own little bow and arrows. Now he was no longer in sight, and he'd been there, just a moment before.

As early as possible, all children took up hunting. Her little brother hadn't shot anything yet, though it wasn't for lack of trying. Many nights, by the fire, he would have to pester his cousins to make him more arrows; for once again he'd lost them all. Sooner or later, after he'd pestered for a while, someone would go with him to collect suitable pieces of willow. Then they'd sit around the fire and start the process by whittling the shaft.

Yaot'l remembered when she'd been learning these same things. She'd sat with her older brother, Charlie, who had—sometimes patiently, sometimes not—shown her how to peel and shape the stick, how to find the tree gum and make the binding from leather or string, how to cut a piece from a can to make an arrowhead. She'd pleased everyone by bringing down a ptarmigan, and she'd done it days earlier than her novice male cousins.

Yaot'l thought about Charlie a lot. He'd gone north and was said to be living near and working close to the kwet'įį mill on Great Bear Lake. No one had had any word of him for months and she knew her mother was anxious. Accidents happened, and the white men weren't too scrupulous about letting people know when the native men who worked for them died.

"Who is in your thoughts, cousin?"

She started. Hardly making a sound, Sascho had sat down on the same log. He had a way of getting into people's minds. He'd always been that way, thoughtful and quiet for a small boy, especially one whose body was so big and strong. Her mother said that was why his Uncle John, who had įk'ǫǫ̀ had chosen him for medicine training.

On all sides of where they sat, people found seats in the shade. As always seemed to happen, without speaking, they'd come to an agreement that it was time to take a break while the stragglers caught up. They took to the water as a group from this place because there was upcoming white water as one lake poured itself into the next. Not that it was highly dangerous, but it did take skill to negotiate, so it was best for everyone to keep together.

Yaot'l shaded her eyes to look at Sascho, for the sun shone at his back, making a halo around his head and shoulders. He was growing every day now, looking ever broader and more grown up.

"Oh, I was thinking of Charlie. You know, it's been a long time since we've heard from him."

He nodded. "I know. Uncle John had a dream of him last night."

She was about to ask what John had dreamed, but just then three black and white dogs came bounding out of the bush to join them. They came in a rush, but when Sascho waved a hand and spoke sternly to them, they all sat and regarded him, pink tongues lolling.

"In the dream, did Charlie speak?"

"No, they were in the Hozìishià, hunting. He saw Charlie walking way ahead. He called to him, but Charlie didn't hear. Then, the caribou came and the dream changed." Sascho leaned and patted the nearest dog on the head. This fellow was a smiling mostly black creature, quite friendly, which many of the working dogs were not.

He offered no more, so she, after a moment's hesitation, finally asked, "What does it mean?"

"Uncle John says we'll soon learn something about your brother."

It wasn't satisfactory. In fact, it was rather frightening, the idea of Charlie walking out into the barren lands and not turning to answer John, a much respected elder. Yaot'l fixed her gaze on the dogs, unable to ask more. Besides, she knew that was the way with ink'on. It would show you a vision, but often you had to wait for the unfolding of time to see the meaning.

"We don't ever know what's to come, so we cannot worry until it gets here." Briefly, Sascho touched her shoulder. She looked up to meet his dark eyes and nodded.

Sometimes he was so wise, more than his years.

"Those are some pretty nice dogs." She decided to change the subject, and return to the present. Besides, she was also discovering that his once familiar presence now unsettled her.

"Yes, they are part of a litter from my Uncle's best bitch. Dolly's really tame. You remember the litter? She's the mostly white one we all used to play with last łık'àdèè k'è."

"I do. That's one smart dog. She let the little kids do anything and she just knocked them over and ran off when she'd had enough instead of biting."

"And in the summer, she feeds herself. She's good at hunting. I hope these pups of hers are as smart and as good workers as she is."

"They didn't stay back at fishing camp with your old folks?" Normally, the band didn't take dogs into town on purpose, but a determined few always managed to tag along. In the summer, the dogs hung around camp, hunting in the brush and consuming leftovers, which were plentiful.

In the winter, though, the dogs went to work, pulling sledges and carrying packs along the trap lines. It was interesting to see the change in them as soon as they were hitched, all ready to set off with their burdens into the snowy wilderness. Instead of the lazy loungers they had been all summer, now they were part of a team. Heads and tails up, they looked proud of themselves and ready to get on with their winter duties. A large part of any winter hunting kit was the dried fish it took to feed them on the way, about three pounds of white fish per dog a day. In the snow blind times of blizzard, man and dog ate—or went hungry—together.

"I tried to make these fellows stay with my Uncle Theo, but I tied 'em with rope instead of using chain because I thought they weren't so very strong yet. I guess they just chewed through and came after me."

Knowing they were being talked about, the dogs all slid closer on their bellies. Sascho grabbed the head of the nearest and tousled him. This dog growled and grumbled, play-biting his young master's muscular hands with his white teeth.

"Soon you'll have a team."

"I do now, but I still have plenty to learn—and so do they."

"You're fortunate to have Uncle John."

"I have the best teacher in the whole tribe. Uncle John thinks these dogs are going to be good ones. He wants me to bring them along when I go hunting with him this year. We are going north, east of Great Bear Lake and out to the edge of Inuktitut land. He thinks I'm plenty ready."

"You went west with him last year, didn't you?"

"Yes, even, for a little, way down into the Dene country to hunt the forest caribou. Cousin Ned had never been that way, and Uncle John said we should both know it, even though the hunting there is no longer so good. We came home through Wha't'i and stayed for a time. We hunted elk, caribou and wood buffalo, but if it hadn't been for my Uncle's medicine, I don't think we would have got much. We were pretty near the Deh Cho."

"What is it like there, way west?"

"Much like it is here. In some places, it's like coming south to Gam`e`t`i, with creeks and ponds and muskeg. The farther we went, though, the land turned strange. He took us to one place that was a kind of high table that rose up straight out of the muskeg. It was flat on the top, but the sides were all cut through with creeks which ran straight down. It was as if someone had piled it up there and then poured water onto the top. Įdaahtı it is called."

Yaot'l wanted to close her eyes to better imagine it, but Sascho sat beside her, so she did not.

"It was boggy, so it was hard to travel. The ground was covered with grass, but under our feet it trembled, for it was water and earth so mixed together that they couldn't find a way to separate. Right in the middle, we saw a perfectly round pool set in the middle of the plain. When we reached the shore, there was a single circle of willows, but on every side, all you could see was flat. There was not a high spot or a rock as far as you could look. The sky over our heads was a big blue bowl; there was not a single cloud."

Yaot'l shivered as her mind flew to the otherworldly place his words conjured. She was accustomed to the endless networks of muskeg; she had seen the wide barrens, and the spruce forests where the caribou wintered, but this place he'd worked so hard to describe was like the echo of some unsettling dream.

Sascho nodded, as if he'd heard her thoughts. "Uncle John says Įdaahtı is a power place."

Chapter Four

The dogs were lying still now, as if they too had been listening. All around members of their families continued to go about their business. A baby cried and was put to his mother's breast. Dried fish was pulled from packs and offered around. They would eat something now, because soon they'd be on the water. Once they'd launched, they'd be paddling for the rest of the day, across this lake and then down the long creek that discharged white-water into yet another lake.

"Ah, there you are, Yaot'l." Her mother came from beneath the spruce shade. She now had Little Brother by the hand.

"Here! You stay with your sister this time, will you? And you, daughter—you watch him until we reach camp tonight."

Inwardly, Yaot'l groaned. Keeping an eye on Little Brother wasn't easy.

"I thought you were out looking for him, you know, and here you are, just sitting and wagging your jaw." Her mother pushed Little

Brother forward. "Now, son, this time do what you are told and stay with your sister."

Beneath her mother's stern gaze, Sascho shifted uncomfortably.

"Where was he?" Yaot'l rose and took her brother's hand.

"Never mind where he was. I was the one who went back and found him."

"I was with Johnny and George, pulling their canoe."

"You were not pulling the canoe. You were being a nuisance, and you know it."

"I was not a nuisance, Ma. I pulled a lot. Johnny said if I helped, I could go with them through the white water."

Johnny and George were still young, near Yaot'l's age, still honing their river skills. None of them, even together, were really strong enough to handle a loaded canoe in the strong current they'd soon be navigating.

"They are not going to take that little boat by themselves through the white water."

"But they said—"

"Babàcho Crooked Hand wouldn't allow it. Not after what happened to Little Joe—and on that same stretch of water, too. You'll come in the big canoe with your sister, Aunt Katie, me and Uncle Ted."

Little Brother immediately tried to yank himself free of Yaot'l's grasp. Not even a reminder of the cautionary tale—told at the campfire just the night before—of how Little

Joe Crooked Hand had drowned in the upcoming passage—was going to deter him.

"No! I don't want to go with you. I'm not a baby!" He stamped, scowling like a thunder cloud.

Young as he was, he could be trouble, especially when he didn't get his way. Everyone in the family agreed he'd been a bossy, demanding baby. Now, he was a child who gave every sign of growing into exactly the same kind of adult. Even his ordinarily calm mother could lose patience.

"I was going to ask Yaot'l if she'd like to go with me." Sascho got to his feet. "Little Brother can come with us."

Her brother stopped his pulling and looked hopefully at his mother. *Even traveling with his sister wouldn't be so bad if he was with an older boy like Sascho.*

"Well, we'll ask your goʔeh." Mother appeared to be considering. "You'll have two of my children in your canoe, Sascho, so only if he thinks it best."

John came through the bush. They saw the white feather in his hat before they saw him, as he emerged through a stand of sapling alder.

"I want to go with Sascho! Uncle John! Tell Mother I am a big boy and that I can go."

John came to join them silently taking in the scene. Little Brother continued to beg and hop up and down. John watched his antics for a few minutes until the little boy, quelled by his gaze, grew still.

"Little Brother, you will go with me, Nàbe and Babàcho." He pointed along the bank toward a large canvas boat stuffed with bundles. The boy, over-awed by this family elder, head low, went to take his outstretched hand. Mother, with a ghost of a smile, watched.

Yaot'l dared a smile in Sascho's direction. He shot her a look, eyes dancing, for now they both believed they would be allowed to travel alone together. They would be paddling through rough waters, but they could talk unobserved. However, just as the idea began to seem a possibility, Uncle John added, "I passed Mamàcho Josette coming through the bush. You two can take her along."

Just as he finished speaking, the old woman appeared, leaning heavily upon a stick. Even though she was bent and lame, she nevertheless packed a large bundle on her back.

"Is there a place for me in your canoe, young Sascho?"

Mother looked, a little uncertainly, toward Uncle John, for this was another kind of responsibility the children would be assuming—the care of a valued elder—but he only nodded and said, "You have come at just the right time, Mamàcho. These two have strong arms. Here," he said, stepping to help her remove the burden. "They will paddle for you today."

John set about making a place for her in the middle of the birch canoe. After she and her bundle were settled, he and Sascho moved the boat deeper into the water. Yaot'l and Mother joined in, wading and holding the sides. One at a time, Sascho and then Yaot'l climbed in with their paddles. These they pushed against the gravel bottom, while John and Mother, one on either side, gently pushed the boat out into the current.

Yaot'l took the front and Sascho sat in the back. The canoe was laden with packs and cook pots. Mamàcho's tiny body wrapped in a brown dress occupied the middle. The water on either side was brown, filled with boggy, ice cold run-off.

The river itself, their elders knew, would keep them busy, especially with a sluggish loaded canoe. There were no rapids right away, but, later, a number came, one after the other. They were not too difficult for a well-handled boat, but there were tricks to negotiating the rocks that experience taught best. Sascho had been down the river with adults before, as had Yaot'l. Neither were novices.

It was, however, a new thing for both of them, to travel together, even at opposite ends of the boat, even with Mamàcho in between. Yaot'l was a little anxious about the responsibility—just for a moment—and she imagined her companion was feeling the same, though he was doing his best to appear manly and in charge.

The air was heavy with the smells of summer, heat and vegetation. An occasional cloud of insects hung over green backwaters. In the middle, the river was deep, but there were more rocks to negotiate in late summer, ones that were not a hazard in spring.

While they paddled, Mamàcho Josette began to sing in a voice that remained surprisingly clear. She sang of the water, and of the bounty of summer. She called for the spirit of the river to keep them safe as they journeyed; she greeted the fish now swimming unseen in the brown water below, calling them little brothers. She called to a large boulder that the river cut a fork around, greeting its spirit by name, and thanking it as they sped past for letting them pass safely.

All her songs made Yaot'l feel ever so happy; for these were songs she'd heard her whole life, during passages along the various waterways of the Tłı̨chǫ dèè. That, and the wonderful knowledge that she and Sascho had been set to work together, that he was right behind her, steering with such skill.

The rest of day passed swiftly as they worked their way down river, keeping clear of rocks, negotiating the white water. Members of other families floated ahead and behind; sometimes boats under power would surge past them, but few were inclined to waste gasoline when it was so easy to go this way, in the direction of flow. Along the banks they'd catch sight of those dogs, running along on shore, trying to keep pace with their master.

Behchok'o, when they arrived, seemed both smaller and larger than the last time Yaot'l had visited the place. Right away she saw that there alongside old, weathered cabins, there were new ones, brightly painted in yellow and blue. These belonged to the Tłıchǫ and Métis people who now made the place their all season home. Still, Yaot'l was no longer the small girl who had wondered at the sight of cabins.

As they waded ashore, pulling in the loaded canoe, the cabins, and in the far distance, the church spire, did not seem so strange as they had the first time she'd seen them.

They offered to hold each other's arms and make a chair to carry Josette to the land, but the old woman shook her head.

"I'm not afraid of water. Just don't get any on that pack." She indicated the one she'd been carrying on her back, all gathered up inside an old blue blanket. Once they'd set her on her feet, she gathered her skirts and waded out. Yaot'l, carrying her cane, followed close behind, in case her Mamàcho stumbled.

Other boats were nearby. Some had just come in. Others were already pulled high onto the shore and were being unloaded. Packages of canvas, bundles of furs and hides as well as cookpots were stacked here and there, all things needed for a visit to a trading post.

"You both paddled well." The old lady spoke as Yaot'l handed her the cane.

"Thank you, Grandmother."

When she turned again, she saw that Sascho had already pushed the canoe against the shore. In a moment, she would help him drag it up to a safe spot among the others. On all sides came the babble of voices, as families greeted one another. Behchok'o relatives were arriving to seek out family members, to help carry packs and admire children that hadn't been seen since last year.

On either side of the canoe, they pulled it onto the bank. Sascho's arms looked strong from the other side of the shared load. Her own arms ached by the time they were done, so she was pleased when he, instead of straightaway beginning to unload, took her hand. A moment later, they were seated on the shore together, side by side, gazing out at the blue water.

"The white water did not last as long as I expected. We are getting stronger."

"Seemed like that to me, too. I expected it to be rougher when we came through that last section with all those rocks, but it wasn't so hard today."

Yaot'l nodded, enjoyed the warm touch of his hand, for he had not let go. It wouldn't last long, this quiet moment, and both of them knew it. Someone would come and tell them to get a move on and carry those packs to wherever they were going, but it was worth risking that, or the likely teasing, just to sit together, with the cheerful chatter of family all around, there on the dusty Behchok'o shore.

* * *

As they approached the site for the tea dance, the sound of drumming grew, quickening like a heartbeat. The swishing stamp of many feet underscored the rhythm. As they entered the circle of firelight, there was, for Yaot'l, the thrill of standing tall and being seen. Families from all over had come together. Everyone was dressed in their best.

The men wore pants, boots and button down shirts like those worn by kwet'ı̨ı̨. Mothers and grandmothers wore new-beaded moccasins and bright scarves from the trading post. The younger women, just entering womanhood, did more. They brushed their black hair until it shone and then braided it with extra care. The ends were tied and ornamented with either new or well-pressed hair ribbons, for this was a time when marriage agreements were made.

To start off, they danced a simple step. Then, as more and more families joined the circle, the drummers doubled the tempo. Chairs and benches had materialized around the big bonfire earlier, so the elders could sit and watch, although some of them danced for a time before retiring. The men danced first, but, bit by bit, the women joined in. A few young men, some nearing their twenties, danced from the beginning, but others stood just outside the ring of light, pretending to be aloof while talking and joking with each another. Shy glances toward the dancers, especially when some particularly marriageable female slowly danced past, gave away more genuine feelings.

Back in the shadows behind them was a cluster of uneasy looking young men, most of whom had short hair—a sure sign that they had been taken away to school. The school boys, Yaot'l thought, always were much shyer than the ones who had not gone away.

Yaot'l's heart gave a jump when she saw Sascho among the onlookers. He and his cousins appeared to be egging one another on to join in. Her mother touched her arm to get her attention, and then directed her gaze toward Jimmy who was already dancing. Yaot'l promptly looked at her feet, now looking very pretty in the moccasins she and her mother had just finished. They were of pale moose hide and decorated with floral shapes in green silk thread and sparkling green beads. Beside her, noting the reaction, her mother sighed.

"Tailbones are a good family and Jimmy will be a good provider."

"I know, Mama."

"Your father will talk to him tonight, I think."

Yaot'l's throat tightened, but she didn't dare to protest. To contest what was, on the face, a sensible plan, at a time when her father was so ill, would be selfish—plain bad, in fact, to not put the good of her family first. Sternly, she stared into the bonfire, hoping to find comfort in the reliably cheerful sight.

Perhaps Jimmy would not want her. He had been spending a lot of time in Sharon Gon's company. It was likely, surely, that he would prefer the handsome widow? She could hope!

On every side, faces were rosy with fire—lines and creases on the elders, smooth shiny cheeks on maidens. On every side there were Tłıchǫ faces. Some families had round faces, other families who had long, gaunt faces, like the Cree or the kwet'ı̀.

The fire was fresh and roaring, so sometimes she was blinded by billowing flames. Then, for a time afterwards, while her eyes adjusted again, everyone was obscured by shadow. It was so familiar, this firelight circle of the people surrounding her. She was not ready for her place in it to change, not yet.

Sascho had joined the dancers, and as he circled past, the fire leapt again. She could not see his eyes, and whether he'd actually looked at her or not, but she felt he'd seen her, somehow. When a line of women succeeded the men, without hesitation or asking her mother, she stepped into the dance. She could see his strong shoulders in a new shirt among those youngsters moving ahead of her. His face in profile was calm and concentrated.

And she too should concentrate. The tribe was together; for so many families to be in one place happened but once a year. In the voice of the drum and the rhythm of feet, in the old song the men sang, Yaot'l lost herself. Even if they were not close to one another, through this chain of life and energy, she believed she could single him out, feel his heart beat. When he made a circle of his dance, in such a way that his eyes could meet hers, she believed that all these imaginings must certainly true.

More and more people joined in. The tempo increased. Overhead, as if by magic, a green aurora appeared, and it too danced, shaking like a flag in a breeze. The dancers, a flock now, flew around one another, negotiating the space between one another, the fire, and the chairs and blankets of the onlookers. This was the purpose of the dance, after all, this melding, and this unity. Yaot'l knew when it happened, the belonging and joy.

Now our minds are one.

Yaot'l felt safe and content, but then, with a thrill, she realized that Sascho had found his way to her side. For an instant, as they danced in tandem, his fingers sought hers and squeezed. Although he did not smile, he sent a long look deep into her eyes. All too soon, the ebb and flow of The People moved them apart.

* * *

Later, as the red and blue bonfire lay dying, beneath the noisome flare of kerosene-and-rag torches, the dance broke up and everyone went to the food tent. People sat on benches or blankets on the ground and talked; small children curled here and there, fast asleep despite the bustle and chatter. There were sugary drinks, bannock, jelly, and cakes. Just outside, over cook-fires with upright metal racks set above them, women turned out fry bread from deep sided black skillets. Nearby, fire-blackened kettles simmered, each filled with hot weak tea, the old folk's favorite.

Everyone else lined for hot fry bread. You could dip it in syrup, or sprinkle on a party-time mixture of sugar and cinnamon. After Yaot'l dipped her bread into the shallow bowl of sugar, she went to stand outside. Here small children played while older boys and girls sidled up to one another, surreptitiously talking and teasing in the shadows. Yaot'l found a place to stand, and wasn't at all surprised to find that somehow or another, Sascho appeared. For a time, they simply stood close, smiling at one another and eating the hot bread and licking sugar from sticky fingers.

"Oh, such good fry bread! Delicious!"

"My Auntie Susie's is a little better, I think," said Sascho.

"Nothing is better than this." Over the hubbub, a boy's prideful voice sounded. "That is straight from my Aunt Joyce's kettle. She always uses lard." The boy spoke out proudly, for such expensive fat was a treat.

They turned to see a thin well-dressed boy in a cowboy shirt, one who had run through the circle of dancers several times.

Sascho smiled, then pitched his voice low and replied, "My Aunt Susie is right over there." He indicated a round-faced matron only a few feet away, with a drooling toddler straddling one hip. His Auntie was enjoying a laugh with a friend. She'd even been dancing earlier, despite the cranky little one she carried.

"And that is my Auntie Joyce." The boy nodded toward a tiny bird-like woman who was busy scooping fry bread from the oil with a basket sieve. The fragrance of the fat, just at the right temperature, and the smell of cooking dough, deliciously filled the air. "She cooks at all our festivals here in Behchok'o."

"I've never been to a festival here," said Sascho.

"Never been to Behchok'o?" To this boy, that appeared to be almost unthinkable.

"I was at Behchok'o once, but I was younger," said Yaot'l. "We didn't come to the tea dance, though."

"Don't your families come to trade?"

"Our Ka'owae comes with my uncles to take care of that."

"So you have never been to school?"

"No." All the time they were giving way to the pressure of eager fry bread seekers, moving well out of earshot of both proud-cook aunties.

"It's the law now, you know, that you go to school. Your family could get in trouble with the RCMP or the Indian agent if they find out."

Sascho said nothing, but he and Yaot'l shared a glance which said 'we better go away from this loud little person.' Anyone could be is listening!

"Have you been to school?" Yaot'l asked. Sascho had begun to glance around at the crowd, senses alert. He was a boy, almost a man, and was suddenly realizing that although this dance was fun, there was also an edge of danger for "wild Indians" like them, if they came to the attention of the authorities.

"No, but I will go soon with Tanis, my little sister. See her?" he pointed proudly to a dainty little girl in a new white deer skin dress."

"She is very pretty—and so is her dress," Yaot'l said. They kept walking, licking the last of Aunt Joyce's excellent fry bread crumbs from their fingers, but the boy seemed to want to go on talking. He followed in that fancy tasseled shirt.

"I'm Kele Stonypoint," he said. "I'm not afraid of going to school."

"I'm Sascho Lynx and I'm not afraid of anything."

"Yes. Who says we are afraid?" Yaot'l, also stung, added her thoughts. "Our parents need us to work with them."

Who does this boy think he is? He is much younger than us, after all.

At the same time, she and Sascho kept moving, looking from side to side as they walked. Where was the family? The Gam`e`t`i visitors weren't immediately obvious in the milling crowd. Yaot'l realized this was the most people she'd ever seen all crowded into one place.

"You don't know how to speak English, do you?"

"I know a little," said Sascho. He knew a few words, about furs and money.

"Well, my family speaks English and they've taught me, so I am ready to go to school. I even know how to read some, so already I'm smarter than you two are."

"That's how it is if you live in Behchok'o, so I guess that's all right for you." With a shrug, she and Sascho turned away from his boasting. On the other side of the bonfire, they'd seen the upright feather that marked the hat of Uncle John, which meant safety among their own kind. Besides, Tłįchǫ got along with all people. They did not go out of their way to argue with strangers.

* * *

"Jimmy thinks that he will be the one to have Sharon, even though he knows that Armand Chocolate is his rival. Armand, I've heard, has already been courting her and bringing gifts to her family."

Lying in the tent between Little Brother and Aunt June, Yaot'l listened while her parents talked outside by the fire. Her father now sometimes spent his nights in the bush, wrapped in furs and blankets. The kwet'įį doctor at the hospital had given him a strong medicine for his pain, but it still kept him awake sometimes. Rene said it made him happy to lie out-of-doors and watch the stars as they, hour by hour, moved over his head.

"Jimmy may be disappointed if he chooses Sharon. He should remember that Yaot'l is a hard worker and never runs after boys."

"I may no longer be here to remind him. What matters is what will happen to Yaot'l if I die soon, as the kwet'įį doctors have said."

"Even if Jimmy prefers Sharon, the Snow Geese look after their own, my husband. Your brother and cousins are at Wha't'i, if my own family is not willing to help us. Our Yaot'l is a hard worker and a fine hunter, too. Some good man will ask for her."

There was a pause, in which Yaot'l imagined her father's gaunt face angling to the sky. He cleared his throat painfully before he spoke. The sound was heart-breaking.

"As you say, she will have a husband, one way or another. Come, wife, let us sleep now. I ache to my bones."

Her parents crawled into the tent. There was shifting and sighing and the give and squeak of spruce boughs as they made themselves comfortable. The smell of fire and summer, of bodies and fresh tree sap, mingled.

Father respects Sascho's Uncle John. All men do, for John is a successful hunter, one who understands the ways of the animals, and who possesses Įk'ǫǫ̀. Perhaps Sascho will ask him to speak to my father, even though we are still so young. After all, Snow Geese and Lynx often marry.

Although her heart soared as she tested this final "what if", Yaot'l, tired at last from the sorrow-to-joy swirl of her imaginings, fell asleep.

* * *

Yaot'l knew she was smiling while she walked into the brush alongside Sascho. It was exciting, going off like this together! They really weren't supposed to, with her parents gone back to the Faraud Hospital, but she had no tasks, and no one, really, was paying attention to either of them.

Little Brother had gone to the trading post with Aunt Kathy, her husband and their kids. Aunt June, her husband and a few friends were finishing up the end of a pot of homebrew, hiding out in the bush nearby like criminals. Actually, they were breaking the law, as it was illegal for Tłı̨chǫ to drink alcohol at this place. Yaot'l knew they wouldn't be paying a bit of attention to anything soon, especially if there was any quantity of brew left within the old enameled pot they'd carried with them. They'd disappeared as soon as a man with a broad-brimmed hat and a pitted face identified by someone as an "Indian Agent" had gone wandering past. He seemed to be on the look out for someone among the visitors' tents.

She and Sascho had been hoping to be alone together and now—they were! Such a good day, too, maybe even a good fishing day, one to be out and away from the bustling settlement, and the watchful eyes of all those Uncles and Aunts and Cousins! Overhead, a slight breeze urged small clouds across a blue sky. Through thickets and around clumps of brush, they walked a path almost as narrow as the trail it once had been, wandering along, occasionally flushing small birds as they approached the creek.

The future, Yaot'l thought, as they paused to study the racing water, could be this good! He and I will fish together, travel together, hunt together—even sleep together in the great open world of the north! A warm glow encircled her heart with the mere imagining of such a wonderful prospect, but then reality intruded.

-If there is a way to evade marriage to Jimmy Tailbone, I must find it!

-Surely my father will not force me?

-Father is worried about what will happen to all of us if he dies.

-If both families agree that I should marry Jimmy, then that will be that...

She'd have to march away into winter with the Tailbones, work with them through the icy trials of the dark time, while her new husband served out the bride price beside one of her Snow Goose Uncles. After all, her father had talked, just the other night, of wanting to see her married before the men went north to trap.

In the traditional way, she would go to the groom's family, work with his mother and aunts, and wait until her husband, his debt paid with labor and furs, returned in the spring. It was also likely, knowing the things her mother had told her, that by that time she would have reached womanhood.

"Our Yaot'l must have a husband by this winter. She is already skilled in woman's ways. You, my wife, have taught her how to work hard." That's what her father had said. It was unlike him to make a decision unless he'd spoken a new idea aloud in the hearing of his family, and before it had been discussed with other members of the band. Ordinarily, new ideas were planted, like seeds with time to grow before the time of decision and action arrived. But his manner this summer, after his weakened retreat from the mine, had changed. Yaot'l understood that death was pressing him, forcing him, a man who usually waited for events to unfold and show him the way, into quick decisions

"You have a long face. Are you worried you will get in trouble later?"

Sascho had stopped and turned to face her. He was still a little round—his Mamàcho always made the tribe's best bannock—but his body had begun squaring as he grew. When the process was over, he would surely own the sturdy muscular form of his legendary Inuit great-grandfather.

"No! I—um—I was thinking—about ...about..."

"Your father and mother have gone to the hospital in Rae, haven't they?"

"Yes. Last night Father was in great pain. Mother was up with him, out in the bush." Her father had not wanted anyone to hear him—a strong man—groan and sigh.

"My Uncle John—" Sascho frowned and hesitated before he went on. "My Uncle says that the land where your father works makes the animals lose their hair. They sicken and die."

"Yes. My father has spoken of seeing sick beaver in the lakes. He says that when he hunts, he hunts far away from those places."

The frown on Sascho's face remained.

"Maybe—your father has not hunted far enough away."

"That is what Mamàcho thinks—and what my mother fears."

Sascho nodded, but he didn't want to think too deeply about what they'd just said to one another. People died, yes, Grandmother Chocolate, Little Joe—a few years ago in the rushing water—and, of course, winter born babies.

Nevertheless, with her beside him, it was hard to dwell on the sorrows of life.

The sky overhead is blue, and I am with this strong clever girl, the one I want to see beside my camp fire forever.

The night of the dance he'd watched her, moving, a young lithe mirror of others, a perfect

90

part of the larger kinship they shared. There was no immodest putting herself forward, and yet how she'd shone, even among all those others...

"Do you—uh—want to...?" He began to move the fish spear restlessly about hand to hand.

"Yes. Let's see what's in the water." She wanted no more sorrowful conversation either.

Better to hunt the fish skipping in and out of the creek beneath a sunny sky! To be where the water sang, to be on Tłįchǫ dèè, with Sascho— well, nothing was better.

"It will be good to have fish when we return, especially because my mother will forgive almost anything for a few nice Inconnu."

"And mine, too, so let's follow the water up this way to a good spot I've found."

The stream still ran fresh, sending many bright fingers racing among gray boulders. Toward the middle, the water was deep and dark blue, capped in places with hissing froth.

Carefully, they began to make their way rock by rock, out from the bank. They didn't want to get too close and risk a fall into the main channel; it was still cold and wild and would drown you for sure. The side branches held the best spots to fish, for there would be shallows where they could stand and spear any stray Inconnu now making their autumn migration. These meaty white fish were prized.

For a time their shared love of the chase blotted out anything else. There was warm sun on their skin and glare bouncing off the rocks and the water. There was enough wind to move the bugs from the heights, but not enough to discourage them from hovering over the water and attracting the fish. Rough liquid music sounded on every side. Moving in and out of the shallows, they successfully speared several Inconnu.

When there was sufficient catch for the family fire, Yaot'l returned to the bank, laid down her spear and sat next to it. It was hot again today. Even the rock upon which she sat was warm enough to make her glad for this afternoon's stiffening breeze.

She removed the green scarf around her neck, shook it out and then refolded it before covering her head. So much sun had made her, suddenly, a little dizzy.

She had finally spoken aloud her fears, shared them with someone else, someone who understood. Of course, he was a boy, but he was also THE boy, the one she wanted for all time.

She watched as he continued to fish, taking up a station between another set of rocks. Spear in hand, his dark eyes studied the moving water. High cheek bones, slanted jet black eyes, his dark hair blowing, he made a handsome picture. There was no doubting his intensity, but he was no longer catching any fish. It made her smile to watch him persist, when it was increasingly clear the run they'd been so lucky to intercept was over. Perhaps he wanted to prove, one last time, his prowess.

Her thoughts were interrupted by the flourish of more silver coming up the creek. At the same instant, Sascho darted forward. She saw the metal tip dart into the water and return, holding a slippery flapping Inconnu of perfect size.

Chapter Five

They walked back to łk'àdèè k'è, proudly holding their string of fine fish, only to discover an unusual silence. Yaot'l wondered what made the place so strange.

An answer did not take long in coming. There were no children, romping with their dogs—no little ones—no 'tweens like themselves—-not anywhere! There were only a few old women and men, slowly going about the usual chores of food or hide preparation. A woman oddly indoors on this fine afternoon, peered out her cabin window and then, when she saw them, quickly turned away. In the distance, some very old men with battered hats sat under a tree where they played cards.

"What's wrong?"

They felt as if they'd come to a different campground. When they'd left, just a few hours ago, it had been bustling with autumn visitors. People were meeting and greeting relatives and some late arrivals were still pitching tents in open spaces. The feeling of uneasiness grew as they hurried along toward their camping area.

Ordinarily, they'd take the shortest way. That meant passing the church, crossing the road and then tramping down toward the widening arm of the river. All at once that did not seem such a good idea.

Sascho put a restraining hand on her arm and they turned as one to see who was running after them. Here came a young pretty Métis woman, apparently the one from the cabin they'd just passed. As soon as they'd seen her, she stopped and began to beckon, urgently signing that they should follow her.

"Come! Follow! The truck is right over there!"

Catching fear was easy. They followed, breaking into a trot. . A man now stood in the open door and held it wide. When they entered, though, they could see no welcome in his eyes.

They startled as the door closed. Breathless, holding the dripping fish and gear, they looked around at these strangers and the inside of the cabin. It was one room with a single window. A bed on one side was over-hung by a baby in a hammock. An oil-can stove occupied the other.

"Didn't you hear the warning?" The woman spoke. Her husband crossed her arms and regarded them steadily. At last he said:

"You shouldn't have brought them in, Donna, and you know it. Don't we have enough trouble already?"

These strangers were kin of a kind, part Dene, perhaps, and they were also married people who would have assumed labor on behalf of their kin group. Younger people now owed them a good measure of respect, so Sascho did not like to speak first.

"We—we do not understand what is happening."

"The call—the goose call! All the others heard it and are gone into the bush." The man was impatient.

"Can't you see? They are visitors; they didn't know."

"Everyone knows the Métis agents come at this time of year, even visitors." He glowered at Sascho. "Didn't your family explain it?"

"We—we've not been here for a long time," Yaot'l said.

"Métis agents?" Sascho spoke. "Like the man with the scarred face we saw this morning?"

"Yes. They're here to take our children to school. Mountie and the priest both say that's the law—all our children must go. People who hide their children are punished. They lose their government money."

He turned an angry face toward his wife and added, "I'm leaving. If those kids bring the Mountie here, expect trouble."

"Don't go my husband." The woman caught at his checked shirt, but he pulled his arm away. The door swung and he passed through, never looking back. Sascho noted how carefully he closed it. Obviously, he didn't want neighbors to notice his departure.

Now there were tears in the woman's eyes. She covered her mouth with her hand.

"We—are sorry to bring trouble! We will go away."

"You can't." She returned to peer through the window. "There's an agent and a big Mountie too."

Yaot'l leaned forward again, in order to see. She scanned what she could see of the street, and sure enough, there in the distance, by the idling truck, was a red uniformed man. He appeared to be speaking to someone through the vehicle's window.

After a few moments, the woman touched Yaot'l's hand, gazing at her with wonder.

"Haven't you two ever been to school, grown as you are?"

Sascho shook his head. "Our parents needed us."

"Yes, we must go find our family at once. They will know what to do."

They edged toward the door again, but the woman stood in the way, extending her arms.

"No! You can't! It's not safe. Sit and wait."

"We—we have made your husband angry," Yaot'l replied. "We should leave."

"He won't return until he's sure the Mountie has gone." Her expression signaled anxiety about the mood of the departed husband. For some reason, though, she'd chosen to risk his displeasure and bring them inside.

"My husband has come from working on the road. It is difficult for him to be away."

97

Sascho had heard stories of the misunderstandings that arose between his people and the kwet'įį. These tales were told in the evenings around the fire. The elders often had ideas about how to resolve such disputes, especially if they might resume next summer.

Just as Yaot'l's father did, more and more men went to work in the mines or on the roads or in timber for half the year. They only hunted now during winter. It was a change in how the people lived, a change Uncle John sometimes illustrated with stories of the old days, when they'd been free of interference and had simply followed the footsteps of Yamǫǫ̀zha on his yearly travels throughout Tłįchǫ dèè.

In the end, they accepted her invitation and sat cross-legged on her floor—she gave them sweet tea and bannock—and they offered her the Inconnu. She refused those, saying they should take those to their own families. She did take the dripping string outside and hang it up on a drying rack right behind the house. Up high, they would be out of any roaming dog's ambitious reach.

"Wait a little more. Then it will be a good time to run back to your folks." She went on to warn that the agents and the Mountie would next scour the campsites of the visitors.

Yaot'l spied toys piled in corner basket and asked about her children. Donna said they were hid with older cousins, all of whom had run off into the bush at the first alarm.

"Still, if we are threatened with losing our government script by that Indian Agent, we will send them. They are so young! One is five and the other is seven. Sometimes I think to leave this house and runaway into the bush beside them. I remember that school."

"Was it very bad?" Yaot'l's heart raced waiting for the answer. The response left her even more frightened than before.

"I was seven. It was hard to be away from my family in a place where they do not like Indians."

Sascho felt he should acknowledge only with nod, but instead he asked another question:

"Did—did you learn English?" Kele's words still rankled.

"Yes, at Fort Providence, where you will be sent if they catch you." Above her gray eyes, Donna's smooth brow furrowed. Her memories were not good. "But mostly what they teach is prayers and songs and proper ways to speak to their god. Now we all follow Him, for He is very strong. We shall never die but instead go to live in his big house in the sky."

Her eyes turned toward a wooden cross hung upon the wall, with the carving of the suffering man. The sight of his torment did nothing to reassure Yaot'l.

"Since we live here, so close to the church, we must follow their ways. If you attend their ceremonies, the priest and their women will sometimes help with food if winter is hard and the men are away for too long and supplies run out." She sighed and then turned her eyes back to that lone window.

"At that school I was frightened without my family, and kwet'įį ways are not like ours. I swore I would never let the school take away my children ...but, my new husband...well, this is his house and he says school is the law."

Donna's voice trailed away. Then, as Yaot'l watched, she straightened and squared her shoulders, a woman resigned to all hardships, both the past and those to come.

* * *

The street stayed quiet as the neighborhood made supper. When she peeped out the window, Yaot'l saw men here and there, seated outside their cabins checking over fishnets. Women prepared food. The only children present were babies, the newest walkers, and infants back-packed inside shawls.

It seemed a good time to go. After studying the street, Donna agreed. Together, she and Sascho gathered up their gear. The Inconnu were not mentioned, so they remained behind, hanging where they had been placed.

They had planned to go back the way they'd come in, and then walk a long arc through the brush outside the town. Perhaps if they did this, it would bring them, unnoticed, to the Lynx campsite by the water.

After skirting the last cabin, they entered an area they'd seen before, a place where old birch bark canoes, now rotting down to the frame, had been discarded. There was an open pit too, where junk was eventually buried—broken household items like furniture and dishes as well as bits of engines, metal, sawdust, and, naturally, rotting food stuff.

It seemed a place more likely to encounter an old half-blind bear than a Mountie, but there he was, a big man, who knew all the good hunting spots for runaways. Shoulders bright beneath that red coat, he stepped onto the path. Gloved hands rushed at them.

"Run!"

Yaot'l took off as fast as she could. She dropped her fish spear; it was far too cumbersome. Even worse, she did not know where she was running to, not exactly—away, she hoped— farther elsewhere into the bush.

She did not get very far, for almost immediately she was grabbed by the Métis Agent, the one with the scarred face. Once he had caught her arm, she couldn't shake him off. Instead, he seized both her wrists and twisted them behind her. It was the same man they'd noticed when they'd left the family shelter earlier this morning.

Before he started to push her ahead of him, Yaot'l had a close up look at his hollow lean face. It crossed her mind to plead with the man to let her go, but she could see from his righteous expression that he would never do that. Her heart sank into a fearful——unimaginable— future.

The Métis shouted something cheerful while he pushed her along, although no one, at first, was visible. As they rounded a large shaggy spruce, she saw that the Mountie walked ahead. He was dragging a tall Tłįchǫ boy.

Sascho!

* * *

"Here's two more for Father McCarthy. He'll be pleased with the numbers this year."

"He should be! They pay by the head, don't they?

* * *

They were ordered into the back of that stinking noisy truck. Here they joined a huddled crowd of other children, most looking frightened. Outside a big white Indian agent laughed and said something scornful as they climbed up. Without ceremony, a tarp covering their view was dropped and the truck lurched away, in a cloud of exhaust. They were jolted along, soon choking from the heat, dust and smoke. The children crowded toward the back of the cab, the only place where any light came through and the best place to escape the fumes.

Sascho held Yaot'l's hand and they hunkered down together as well as they could, on the metal floor. Pressed around them were smaller children, all with teary faces. Yaot'l gently touched the shoulder of the small girl who was packed against her. "You're Kele's little sister, aren't you?" The round sweet face turned anxiously toward hers. "Yes," she said. "The priest said he'd take us in his car and Kele climbed right in. He wasn't afraid, but I was. I tried to run away from them and go home, but that mean man caught me and put me in here."

They bumped up and down, grinding in and out of holes in the dirt road. Dust and stink blew in whenever the tarp flapped, as well as a tantalizing breath of fresh air. The engine made it mostly too loud to talk, but a few friends managed to find one other. Family groups settled, the older children holding little brothers and sisters in their arms.

As the truck plowed on and on without stopping, there were a few who had to relieve themselves. This, with some difficulty, they managed scooting to the open back of the truck. The boys could stand, brace themselves with one hand on the wall; some of what they let go went out onto the road, some inevitably onto the tarp. The girls had to squat as close to the back as they dared while the truck climbed a grade and hope it would spill out. Everyone was grateful for the darkness which hid their shame.

* * *

The truck finally stopped with a lurch and a loud grinding of gears. Outside, they heard babble, but Sascho had already made up his mind about what to do. He pushed the tarp aside and jumped out.

The daylight was strong, nearly blinding. There was not a tree in sight. He stood on what at first appeared to be rutted plain of dust. That alone might have stunned him, but the view on every side was alarming. They were in a bigger town, next to a ramshackle clapboard building. A pump and a horse trough stood nearby, things he recognized from Fort Rae. However, it was the people on every side—all kwet'ı̨ı̀, wearing their strange garb, the women's heads and the men's too, covered with hats, like buckets on their heads. A white boy, perhaps his own age, stared back at him, drop-jawed. The kwet'ı̨ı̀ mother, noticing, roughly grabbed his hand and pulled him away, looking over her shoulder with distaste.

A big rough hand landed on Sascho's shoulder.

"Where you think you're goin'?" Pierre, the Métis agent, his brown face impassive, spoke in Sascho's language.

"We need water. And, uh, we need …"

"Need water and to make water, huh?"

Sascho nodded. *This is a terrible dream...*

"Stay here. Tell 'em not to drink that stuff in the trough. I'll get something better." Pierre removed a pail which had been banging loudly against the side of the truck.

Then a big kwet'ı̨ı̀ climbed down out of the front cab and came striding up. He spoke in a rough tone. The Métis shrugged and said a few words. Then, bucket in hand, he went to the back of the truck and pulled the tarp back, revealing the children, huddled together inside. Fluid leaked at the back of the bed. The white man spoke angrily and spit dismissively onto the ground. His spit was all brown, as if he was rotten inside.

"What a stinkin' load of pups!"

Sascho understood, for the insult was delivered in his own language, a feat the man had probably rehearsed many times.

If he wants to scare me, Sascho thought, gazing at his burly captor, he's doing a pretty good job."

The Métis led them to a little shack which stank mightily. Inside was a hole in the ground with boards laid down for them to squat over. It took a while, the children going in a few at a time. Everyone complained of feeling dizzy and their heads ached. Mouths were dry. Fortunately, a woman came out lugging a brimming pail of water and a dipper. It was hard to wait, but Sascho made sure the littlest ones drank first.

"Stay by this tree and don't go anywhere." The Métis pointed to a lone, half dead spruce that stood behind the building. Soon they were all crowded underneath, squatting down among the fallen needles in what shade there was. Behind the place, keeping them company, was a leaking pile of manured straw. Flies buzzed, and some sad looking cattle stood in a muck-filled pen.

Yaot'l, at last not focused on her need to relieve herself, began to look around. So many people! No trees, just the wooden houses, the white people. The few who took notice of them quickly looked away, as if willing them invisible.

Some ragged boys appeared. First they shouted and made faces at them by pushing fingers into the skin beside their eyes and pulling. Next stuck out their tongues and whooped. When no one responded, they began to throw stones. Yaot'l wrapped her arms protectively around the nearest little one. With one hand, Sascho deflected a missile that had come in too close.

Yaot'l bent and picked up a rock. She had just winged one of their tormentors when Pierre came around. Seeing what was going on, he roared and ran at the white boys, as if he intended mayhem. Hollering, they ran away.

"Cowards." Sascho eyed their backs with scorn.

"You don't mess with them, though," said Pierre. "It'll just make more trouble if you do."

He held a sack in his hand, the sort white storekeeper's used, a thin brown wrapping material stained with grease.

"Here's something to eat."

It had been a long time in the truck, and although everyone was still queasy, they could also feel the pangs of hunger. It had been a long time since the bowl of yellow gruel they'd been offered this morning.

Sascho and Yaot'l moved the younger ones forward to receive what food there was. It proved to be broken bits of hard bannock which must have been several days old, but it was better than nothing.

Crouching as soon as they received a piece, the children ate.

"Where are we?" Sascho asked Pierre when they'd all settled down to work their jaws upon the hard bread.

"A diggin'. Stuff in the ground kwet'įį wants."

"So many!"

Sascho had never seen, in all his years, so many kwet'įį! It was beyond dismaying—it was frightening. As if all the shadowy monsters he'd heard about in so many night-time stories round the fire had suddenly walked out into the daylight and said hello. He now understood why the older head men, the Ka'owae, those who went into the towns to trade on behalf of the band, were looked up to for their strength of will, their knowledge, and courage.

"Yeah. They just keep comin' and comin' up from the south and over from the east," Pierre? said. "That's why you have to go to school. You must learn to be like them, to think like them, talk like them, do what they say, 'cause pretty soon there won't be no other way for you to live. If there's trouble anywhere, if your skin is red, you're the one they will blame it on."

"Did you go to a school?" Yaot'l dared a question.

"I did." Pierre's face drew down. "It's tough. I won't lie. Real tough. It's lonely without your family. There'll be bigger kids who will push you around and some of them Chekaa—teachers—are ...real mean." He paused for a moment, and then looked away as if it was too much for him to continue to meet their eyes.

Yaot'l felt a chill at his evasion.

So much this man doesn't say!

"It's all that's left for us Indians. We have to do what they say if you want to get on." Reflexively, he touched the big wooden cross he wore around his neck. "You must be a Christian and get saved, too, follow their ceremonies, learn their chants. That helps you get along."

Yaot'l and Sascho shared a fearful look. Hadn't they just—a few weeks ago—spoken of Yvonne and Andre? No one knew what had happened to Yvonne or when—or even if—she had died, but they all knew how Andre had returned to his family, so fatally changed.

* * *

They were at last in Yellowknife, driving through a jumble of buildings and people. Sascho was tall enough to peer through a hole in the tarp.

"There are lots of trucks and cars and wagons with horses and many people."

108

When they came to a halt at last, they could hear, over the roaring engine, the shrill screech of shore birds. This time, when they climbed out of the back, they found themselves standing in a chilly breeze, with the breath-taking sight of a wide blue lake spread before them under the sun. In the distance, kwet'įì boats, ones with chimneys on their decks, trailing smoke, their insides roaring, plowed through the harbor.

* * *

Sometimes Yaot'l could smell the breeze and the watery smell, but in her mind, the aroma that overpowered every other scent was the smell of fuel. It was far worse than the gasoline that powered the familiar putt-putts.

"What is this big water?" She asked, shading her eyes with her hand as she surveyed the gray sea.

"This is Tındeè. Pierre said we will travel on a boat to Dehcho, which the kwet'įì call Fort Providence."

"We will float on that water?" Yaot'l shivered. Tındeè, the big lake, was well known to be a dangerous place, not only for its sudden storms, but because their ancient enemies, the Yellowknives, lived beside it.

"Yes. You will go in a boat." Pierre pointed. "On that one tied up right over there."

One of the kids who had been to school before, hooted and then cried out: "Wait till you hear the noise it can make!"

* * *

They were marched in two by two, now following a priest in a black robe. The children who had been to school before seemed happy to see him. He'd given them sweets from a bag, smiling and greeting them, tousling ~~the~~ one boy's hair. He was the one who'd taken Kele, and, it seemed, some other returning students as well to ride with him. Now, he took Tanis ceremoniously by the hands and spoke softly to her, all the time shaking his head. Yaot'l could not understand his words, but he seemed to be telling her how foolish she'd been to run away. Tanis hung her head, and he stroked her thin back. He seemed tremendously pleased with Kele. From a pocket, he kept producing sweets which were handed to every kid who came up to greet him.

Pierre brought up the rear, counting heads over and over again. Yaot'l wanted, more than anything, to turn and run from that great lake spreading so endlessly before her. She had never seen so much water. Besides, she had been taught that some big lakes required an offering before you crossed.

When she, with increasing alarm, had whispered it to Sascho, Pierre overheard.

"Kwet'ıì make no offerings to spirits of land or water. Their holy men say they are false gods, not to be honored. You must instead pray to their Jesus." The man rubbed ragged fingers

110

nervously back forth against his cross. "You must not think of those evil spirits anymore."

When they stared at him, faces blank, he said, "Here, I will show you the right way to say a prayer. These children here know what to do." Pierre called to a group of English speakers. At once they stopped talking among themselves and came to obediently make a circle around him.

Next, they all closed their eyes, bowed their heads, and templed, resting their index fingers against their noses.

"Do as they do." Pierre directed. He closed his eyes and put his hands together exactly as the children had. Next, he solemnly intoned a great many unknown words.

Yaot'l did not close her eyes. Foreign phrases spoken to a power she did not know could not make her feel any safer.

Under her feet, the boat gently swayed. From every side came a relentless babble in another tongue, fractured by the crashes and bangs of loading. Ordinarily, in a canoe, she glided softly, feeling kinship with the spirit of the waters. Here there was nothing but noise and confusion.

When Sascho took her hand and guided her to a spot against a stack of canvas covered trunks, she was grateful. Here, they sat down together, backs against the boxes. Leaning close, so as not to be overheard, he whispered, "I will say a prayer Uncle John taught me, one which he says to Wekweti. That is not such a big lake as this, but perhaps if we say 'Tɪndeè' instead, this water will hear and understand."

Resting hand in hand, hidden behind the boxes, Sascho asked the big water to allow them to travel in safety. Yaot'l followed, repeating after him. At once, she felt a little better about the journey they were about to undertake.

She'd just exhaled a sigh of relief, when the screech of the whistle slammed against her eardrums. The duration, the volume, too, was deafening. On the other side of the boxes, they could hear kids whooping—some with delight at the noise, while others, the little ones who were as fresh from the bush as they were, screamed.

"Ah, there you are!" Pierre's narrow head poked around the canvas. "You two come on out and stand where I can see you. Boys and girls are not supposed to be alone together, especially if no one else is watching. Good thing Brother Corbeau didn't find you. He'd thrash both of you."

He stood and waited to be sure they'd obey, so they got up and reluctantly joined the others. Little boys, Kele among them, hung on the rail, watching in wonder as the water sped past. The ones who'd been at school before had gathered into small whispering groups.

The heat today would have been terrific under the late summer sun, but out on the water the wind blew wildly. Sometimes that was pleasant, but all too often greasy smoke blew down upon them on them from a forward stack.

Chapter Six

Fort Providence, Sacred Heart Residential School

The school was a large building, two stories made of flat-cut boards. It was like others she'd seen on the way here, only this was the biggest. It was a ramshackle, lonely place, with a peeling coat of whitewash set high on a treeless shore, fortified by piles of rocks. The children were herded up the bank from a low dock and entered a fenced in area where neat rows of plants were being tended by head-down gray-clad children. Some were hoeing, others were on their knees weeding.

They grew a few things at Gam`e`t'i` every summer, but there was so much food in the bush that the labor involved to grow these new, tender plants seemed a waste of time. In Behchok'o, at her Aunt's house, Yaot'l had seen the tools they used, as well as some of these same foods. She recognized the plants at the school – beans spiraling up poles.

A stiff breeze off the river sent a flag in the yard galloping and popping. The design upon it was familiar now, the kwet'įį saying they owned this place.

"Like every land they set their eyes on…" Mamàcho Josette's voice, a sad memory, sounded in her head.

The place felt lifeless, not at all like the bustle which surrounded the trading post—or an autumn łìk'àdèè k'è. Even the shed and a small barn behind appeared full of shadows. Somewhere an unseen animal let out a *bawaaa*, but no answer came. It was a lonely sound, as if there were no others of its kind. The new arrivals stared at one other in dismay.

"Why dwell in such a windy place?" Sascho whispered. Yaot'l's next thought, besides the coldness of the scene, was of what winter would be like here.

So cold, between the wide lake and big river, this place of no trees! That was certain.

All the children they saw at the school were dressed alike, in gray kwet'įį clothes. They did not speak a word to the newcomers, just watched in silence as they were led by an angular Métis woman who guided the newcomers into a hallway. The gloom made it, at first, difficult to see, especially when someone closed the door behind them, shutting out the sunlight.

When it happened, the ones just returned lowered their eyes, like sad dogs.

They know what comes next.

Fear rose into Yaot'l's throat as she saw those faces and heard the door, with a sullen thud, close.

Women in gray robes and tall white headdresses separated those who had been to school before from those who had not. Sascho and Yaot'l, still holding hands, were sent, along with the other newcomers, farther along the hall. As she walked, Yaot'l had momentary flash of wonder at the size of the building.

How big the inside, and so many doors!

The next room they entered had lines of long slanted tables, what they would learn were 'desks'. Each table had an equally long bench set behind. Yaot'l had seen something like this the one and only time she'd been inside the trading post. She remembered standing and watching while a kwet'įį man with a great bushy beard had made a series of black marks on a 'paper.' At that time, his long bushy beard had been the object of her interest, because her own people didn't grow much facial hair.

Black boards covered with white symbols overlaid two walls. These were also like what she'd seen at the trading post. Here, however, two women in gray robes and that strange headgear stood and regarded them. Their long narrow faces expressed little beyond weariness.

Two stern men in black robes took the boys by the shoulders and directed them to the other side of the room. Yaot'l felt Sascho squeeze her fingers before he let go. It was a reassurance, that warm hand, of the love he felt for her, even as he left her side. Neither would have accepted this parting so easily if they'd known how things would be, how boys and girls were not permitted to speak to one another. The two kwet'įį men shared a look, and Yaot'l had the feeling that they were relieved because Sascho, big as he was, had been willing to obey.

This, Yaot'l would know later, was the first sorting. Next, they would be sorted by age. The smallest newcomers were dazed by the loss of their siblings. They cried and clung to their older brothers and sisters, but to no avail. They'd never been away from family and friends, but here they were being separated by strangers, their brown fingers were pried apart, if necessary. It was clear that the children's feelings did not much matter to the Chekaa, although there was one gray nun who picked up one of the very smallest girls—now bawling at the top of her lungs—and attempted to give her some comfort even while she was being carried away.

Tanis, now distressed by the loss of her brother, had found her way again to Yaot'l's side. Yaot'l quickly put an arm around her, but this did not last long. Tanis's dark eyes welled as she looked up. On the boat, she and her brother had stayed together—Tanis like Kele's pale shadow. They'd spoken English with some other kids from Behchok'o who'd been to school before. Now, with her brother gone, she'd attached herself to the nearest person who'd been kind.

As they stood there, waiting for whatever would come next, Yaot'l noticed onlookers, school girls peering through the open door. All of them wore gray smocks covered by aprons. On their feet were battered leather shoes. They seemed amused by the spectacle of the anxious new comers. One was a Métis girl, her face puffy and pale.

"Hey, you!"

This apparently was the leader. Her rude salute was addressed to Yaot'l in a tongue that, despite the odd accent, she could understand.

"You are the tallest, so I'm talking to you. If you do what Sister Louise says and help keep the others in line, it will be easier for you. It's time for you new ones to change clothes—into nice, clean kwet'įį clothes, and get rid of that dirty, stinking hide."

"Deerskin smells good."

As Yaot'l spoke, she remembered the punky smoke from the spruce that she had used to cure a skin. The dress she wore was a memory of home—in fact, she had helped her mother make it. Earlier on that same day she had also helped to butcher the fine doe from whose skin it was fashioned.

"All the Sisters say those clothes stink. I thought like you when I first came here, but I learned to think different, and you will too."

"She's wrong—and so are you—whoever you are." Yaot'l hoped to sound brave, but she heard her voice quiver.

"I'm Charlotte. I'm the head girl and you better pay attention to me."

"I am Yaot'l."

"No, you're nobody." Charlotte took a step forward. "You don't have a kwet'ı̨ı̨ name."

Yaot'l felt dislike rise in her throat, but before she could frame a retort, the smug girl spoke again.

"I've been here for nine whole years now, so I'm the one who will say what you do. The Chekaa teach us their language and their ways so we can be like them. You are lucky to be here, so you'd better shut your mouth and do what I say, you dirty wild thing."

Dirty? Wild?

Yaot'l stared at this person in her starched kwet'ı̨ı̨ dress.

How free she is with insults!

Unlike the scorn from the whites she'd experienced on the boat, this girl spoke in her own language.

At Gam`e`t`i, everyone would look down on you, Charlotte. I can see by your pale face you are a Métis and one who doesn't know how to spear a fish or tan a hide.

Still, she spoke words Yaot'l could understand, so she held her temper and decided to learn whatever she could about what was to happen.

"Nine years?" Yaot'l's heart sank even further as she repeated the words. "You have never been home to see your family?"

She remembered what Pierre had said about summers.

He said we could go home. Had that been a lie? An entire winter here will be bad enough— but to never see mother or her brothers or cousins—for years?

Across the room, one of those gray women shouted. For emphasis, she struck a long flat stick against her palm. Charlotte startled and turned. The scolding sounds—whatever they meant—carried a distinct threat. The woman's face, pinched between the two stiff white wings of her bonnet, was angry. Some of the kids, the ones who understood her, hung their heads and studied the floor.

Charlotte only waited until the grey-robe began to speak to one of her kind.

"Just listen and do what I say. If you disobey, you will only get the strap, and that makes things worse for everyone else who is new."

The cloth of Charlotte's dress was smooth, creased, with not a single soft fold anywhere, just like the robes of the kwet'įį holy women. Although it was obvious she was afraid of those gray women, she was not at all afraid of Yaot'l because she began to taunt again.

"You are the dirtiest of all of them."

Her two friends traded glances and smirked. Although Yaot'l could see that they had played this game before, she made a calm reply.

"There was no place to wash on the journey."

"Maybe all that Indian dirt doesn't come off." Charlotte appeared to relish the words, rolling them across her tongue. She turned for approval to her friends, who grinned and nodded. It was all done as quietly as possible, while the teachers or whatever they were talked among themselves.

Yaot'l narrowed her eyes. "You're Indian too."

"Only part! Me and my friends are civilized now, so if you don't do what I say, I'll get Sister Louise to beat you—and I can do it."

She smiled, clearly daring Yaot'l to challenge her again.

Behind the mean girls, Yaot'l saw that a few others had gathered to watch, hanging back in the shadows. They did not mirror the Charlotte's contempt. Instead, one with beautiful long black eyes signaled caution with an elaborate gesture, by covering her mouth and shaking her head.

Yaot'l took the hint. She lowered her eyes and said no more.

The gray woman who had been so cross earlier reappeared. That flat wooden stick was still gripped tightly in her hand. Again, she shouted something. Yaot'l could not understand the words, but she caught the gist because her antagonists, grins dispatched, hastily slipped away.

* * *

"Charlotte! I expect better of you and your friends here! Doris! Marie! All of you!" The woman advanced, stick in hand. "Get out of here, all of you. I know every one of you has work— and you'd better hurry and get about it."

The flat stick slapped once more against the open palm. At this, everyone fled and the open door was firmly closed behind them.

* * *

Next, they began to undress the little ones. Any clothing from home was tossed onto a pile. Tanis shivered as she removed her dress and sadly stepped out of the beaded, fringed moccasins she'd worn. Yaot'l's deer skin dress was old, but she still felt sad to relinquish it.

Any clothes that were Indian made was gathered and placed in a box. The kwet'ı̨ı̨ clothing in which some of the children had worn on the journey—print dresses and pants—were also taken. Marks were made at the neck holes and then, these too were put away into a separate container.

The younger children were placed on stools and then the tears began in earnest. One of those women, gleaming silver scissors in hand, cut off their hair. Child after child, without the least ceremony, had their braids shorn away. The first little ones crouched down, shrinking their skinny necks into their shoulders, like poor little turtles about to be beheaded. Their round cheeks trickled with tears when those long plaits hit the floor, creating an ever-growing heap of black. Some children, those with coarse hair, found that the short cut sent it sticking out on all sides, like the feathers of an outraged bird.

Yaotl watched with alarm. She was proud of her long thick braids, proud of the way, when she combed them out every the morning, her locks turned smooth beneath her practiced hands. "Why are they cutting our hair? Why?"

Charlotte had returned again, now with a pan and broom. Keeping her eyes low, as if strictly set upon her task, she answered softly, just loud enough so Yaot'l could hear.

"Because you are dirty, lousy Indians, that's why."

The gray woman turned. It seemed she'd over heard. Once more she spoke angrily to Charlotte. A torrent of the new language followed. Charlotte, at last appearing alarmed, got up then went to collect a basket, one into which she piled the hair.

While her tormentor was busy, Yaot'l, hoping no one would notice, quickly slipped the knife Charlie had given her into the pocket of the apron she held.

While this went on, the smallest children were redressed in kwet'įį clothing, which came in several pieces. First was something like men's pants and an undershirt. Then, over that, went a blousy dress covered by an apron. The material was made of some rough cloth, which was even scratchier than the under things.

The gray woman with the scissors now beckoned to Tanis, who'd been staying close to Yaot'l . Head down, Tanis stepped forward. Yaot'l signed "no," but Tanis only shook her head before fearfully approaching. She looked like a beaten dog creeping to the feet of a cruel master. Roughly, the gray woman seized her by her skinny shoulders and spun her around. Brandishing those gleaming scissors, she grabbed one of Tanis's thick plaits.

Tanis began to cry as soon as the scissors started to chop their way through. The woman paused as the girl's shoulders heaved, just for a moment, but only to slap her and admonish. Then she grabbed the other braid and returned to sawing away. Tanis stood, still as a stone. Her whole body quivered. She looked astonished and terrified, as if she'd never in her life been struck.

Yaot'l's heart swelled with anger and dismay, and the last of the new girls grouped and shrank behind her. She knew that as the oldest new comer here, she was the one the others looked to for guidance. She had no idea how to help them—or herself. She felt like a stick, swept and tumbled inside a spring torrent.

The woman finished her rough treatment by tossing some white powder all over their heads.

The flying cloud made Tanis to choke. When that was finished, she was shoved aside and the woman pointed to Yaot'l . From where she stood against the doorsill, Charlotte nodded giving her the look that said as clear as anything: *Your turn!*

When Yaot'l did not move, the woman angrily gestured. Yaot'l simply fixed her with a stare, but she did not budge an inch. Beneath the new dress, she still wore her moccasins, ones she'd worked herself, these decorated with green beaded porcupine quills. She'd worn them on that fatal day so that Sascho could see the fine handwork of which she was capable. Now, here, where everything was so frightening, she'd been hoping that, somehow, she could keep them.

The gray woman called out again, cawing like a crow. When Yaot'l did not obey, she gestured ever more widely, her mouth a grim line. Though the furious look was frightening, Yaot'l did not move. Her own hair was beautiful, thick and long, black as a raven's. She understood that she would be punished, just as warned, but she remembered her name—'warrior'—and what proud meaning it held.

Behind her came the sound of hasty footsteps. When she turned, she saw two more gray women approaching. The skin of one was freckled with orange and her eyes were exceedingly pale, like glass panes. She was big, too, and she shoved aside those close to Yaot'l and then grabbed her arm. Fingers of steel punched into her flesh from the other side too, and she was dragged to the stool.

She couldn't move her arms, but she could still use her legs. Aiming a strong kick at the spotted woman's skirts, she was pleased to feel her foot connect. A loud cry and the grip on her arm lessened. Yaot'l, using all her strength, jerked that arm free. She twisted and turned wildly, trying to get loose; girls on every side scattered. There were screams and shouts. Yaot'l grabbed the stool and swung it around. After she hit one of the gray women, hard, in the shoulder, she discovered she'd cleared a space all around.

This moment of triumph was short lived, however, because a big fat kwet'įį, this one dressed in a long black dress like a woman, entered the room. All the gray women gathered around him, gabbling and gesticulating. He must, Yaot'l thought, be the big boss here—— dressed like that fellow whose church she'd attended so long ago at Behchok'o. He didn't look happy. She knew there would be severe consequences for what she'd done—still, hitting those bullying women had brought her a surge of satisfaction—even though it was clear her resistance would only bring on more terrors.

The fat priest seized Yaot'l and threw her against a desk where she was pinned, slapped, and beaten, first with hands and then with a strap till the pain was too great not to cry out. Next, still held by the arms, her hair was roughly cut away. Lastly, they threw white powder all over her head. It fell in a choking cloud, stinging her eyes and leaving a bitter taste on her lips.

Afterward, she was dragged up two flights of stairs, and thrown into a big room. The door slammed and locked behind her. She had done her best not to cry while they beat her, but now, finally alone, she could let go. Tears poured down her cheeks, streaking the white powder, while she, crumpled in that corner, felt her shoulders shake with rage and anguish. On the way up the stairs, she had bitten one of the gray women in the arm, as hard as she could, and the sour taste of that cold white flesh and the long shriek she'd elicited, was another memory she would hold onto with all her might, despite the second rain of blows with that leather strap which had come as soon as they'd reached the landing.

At last she found the will to look around. Light came through the cracks here and there. At either end of the building there was a pair of dusty windows. On every side the room was full of trunks and boxes and lines of hanging clothing. Slowly, hurting, she got to her feet and hobbled to peer out. She put her hand into her apron pocket, but somewhere, perhaps on the stairs, her knife had been lost. Gone! Now not only her hair, her deer skin dress, but the beautiful knife with the carved bone handle her brother had made. All she had left of home were those pretty moccasins…

The glass was dusty; she brushed cobwebs away. Brown dirt yard and rows of beans. A little fresh air came in around the sill, but it was hot—maybe the last of summer. She looked up through the cobwebs toward the blue sky overhead. It would be time the feathered Golika Xah moved south again, time for The People to hunt moose and walk north to meet the caribou.

Her heart ached as she thought of her family—her mother, her dear Mamàcho—even Little Brother! She wondered if they were mourning for her back at Gam`e`t`i—as the Lynxes would be mourning the loss of Sascho.

When would they know what had happened to their children?

Nothing moved in the dirt yard. Not a dog, not a person.

"It will be tough. " Pierre had said that, but this was far more than "tough." I was as if she'd been carried away captive by the Cree or Yellowknives or by some other fierce enemy from the olden days.

No. No. This is worse.

Remembering her mother and her aunts, and all their days of working and walking in the sunlight of the dèè, beside the shining waters, she began to cry again. How she wished to be with her family! A vision of their brown faces, almond eyes, firelight shining all around, stories told, arose in her mind.

There in the attic, alone and hurting, she wrapped her arms around herself and rocked back and forth. She didn't know when it was, but finally she fell asleep on the floor, curled as tight as baby fox hidden in an esker den.

Yaot'l awoke when someone opened the door. The long twilight of the north trickled through the window. A sliver of light grew into a wedge. She tried to get up quickly, but she was unsteady and stiff from sleep on the floor. As she did so, something was pushed in, across the floor. Then, the door slammed again. On her feet at last, anger sent her to the door, where she grabbed the latch and rattled it.

She stopped, however, when she heard sniggering from the other side.

"Told you so. You better be quiet now, or you'll never get out of there."

She froze to the spot. From farther down the hall came a loud command, more words she could not understand. Charlotte replied in return. Then Yaot'l heard the tread of feet shod in hard shoes moving away, heels tapping against the floor.

In the sliver of light from under the door, she saw something had been left inside—a bucket. In it was a lump of something white and what proved to be, when she got down on her knees and picked it up, a canteen.

Water! This was what she most craved. It was hard not to drink it all in one go, after all the tears and the time she'd been without. The white thing was a dry lump of bread. After a single bite, she set it down atop a trunk. Eating that, she decided, would only make her thirstier.

She had to pee, so she struggled out of the unfamiliar underclothes and used the bucket. Then, she pushed it to the wall adjacent to the door. Time passed and below her, occasionally, she could hear those hard soled shoes coming and going. It had been such a pain blur when she'd been dragged here that she couldn't remember much. She had a notion that she would be here a long time, so she did what Lucky did in the winter snow; she curled up and lay, shivering. Her body ached; her nose was crusty with blood; her mind drifted.

I am a prisoner, just like prisoners in the old stories, carried away by the fierce Yellowknives to be a slave. She wondered what work they would expect. Pierre had said there would be plenty of that as well as the learning of the language in this place called "school."

They had fenced her, cut her beautiful hair—so much a part of who she was. They had beaten her. Again, she wondered when she would be let out, or if she ever would be? Did they intend to starve her and bury her somewhere in that dirt yard?

Is this what happened to Yvonne?

She promised herself she would be quiet from now on, learn what she could of these hard people. She would watch and wait. It might take time to find a way to escape, but, somehow, she would. She would walk free on the land as did all the members of her Sho'ti. Then, she would again travel with the seasons. She would follow, alongside her tribe, the journeys of fish and caribou.

But how?

Fear surged. Her dry throat tightened. Next came the ache and sting of more tears, but soon after that came Grandmother Josette saying, "Remember you are called Warrior and what you must do. Now, you must sleep, tomorrow, endure and find your strength. Later, you will escape."

I hear your words, Grandmother.

Yaot'l curled tighter, rested her head on her hands. After a little, she dreamed, of blinding sun on the snow. Then, the snow geese entered her dreams, with their black and white wings. Her heart was comforted by the creak of their feathers and by their sweet cries. They flew north every year, into the wide open land—yes, yes! Somehow or other, when spring came, I will join them!

I am Yaot'l, born to Golika Xah. No matter what these kwet'įį do to me, I will not forget my own ways. *I will reach my home again.*

* * *

Days passed. Yaot'l became familiar with that brown dirt yard and the distant glint of the great river. A little fresh air came in, though the afternoon heat could be bad.

And—where was Sascho? And what had they done to him? That big man had had a whip in his hand...

130

She slept and had bad dreams. Her stomach ached. The light under the door appeared and disappeared; the noise in the hallways came and went. She heard chanting, a sound which came early in the morning, in the middle of the day when the light outside was brightest, and late in the evening, when the only lights she saw moved quickly by. She awoke often, changing position. She was always stiff and sore, rediscovering pain every time she moved. It was terrible to wake up and find herself still locked in, to face another day of hunger and thirst.

Now, when the door opened, she didn't even move, though she did open her eyes. Filtered light came through the dusty windows, which proved to her stunned gaze that Mother Sun was still shining somewhere.

One day, there was a change. By the door stood the big fat kwet'ı̨ı̨ accompanied by a lean woman in a stained apron, her nose long and thin and spotted. The skinny one retrieved the bucket. At first Yaot'l had left most of the bread, but now she ate it all. She'd always drunk every drop of the water, swishing it around inside her parched mouth. The big man looked stern and said something.

Yaot'l backed herself against the far wall, hoping to hide her fear. Her legs and back began to throb, as if recalling his blows. He turned his head and barked something which caused the woman to go away. A new bucket, her clearing vision allowed her to see, had been placed inside the door. For this, she was thankful.

The fat priest continued to stand there, looking down at her, his eyes studying her in a way which caused Yaot'l to tuck her moccasins beneath her dress. At this, he smiled slightly, although the change didn't make him appear any kinder. Then, slowly, he extended his hand, and she saw that something dangled from it— that necklace-like thing called 'rosary.' She'd seen these in Behchok`o, where the people chanted prayers. Words, Aunt Francoise said, for each bead. To please Auntie Francoise, and to learn something of Kwet'ı̨ı̨ ways, Yaot'l had memorized the sequence of sounds. It didn't matter if you didn't understand, Aunt Francois explained. It was Kwet'ı̨ı̨ magic, like some of the oldest Tłı̨chǫ songs.

At least, Yaot'l thought, I know that kwet'ı̨ı̨ believe these beads are for prayers. Her old Behchok`o auntie had explained that each bead was counted between your fingers so you could remember to speak to their god the correct number of times.

The priest came closer and she could not hold the feeling back—the sight and smell of him, so strange, and now in her mind so entangled with the beating—made her shudder. She longed to press herself into the wooden wall, to disappear into the grain of the planks. She would have too, if that had been possible.

His narrow ghostly face was in shadow, but his gray head bobbed up and down in a way that might indicate pleasure. With a plop, the white beads landed in her lap.

He spoke a few words—she thought they were Yellowknife—s language near enough to hers to understand.

"Pray to be forgiven."

Then he turned and went out. The door closed and locked behind him, and she was left in the dark again, with the glimmer of those beads in her lap.

His direction to pray for forgiveness puzzled her at first. The most important Tłįchǫ laws, the ones Yamǫǫ̀zha had taught, concerned sharing what you had—food, tools, dogs and canoes—about cooperating and helping the Seho'ti—your family.

It must be, she thought, for disrespecting her elders that she was being punished—and she certainly had sunk her teeth into that gray woman! At the same time, however, her heart rebelled against the shame of calling that a "sin."

These women are not my elders! How cruelly they had bullied the girls even while they'd chopped off their braids!

No, I have committed no sin. I have only fought my enemy.

* * *

Days and nights circled, cold nights, hot days. She heard feet coming and going below her, the orders of the gray women, and then, later, speech in her language—and sometimes in the languages of other tribes, like and yet unlike her own. She'd hear the murmur fall silent too, and the muffled sound of feet striking the floor in unison after the morning bell rang.

Sometimes she heard the strap crack, followed by distant wailing. She wanted to be brave, but the mere sound cut through her as her body remembered the pain. The bruises on her arms and weeping welts on her legs diminished, but it seemed her flesh kept its own counsel, for just the sound of a beating made her ache all over again.

Bells rang, feet marched back and forth. Several times she thought she saw Sascho chopping wood near the barn, but she couldn't be sure. There seemed to be more than one Native youth working over there.

The bucket came and went, once a day. In it, always, came the water bottle and a single hard piece of bread. Sometimes, the bread had a mottled look and the sour taste of mold. It didn't matter, after a while, and she ate whatever the bucket contained because she was increasingly hungry. She was careful to ration out the water, and on hot days, it was hard not to suffer from the torment of thirst. After days, she'd begun to wonder if they would ever let her out, or if she had been left to slowly die slowly.

Now, whenever she heard those footsteps on the stairway which led into the attic, she'd pick up the beads and kneel and begin to murmur whatever she could remember of those chants, so that she'd be seen, apparently praying.

Perhaps if I do that, they will release me.

For days, though, the exchange of buckets took place quickly, just a hand coming in and going out. Once it was Charlotte, who only laughed and slammed the door. Another time she was fast asleep, curled behind some boxes when the door opened. She was too weary, weak and full of despair to even try to get to her feet and put on a show for whoever it was.

She began to dream awake, watching the sun slant through the dirty windows and slowly make its way across the floor before vanishing again. The moon outside the window, which had been just a hair past full when she arrived, was now a thin rind, nibbled away night by night.

One morning before dawn she awoke to a familiar sound, a sound which struck her ears like a melody, coming from far away. Pushing herself upright, she went to the window. Stars alone illuminated the empty, stripped off yard. She heard the marvelous, musical sound approach, ever growing. Her eyes strained to see into the sky.

Then, there they were! Sparkling white, in two great V's, calling to one another:

On and on we fly and fly and fly!

Now you lead! Now you! Now you!

Now you, my cousin! My brother, my sister, my husband, my wife!

Lead and break the wind for our clan!

We are Golika Xah, chasing the sun, going south!

Wordlessly, she stretched her arms out to them, those thousands of snow geese passing above her. For a time, there were so many, she could hear the creak of their strong wings.

I am here! I am here! Oh, I am here! Golika Xah! Oh wait! Please let me fly away with you!

It was all she could do not to shriek. With all her might, she willed her spirit up and out the window, willed herself to fly. Their journey, she knew, was long and dangerous, filled with hunters whose guns might bring them tumbling to a painful death, falling in a whirlwind of feathers, spiraling to the ground. Still, anything, any end, was better than this, this caged captivity. Tears cut new trails along her cheeks.

So many! My own feathered family, strong and free!

The geese turned to specks and then disappeared, along with their ghostly song. Yaot'l's knees failed; she collapsed onto the floor and for what seemed the hundredth time, she sobbed.

Chapter Seven

When they finally led her from that place, Yaot'l was thin, pale, and silent. One of the big white women, holding her wrist in a vice grip, marched her out and down two flights of stairs. She felt her feet going down, down—they were still in their moccasins, with the quill decoration she herself had sewn—dearer to her now than she could have ever imagined. She was in a dream, she thought, watching the others watching her—the big white women with their cold eyes—sometimes their eyes were brown, these white women, or muddy—but always, always the only feeling that came from them was cold—as if she was something unclean.

The dream feeling persisted, until they pushed her under the icy shower and stripped off her clothes. Then she began to scream. A few hard slaps, though, and she fell silent for each blow made her body remember pain. Chattering, she was roughly dried. Then, with the big red face close to hers, the woman held up a fresh dress, pointing to the inside. On the neckline there was a symbol in black: "twenty-nine". It meant nothing to Yaot'l, but when the woman showed her another piece of the strange clothing, she again pointed out the same marking. Red Face said something in her language, pointing to the marks and then, after poking Yaot'l in the chest, she made the sounds again. She repeated this rough action a good many times, until Yaot'l tried mimicking the sounds. That appeared to satisfy her.

The process was interrupted when one of the gray women opened the door and said something which sounded urgent. Red Face pushed the clothing into her hands, barked something, and then followed the gray woman. A sloe-eyed girl, seemingly appearing out of nowhere, stood at her shoulder and whispered urgently, "That sign means twenty-nine! Twenty-nine! That's how the gray women will call for you, so don't forget. These are clean clothes."

Yaot'l suddenly realized that this was the same girl who had stood in the doorway and had tried to help when Charlotte had been bullying everyone.

"What is your name?"

"Clare—now shussssh! Put these on right away—there are shoes in that box over there. Choose carefully so they fit—but don't take too long, or we'll miss supper."

Yaot'l did as she was told. The hardest part was trying on the unfamiliar shoes, but Clare helped her with that.

Red Face returned just as she finished. She took Yaot'l by the shoulders and marched her along a hallway where a line of girls stood. Here, she was pushed into the line. Clare, with a look of sympathy, walked to a place farther up, nearer the door. Yaot'l had hoped, momentarily, that this girl might be next to her, but it was not to be.

Red Face glared and raised her voice—a threat—Yaot'l knew by the woman's expression and the volume. She moved carefully, following the others. Her feet, now tied up inside stiff, hard footwear, felt stupid and distant.

The others had anxiously moved away when she was been pushed into the line, only daring to steal a glance. Everyone was dressed alike, only their dresses were wrinkled from days of wear. She smelled kwet'ı̨ı̀ food, too, the boiled sour smell that had hung over the hospital when they had taken her father. She leaned against the wall, but was soon pulled straight and loudly admonished by Charlotte. It was her job, apparently, to patrol the line and bully everyone.

Eventually, they filed into a white-washed room filled with benches and long tables, each set with a line of bowls and spoons. A big blackened pot sat at each end. This, she'd learn, was oatmeal gruel in the morning or some greasy undefinable liquid for supper. Fortunately there was often bread, with white lumps of canned shortening to spread on it. If they were very, very lucky, there were bacon grease or drippings from the meat served to the cheka, or, what they had in Gam`e`t`i sometimes, real lard.

On that first day it didn't matter. The thin gruel was enough. She felt strangely removed from herself, almost as if her eyes now floated a few feet above her body. The sight of the fat priest, marching up and down between the tables, his eyes boring into them, made her shiver, for he was the one who had beat her and locked her away. When his eyes found her—and they did every time he passed, she lowered her head.

Yaot'l had never slept in a bed before. The room with the cots all in a row, carefully set at an equal distance from one another, did not, on first sight, make her think of sleep. The padding was of straw and ungenerous, and the students had all learned to take the cloth they used for bedding and fold it around the straw-filled mattress as if making a package.

That night, in the dormitory, she huddled under a thin blanket, trying to sleep and wishing, as she had every night in the attic, for a nearby body to warm her. It was strange to sleep alongside other people without touching anyone. Each child was held separate upon a rickety narrow bed frame. The tight white sheet which encased her and the worn and lumpy straw mattress were a poor substitute for the familiar creature comfort of a night spent in the family shelter.

Yaot'l was exhausted, but for a time she lay awake, listening to the night sounds of this new captivity. So many people breathing all around, some snuffling, some coughing!

It was a little like the first night they spent in łık'àdèè k'è, surrounded by many other tents, listening to the sleep sounds of the neighbors, but here was no fresh air, no owls, no distant cry of the fox or the homely barks of the dogs. The only good thing here was the gentle creak of a stove, giving up the last of what had been a hot fire. She was glad that she was not too close.

If she lifted her head a little, she could see, dimly lit by a kerosene lantern, other bodies like hers, young women curled beneath old blankets, sleeping on pillows filled with straw and a few chicken feathers. Smells of kerosene mixed with wood smoke. There was also the scent of many bodies washed with strong soap. On other nights, when the strap or the rod came out because one of the gray nuns had lost her temper, the smell in the room would be tinged with fear.

In the morning, a nun with a bell started their day with a head-splitting clang. Everyone leapt out of bed, and Yaot'l did too. One who did not, a girl who had coughed off and on through the night, was yanked upright and given several whacks with a leather strap. This, she soon learned, happened every couple of days, for someone was always caught lying just a moment too long within the warm cocoon of bedclothes.

To Yaot'l, on this first morning, it seemed just minutes ago that she'd fallen asleep. Now she was suddenly jerked awake with this clamor! In the attic, certainly, she'd heard these sounds, but they were a muffled noise just before dawn. So near now, it was head-splitting.

The sight of that big gray woman marching along the central aisle between the beds, the leather strap in hand, remained a fresh memory. She'd fairly shot onto her feet, straight from sleep, for she'd been dreaming that she was home again, back in the tent village in Behchok'o. The bell had invaded the dream, and at once it had all gone sour as she, with a sick feeling, relived the fatal instant she'd encountered Pierre on the path by the dumping place.

Trembling, feet on cold floor, she stood in a room where dawn, the color of an old stain, colored the windows. She was afraid, uncertain, but no eyes, she soon realized, were upon her. Everyone was focused on themselves and on the task at hand. Girls raced around on every side, making their beds, collecting basins and washcloths, hurrying to form a line which was marched away into the hall, toward where the water closet—another new experience—was located. They were the ones whose bladders were ready to burst after the long night's wait.

Charlotte appeared and began to give Yaot'l orders about folding the sheet and blanket around the bed in the right way. She shouted words in English and pointed to indicate what she wanted. Yaot'l followed the instructions with no trouble. She saw at once that the object was to make a kind of package out of the mattress, using the sheets and blankets. It was not hard.

Later, at the wall peg where she'd hung her clothes the night before, she dressed, gathered her basin and joined the end of the line, as the next group readied themselves to use the water closets and the sinks. Clare, passing her by, nodded in a friendly way. She leaned in and whispered, "Remember——Twenty-nine!"

Next they were shepherded down the hallway and into another big room, one which resembled the inside of the Behchok'o church. The kwet'ìì dying god hung on the wall. In a niche beside him was the carved figure of a woman. She wept wooden tears, and her heart, painted to show that it dripped with blood, seemed to have been excised from her body. Yaot'l thought of a slaughtered animal.

There were candles here, as well as the gray women, the priests, and others, who, she'd learn were the cheka. Everyone knelt and prayers were said, on and on, over and over, while her stomach ached and her skinny knees throbbed where they were pressed against the hard cold floor. After, when she was so stiff she could hardly stand, she lined up again, walked down another hallway, this time one which led to the tables, again set with bowls, spoons and big pots. Another ladle of oatmeal gruel and a piece of white bread later, they were marched off to learn.

Yaot'l was sent to a bench beside much younger girls. A gray woman said words in English, and, at the same time, pointed to pictures in a book. This, at last, and after everything, was "school." She watched the pictures and mimicked the others, calling out the sounds at the appropriate time. Then, sitting on a bench in front of a sloping sort of narrow table, chalk in hand, they were set to scratching signs that she learned were called "letters" onto squares of slate. A rag wiped it all away, and you were to begin making the marks anew.

Sure enough, the gray women called out "Twenty Nine!" When Yaot'l stood up—not knowing what was expected—it seemed to please her. She gestured for her to sit again and then drew more of the strange marks at the top of her slate.

Yaot'l would learn that the gray women would often come, lean over her shoulder, and study what she had drawn. If she approved she nodded and smiled; if she didn't she'd frown and erase her work so she'd have to begin again. If the latter was the case, there was often a slap or an ear pull, or, perhaps, a pinch. Perhaps, she thought, this was the purpose of cutting away her hair so high up on her head—it made ear pinching pretty easy to do.

Before a midday meal of greasy broth, they prayed again, though not for as long as they had in the morning, much to Yaot'l's relief. Then, they were marched out and given work to do. These tasks changed daily, but on that first day, they were "house cleaning" the inside of the kwet'įį building—sweeping, mopping, wiping dust and dirt from surfaces, or washing stairs and handrails, with a wet rag and a bucket of water. Each task was new, as she'd never spent time inside this kind of dwelling. Here again she endured many more slaps and corrective pushes and pulls, all accompanied by shouting.

Later, they marched into the yard. As soon as they were out of doors, some girls ran and whooped, others bunched into quiet groups. A few others, those who appeared sickly, straggled away along the sunny side of the building and sat down in the dust, as if they didn't have the strength or will to do much else.

On her first day among the others, sun shone onto the dirt rectangle. Yaot'l looked around and finally saw Clare, but she was among a group of girls who appeared absorbed in some game.

On the other side of a long wall, she could hear the shouts of boys. Walking the fence line, ignoring the others, Yaot'l walked down the slope to where there were still a few tufts of grass. From up top, as she'd come out of the door, she'd seen that this fenced in yard ended by a weed and willow patch near the river.

As she approached, she heard: "This is our place. Go away, Trouble-maker, or we'll beat you like Sister Louise and Father Tremblay did!"

Yaot'l stopped and studied them. Five girls, all were younger, though not by much. Two were the ones she'd seen with Charlotte on her first day. Their leader, though, was not present. She'd seen them again this morning, busy bullying some smaller girl while the nun turned a blind eye.

She didn't move at once, though, because it was important not to turn too quickly and provoke a pursuit.

I will fight them. Yes I will. Fighting, though, is not for today.

"Go Away! Didn't you hear us, Crazy?" The tallest, Marie, took a few steps forward.

Yaot'l allowed her eyes to move slowly across each face before she turned.

Know your enemy!

Hoping they wouldn't chase her anyway, she slowly began to walk away. Almost at once a rock struck her between the shoulder blades. Although it hurt and she couldn't keep from wincing, she didn't increase her pace, just continued a steady retreat up hill.

She continued along the fence line, hoping not to encounter more hostility. She kept her eyes down, though all her senses remained alert. The shouting of boys on the other side came through the boards clearly. Large cracks between slats provided a view, but as she walked she saw, directly ahead, Charlotte shaking some girl who'd been caught peeping through. To whisper to the boys, it appeared, was another "forbidden."

After the shaking, the younger girl was released, but Charlotte continued to loom. The girl stayed on the ground, but Yaot'l saw too that she'd stubbornly remained close to the fence.

It was Tanis. Yaot'l thought that she might have been talking to Kele, now trapped on the other side. Tanis recognized Yaot'l, but immediately pretended she saw nothing but the ground. All the time, Charlotte continued to poke with her foot.

"Stupid baby! I'm gonna tell Sister Louise!"

Yaot'l kept moving forward, very slowly. She didn't want to attract any more unwelcome attention, but she did want to talk to Tanis.

At last, Charlotte lost interest and walked away.

When Yaot'l was sure Charlotte's attention had been drawn elsewhere, she sat down beside Tanis.

"Yaot'l! I'm so glad you are back! Everyone is talking about you. Some said you were brave, but Charlotte and her friends said you were bad and deserved it. I didn't dare say anything, but I think you were brave. I wish you hadn't gotten in trouble because of me."

Yaot'l considered. She hadn't felt brave at all while she'd been locked up.

"Was that Kele?"

"Yes. We aren't supposed to talk, but sometimes we manage. Only that horrible weasel saw us. Now she will report me and I will get the strap." Her tear-stained face angled to glare after Charlotte. "She's the meanest of all these mean people, right beside the nuns and the teachers."

When Yaot'l didn't reply, she asked, "Did they starve you? You were gone so long and now you are so thin."

Yaot'l took the little hand between hers. Then, she gazed away, south across the broad river. It was good to sit beside someone she knew, here on this dusty hillside. There was pleasure in the sun as it touched her skin and in the afternoon breeze as it lifted what remained of her thick hair.

* * *

Yaot'l removed her dress, following what was happening on every side. Clare passed by, acknowledging her with a nod and a smile. At this kind gesture—even from one who'd been present at her humiliation by water and the strap-Yaot'l was grateful, although she did not respond by any more than a slight inclination of the head.

As she returned to preparing herself for bed, though, a thin, wiry girl—one who slept right next to her—appeared. She walked straight up to Yaot'l, grabbed her by the shoulders and pushed her backwards, so she stumbled toward the wall. Yaot'l, thinking another attack was coming, crouched and readied herself. Instead, the girl stood back, grinned at her and announced cheerfully, "I'm crazy too."

When she extended a hand, Yaot'l realized this had been a kind of welcome, so she accepted the hand up. While she gathered her dress, the girl, who did not look back, walked away and pushed into another new forming line.

No one challenged her intrusion. What's more, Yaot'l noted, they gave her wide berth.

While she hung up the dress, she heard Clare.

"Hurry! Get in line."

"Who was that?"

"Patricia. She's been locked up too."

Before Yaot'l could ask what crime she'd committed, Clare caught her wrist and moved her into the aisle that ran full length of the room. She made Yaot'l go first, ahead of her until they'd joined the back of the line.

As they moved, along with the others, Clare leaned upon her shoulder and whispered, "Pee now, because we won't be able to until dawn— and tomorrow's Sunday, and we'll be on our knees for the whole morning."

As they shuffled forward in nightgowns, on every side there was whispering in forbidden languages.

We are, briefly, unguarded.

Clare said, "The boys will be on the other side of the church, but I hope that this time I'll see my little brother. He's new, like you, but he had a cough when we left home. I can't talk to him here, but if I see him, at least I'll know he's better."

Yaot'l wondered if Sascho would be there, and if he would see her. She wondered if, for just a moment, their eyes would meet. She had thought of him so many, many times.

Later, there were the sounds of sleepers, dreaming and tossing, on every side. It had been far worse in the attic without a bed. Here were others of her age, some even from her tribe, though, for the first time ever, she'd seen people from other tribes, Yellowknife, Slavey, and even Cree.

Perhaps some of these young women had also been to the Behchok'o tea dance, where, in the circle of life, she'd danced beside Sascho. Her eyes had been so full of him that night she had not paid proper attention to anything but the drum beat of her own heart.

* * *

The church day was long and with too much kneeling, just as Clare said. When they entered the gloomy room filled with the sweaty smell of tallow, with the pictures of the new god—girls sitting on one side, boys on the other—there was very little time to recognize anyone among the lockstep crowd. Everyone now looked much alike—sheared hair and gray uniforms. There were a few pale faces—Métis children, some of these marked out by kwet'ı̀ı̀ as 'better." Before they knelt, Yaot'l knew Clare

150

was straining to see if among the little faces turning backwards from the front benches, one might be her little brother.

Down on her knees before the flickering candles! Here was the carving of the tortured man, that bloody torso confronting her everywhere. Yaot'l would learn that she must stay and stay and stay kneeling until she thought her knees would shatter.

Yaot'l had seen the bloody man before in the white man's church when she'd gone with Aunt Francoise. They'd all bowed their heads before that kwet'įį holy man—"Father" they called him—watching while he marked the babies with water and spoke to people in his own language. He'd smiled and seemed kind. She'd often wondered why her own father had been so adamant about keeping her away from kwet'įį school, but now she understood.

The stick, the strap, and those pale cold hands wielding it, the stern faces, the blue eyes, hearts as cold as winter ice!

Her heart froze—but then, when they could finally stand again, she caught a glimpse of Sascho right on the center aisle. Among the despondent boys, he alone stood straight. He never looked back, but the simple sight of his square shoulders buoyed her, kept her from drowning in despair.

* * *

One thing she already knew how to do was to sew. After hours spent in the schoolroom where everything was so unfamiliar, the sight of cloth, of thread and needles was a relief. Here, though, some of the girls used machines—these too were devices only seen once before in Behchok'o, at her Aunt's house. She had been so small back then, watching her Aunt whirling the wheel and entranced by the silver needle which drove up and down ever so fast.

The gray woman had set her to hem handkerchiefs. She'd been grateful for that, for it was something she could easily do. The woman, after observing for a time, had nodded approval, said something, and then set her down at a table where a dress was laid out. More words she did not know, but she could see what was being pointed out—lost buttons—so she threaded a needle and began to work on that, using the box of buttons set beside her. This, on her first day, was the only place where she didn't receive a reprimand.

One day she was sent to train in the laundry with kwet'ı̨ı̨ women with big red hands, their arms as muscular as the back legs of a moose, working on heavy wet sheets, and cranking devices called "mangles" which squeezed the water out of the cloth. It was first done to soapy garments. Then, after the tubs were drained and refilled with clear water, the entire process was repeated, the object now being to rinse away the soap and any lingering grime.

A good job—at least, in the few warm days that remained—was hanging clothes. Here she could see the sky, and the eroded earth which stretched away to the river. In the distance lay the lake upon whose breast she had been carried. In the coldest times, the last trip through the mangle would send the workers to carrying baskets upstairs into her old prison, the attic. Here, on lines, the clothes were hung. It didn't quite freeze up there, but the wind blew through every crack, and the clothes did eventually dry, though the material, when taken down, was rough and stiff.

Ironing was another thing she'd mostly seen in Behchok'o. As a little girl, she'd watched and even had a lesson. First, you sprinkled water; next you pushed the iron. She'd stood on a chair beside her soft-spoken Aunt and helped. That was one of the ways Aunt Francoise made script, by ironing for white women.

"I am the best of all in Behchok'o who do the work, for I learned at school...the school where all your children should go, Rene."

How strange to think that this was what Aunt Francoise, so quiet, so generous and kind, had wanted her to experience! The unkindness, dished out every day, and all this work—and bad rations, too, stuff she wouldn't feed a dog.

* * *

153

As the days turned into weeks, Yaot'l awoke one morning to a cold wind blowing in through chinks in the walls. It was now far too late to dream of escape.

Like the woman who returned from captivity, Wetsi Wek'o, she would do her best to study the ways of these people and then find a way to leave them. It would be easier if she could make friends among her captors, as Wetsi Wek'o had, but the memory of her teeth on that woman's arm, Yaot'l knew, would never be erased. She continually hoped to find allies among the other students, though. Most, wanting to stay out of trouble with the nuns, avoided her, but there were a few who were not afraid to be seen with her, genuinely kind girls like Clare.

Patricia was the only one who constantly stood by, although Yaot'l hadn't been sure at first that a "crazy" would be the best kind of friend to have. In the end, Yaot'l found a reputation for madness was in some ways an asset, and besides, Patricia's beautiful wide smile warmed her heart. Best of all, when the two of them walked the halls together, the bullies weren't likely to try anything. When attacked, they ably defended themselves, punching and tripping with the best.

Although they were always the ones strapped for "causing all the trouble," even Charlotte began to look for prey that didn't leave her with quite so many bruises. Patricia had nothing more to lose, to which the bruises on her pretty legs testified. Sometimes other girls would giggle behind their backs, whispering that they were "the crazy ones," but if this happened, an angry glare was usually sufficient to quell it.

Outwardly, to the Chekka, Yaot'l was obedient. She did what she was told; she tried to stay out of trouble; she listened to and tried to pronounce the strange language until her head, by the end of day, ached. None of this was easy. It was difficult to learn so many unfamiliar things all at once.

Yaot'l's given name had been changed, along with those of the others who had just arrived "without proper Christian names"—in one of those mysterious ceremonies in the church, with all sorts of chanting and singing and getting up and kneeling down—until finally there came a touch from the priest with water and a prayer over her. There was not a word of it she understood.

So, after that, I am not only "twenty-nine" and I am also kwet'íí God-named "Barbara." They keep trying to make me forget who I am, but they will never do it-no, they won't.

Others girls walked around her carefully, even the older ones who had become full time servants at the place. To Yaot'l, the hours seemed endless. A device called a "clock" marked the duration of each task. Pointers moved to numbers—these called hands-went slower and slower the more she watched them, jerky jumps from one black mark to the next.

Kwet'ı̨ı̨ broke his day into tiny bits, like a man with a hammer. Each piece had a task to busy it. Yaot'l felt as if the great world of sky and earth of which she had always been a part was banished. She now an indoors creature, penned in dark rooms and fed strange fodder.

There were days when she ached to be out-of-doors. Even after it turned bitter, Yaot'l would stand in the yard gazing upward, allowing the low sun to beat upon her face until red circles spun behind her closed eyelids. Even the icy winds searing her cheeks were welcome. Patricia, with mischievous bright eyes and her sweet wild oval face, would huddle in the snow with her. They'd dig down into the white stuff in order to endure the time out-of-doors.

"Maybe kwet'ı̨ı̨ wants to turn us into Nakan who hides underground all winter." The thought passed through Yaot'l's mind as they sat inside their wall of snow together, fighting off shivers.

"Maybe kwet'ı̨ı̨ *is* Nakan," Patricia suggested, which made Yaot'l laugh at the strange notion that these tense, numb white people could somehow also be the legendary shaggy monster of the bush. Patricia sometimes made odd remarks—shocking—but they always made her think.

"But Kwet'ı̨ı̨ also carries women and girls away to his lair." Patricia waved a snowy mitten at the big house. "He hides in there all winter. He smells—weird—and he is—wicked—and does terrible things to those he captures—before he kills them." Patricia's lips had drawn into the familiar wild grin, but when she came to the end, everything changed. To Yaot'l's dismay, Patricia suddenly shrieked, then began to beat fists inside icy mittens against her high forehead.

"No, Nakan! No! No! No! Get away from me! You get away!" Patricia fell backwards; she stretched out her legs and kicked snow, pounding her heels against the frozen ground.

"Patricia! No!" Shocked, Yaot'l sat back and stared. She did not know what to do. She wanted to hold her friend in her arms, to keep her still and tell her there was no Nakan here, but the violence of her friend's thrashing held her at bay. It was as if Patricia was having a fit. Yaot'l had seen one of her own small cousins fit with great violence—so much so that the child died.

"Patricia!" Despite fearing she'd be kicked, she grabbed her friend's shoulders and shook. Patricia's eyes had rolled up and her face pulled into a hard mask. Her eyelids fluttered.

No! Patricia must not die!

Yaot'l was holding onto the girl's arms, tight as she could, when Patricia's body suddenly relaxed. She heaved a great deep sigh. The exhalation appeared as a cloud of moisture carried away at once by the chilly wind.

"Patricia?" Yaot'l sat back on her heels, regarding her friend, now lying quietly beside her. She looked around hoping none of this had attracted attention.

Closer than she'd like, there was a chorus of cheerful shouts. The senior girls had picked a few sturdy sheets of cardboard out of the trash and were now using these to make a slippery slide down the steepest part of the school yard. Others less popular girls stood around, hoping to be included in one of these downhill jaunts.

Yaot'l knew that she'd have to lie down and hold Patricia in her arms to keep her warm if she didn't get up soon. She also knew that if Doris or Marie, or—worst of all—Charlotte, saw them like this, they would be punished for some sin or other, even it was good sense to warm someone who was out-of-doors and unconscious. It was a sin, too, if the touching was motivated by friendship or affection and that of course, she knew, was what she'd be punished for.

She'd just finished thinking of all of that when Patricia opened her eyes. For a moment she stared up at the sky, as if trying to make sense of where she was.

"Was I dead?"

"No. I think you had a fit, like my cousin."

"Help me sit."

Yaot'l offered her an arm, pulling her upright. As she did, Patricia, now coming back to herself more fully, began to shiver.

"I'm really, really cold."

"So am I. Come on. Let's get up to the door where it's not so windy. It shouldn't be long until the bell rings."

158

Slowly, they got to their feet, both of them covered in white. Slowly they made their way toward the shelter in the wake of the building.

"What happened to the two of you?"

Both girls startled, but, fortunately it was only Clare walking up behind them, not one of their tormentors.

"She fell down."

"Yes. It's slippery over there."

Patricia, still dazed, only nodded.

"I'll take your other arm," said Clare. "Are you faint?"

"A little."

"Well, come on then." Clare put an arm under Patricia's. They walked on together, but as they came over the crest of the hill and saw that a small crowd had already gathered by the door, all in foot-stamping, mitten-slapping anticipation of getting inside, she asked, "Patty—do you think you can get in by yourself? If Sister Mary Margaret sees us like this, she'll be sure to ask questions."

"And then find a reason to beat us all too, probably," Yaot'l reflected grimly.

"Go on ahead then," Patricia said, "you and Barbara."

"Are you sure?" Yaot'l asked.

"Sure. I'm okay. I'll just come along real slow. Anyway—" Patricia managed a wink and gestured at the sniffling group huddled by the door, "That pathetic bunch won't bother me."

* * *

"She had a fit, didn't she?" Clare whispered as she and Yaot'l walked away together.

"I think so."

"She was talking about Nakan, right?"

"She made a weird joke about kwet'įį̀." Yaot'l shrugged again. "You know Patricia."

"Better than you do." Clare's forehead wrinkled with worry.

The bell rang. It seemed louder than usual.

A line was already forming, and stout Sister Mary Margaret trundled out onto the steps. Her coat had a nice fox collar, head, feet and tail, that some of the younger kids were always trying to stroke. Yaot'l turned back one last time to make certain that Patricia was still on her feet.

There she came, upright and walking slowly. Her shoulders trembled, while fine wind-blown snow whirled around her. She seemed unstable. On and off her progress slowed, while she strove to keep her balance. Meanwhile, the line pushed forward through the open door. Sister Mary Margaret counted heads, lips visibly moving.

"You go in now, Barbara." Clare spoke loudly, adopting a bully's tone, apparently for the benefit of Charlotte, who'd appeared nearby. After their enemy pushed past—she too was covered in snow and shivering because she'd fallen off the "sled"—Clare whispered, "I'll make sure Patricia gets inside."

* * *

They wanted privacy to talk, but punishment had not been part of the plan. Only a few hours later, Yaot'l and Clare were caught whispering in their own language in the kitchen, a place where the clatter of the nightly wash up was generally sufficient cover.

Sister Angela, who was supposed to be minding them as they took their punishment—as well as attending to her own prayers—had slipped away soon after Sister Renne dashed in to whisper something in her ear. Now they were unwitting allies to the girls who had been sentenced to prayers on their knees in the dark, cold chapel.

As soon as the door closed behind the nuns, they got up and went to a bench to sit side by side.

"Finish what you were telling me." Yaot'l shot a quick glance over her shoulder as feet went stumping past in the hallway. Everyone knew the heavy tread of Sister Louise—and feared it. Sister Angela, Yaot'l had recently learned, was far from "obedience and submission." She was often in trouble, either with Sister Louise or with Mary Margaret.

"About Patricia?"

Clare's face tightened with reluctance, but in the end she said, "I—think Brother Murphy behaved toward her—like—like Nakan, that time when she was shut in the attic."

More footsteps approached. They readied themselves for flight, but the sound went past.

"Who is Brother Murphy?" Yaot'l, now shocked almost to speechlessness, had never met this Chekaa. And to link a white person to the legendary Nakan? Monsters that killed their women?

"That Murphy's gone away to another school—bad for them, but thank-you Jesus, Mary & Joseph for us!" Clare fervently crossed herself. "But if Patricia talks about Nakan, you better be ready, because—because—when she mentions his name, something always goes wrong in her head."

A raised voice from the hall cut off anything further. They both jumped to their feet because they'd also heard that signature heavy tread.

"Sister Angela? Sister Renne? What are you two doing, lurking over there?"

The time to talk was at an end.

When the door opened and Sister Louise looked in to check on them, what she saw was what she'd expected—two girls meekly upon their knees, heads bowed in prayer. They were right where they were supposed to be, too, at opposite ends of the altar rail.

* * *

There were many rules, the first being: Don't talk to boys!

Not even whispering through the fence at recess to your beloved friend.

Speak English—or don't speak at all.

Words still came boiling up inside, like bubbles in a pot, her own language, forbidden now but always struggling to escape...

Sit still!

So strange, to sit up straight on a bench and pretend to be a stiff kwet'ji, all the time blood pooled in her feet...

Hold it this way!

A thing called "chalk" in her hand to make marks on slate...copying what was on the board, those signs and marks which she didn't understand.

Repeat after me!

Squawk like a crow, growl like an angry dog, roar like a bear...

Look at me when I'm speaking to you!

I'd rather not see the contempt in your colorless eyes...

* * *

Yaot'l was sometimes backed against the wall to be kicked or punched by Charlotte and her friends, but if she defended herself, Charlotte (or whoever) would burst into noisy tears and run to the nearest nun, who would come directly, strap in hand ready to beat the Indian out of that child.

Yaot'l raged whenever that happened.

"They don't pay attention when Charlotte and her pack are beating us, only when the nun's little darlings cry!"

"That's how it is here, so just try to stay out of their way," Clare said. She handed Yaot'l her handkerchief.

"I can't, and you know it. They wait for me. If Patricia and I aren't together—"

"Yes, I know. Everyone is saying that you are very brave, that you are tougher than anyone—even tougher than Patricia. I don't think I could keep from crying as long as you do, but, remember, things can get worse."

"If I'm around the next time," Patricia said, "I'll give that baby Charlotte and her stupid friends something to cry about."

"No, Patricia." Clare, worried, put a restraining hand on Patricia's arm. "Don't do that. You'll just end up in trouble again."

"It's bound to happen anyway," said Patricia. She grinned briefly, though it looked more as if she was baring her teeth. "Barbara and I—we're in trouble no matter what we do." With a mad expression, she cheerfully punched Yaot'l in the arm.

Clare went home over Christmas. She was lucky to have some distant kin living near Fort Providence who were happy to open their house to her.

"Two weeks of freedom!" She'd waved at them as she'd gone off in a car crammed with other kids heading home. Local families pooled money to pay a driver to come to fetch their young relatives. Clare had promised to bring back treats.

Now that so many were gone, the school was quieter, but there were still plenty of daily chores and even more praying. Ordinarily, Yaot'l would have been snow bound in the bush with members of family and friends—the women and children together, while the men trapped farther north.

But Patricia was there, along with children like Yaot'l whose families lived far away, so that was a good thing. Today, outside, in the biting cold, they walked around the yard, kicking through the dusty dry snow. Charlotte and Marie were again sliding, now using an old inner tube. The rest were looking on hopefully, or using weary pieces of cardboard.

Yaot'l and Patricia walked fast to stay warm, talking as they went.

"Kwet'ıì god born in the long night. He maybe no live if he born out in—wide open country. Maybe kwet'ıì not have winter."

"I do not think they do," Patricia said. "Sister Mary Margaret told us a story about Jesus fasting in the desert seeking a vision. A desert's all sand, you know. It's always hot, like our summer."

Yaot'l continued to follow her own thoughts.

"Sometimes our old people die when sun comes back. Aunt Katie say they melt like ice."

Patricia managed a smile despite her chapped lips. She loved this exchange. They spoke in English today, to help Yaot'l learn it quicker.

Patricia enjoyed Yaot'l's stories of her old life. She seemed to yearn after her own past almost as much as her friend did, although it had been four years since she'd lived in the bush. After an epidemic had swept through the area, she'd lost everyone. Patricia said a very old man, a stranger, had carried her, still half sick with measles, into a church service. When, she'd fallen asleep in the unaccustomed warmth, he'd abandoned her there. That was the story of how she'd ended up in the school, as "orphan and charity child."

A dream dear to Patricia's heart was that she had some long lost kin who might, some day, appear and take her away.

"Maybe Clare's aunt will let me come home with her for the summer. It would be so wonderful to leave here. I would work as hard as I know how if she would only do that."

Clare had mentioned this notion before she'd left for the glorious two week holiday. Now, most of Patricia's waking thoughts circled around the idea. Yaot'l, now facing the same fate, understood what such a dream meant to her friend.

Somewhere, though, I do have a family, a family who misses me, a family who may not even know where I am. They are still alive—somewhere.

166

Yaot'l's heart ached as she imagined what it must be like to be Patricia, left all alone among the enemy.

Chapter Eight

Sascho knelt on the cold floor, putting wood he'd split a few weeks ago into a stove. He was tired, but he was always tired here. He slept in a big room with other boys near his age, in a bed set beside the door. Every morning, in darkness, though, he'd feel a tug on his blanket. He'd learned that this was time for him to rise, gather his clothes from a nearby hook, and go into an alcove to dress. He and another tall boy, a lanky Yellowknife, David, had tasks to complete before the others awoke. There were stoves to stoke downstairs, water to pump and set to heat, and, always it seemed, more wood to chop.

Then out to the barn to tend the horses and the cow that belonged to the place, shoveling manure and carrying water and hay. As it got colder, the ice had to be broken in the stock tank and more pumped in. Only then would they have time to scrape the stable off their boots, and wash up before prayers and breakfast. The last task of the day was to haul out the garbage, lug it around to the back of the barn and dump it into the pig trough.

Snow blew in the door even as he hurried to close it. Mittens barely kept out the cold as he and David crossed the yard. Neither spoke; no need, for they knew what lay before them. If it wasn't done quickly and well, there was always the dog whip that the Métis overseer, Guy, habitually carried and sometimes used. Guy was the one who cared for Father McCarthy's horses. The woman with orange freckles, Agnes, took care of the cows, geese and chickens. Agnes also worked in the kitchen, scrubbing, cooking and making butter and cheese—delicacies for the kwet'ı̨ı̨ staff. Guy, and another Métis, Frank, bunked in a little shack backed up in the lee of the barn.

Sascho learned that both these men had been to school here. They'd gone back to their homes in due course, but, eventually, had returned—a decision of which Sascho could make no sense.

Mr. Frank, he learned, had worked on the river for a time and acquired some useful kwet'ı̨ı̨ skills, for he kept the truck, pumps, and the pipes at the school in order, and he also did carpentry and other fixes to maintain the property. In the big stand-alone shed where the prized truck sheltered, there were boxes of tools, a big work table lit by kerosene lanterns, wrenches, vises, chisels, saws, and a long bench. Now, in winter, when Frank was at work there, an oil drum stove kept him warm. One of

Sascho's tasks was to be sure that Frank had plenty of wood piled close to hand.

He and David fetched and carried for these men, as well as for the school. Both older men had short tempers, so he'd endured plenty of knocks and head slaps during the time when he'd been struggling with understanding. It seemed that an earlier boy, one who'd just graduated, had filled the bill to perfection, and he often had to listen to lectures, in a mix of Slavey and English, about how good the absent Leo had been, how smart, and how willing. As Slavey bore only a passing resemblance to Tłįchǫ, he was often in the dark.

"Cold this morning, eh, Bernard?" David, breathing steam in lantern light, slapped his hands together heartily.

Sascho got along with David. In fact, Sascho understood that David was pretty happy now that Leo had gone, because that made him "lead dog."

Some time ago, Sascho too had been renamed. Initially, it had been hard to remember the name (as well as "twelve," the number he'd been assigned) along with everything else which was new. The knocks he'd received during the first weeks, though, when he'd not responded to "Bernard", had soon worked their rough magic. The number was mostly used in the schoolrooms or on laundry day, when they received a clean package of clothes.

On the morning when they'd hung a cross around his neck and—after a lot of chanting and getting up and down—put water on his head, he'd felt nothing like Father McCarthy had said he would. There was no light, no warmth, no change within his angry heart. He had learned to mouth the prayers, but as none of that prayer language was translated—it, like just about everything else, was forbidden—he had no idea what any of it meant. The priests and nuns were the ones who knew what the words meant.

* * *

It was still dark, and would remain in a long twilight now until well after breakfast. At nine, when lessons began, the sun would at last be above the horizon. Despite that welcome presence, a cold wind had slipped down from the north overnight. This morning was snot-freezing.

When he and David were alone together, they did not speak English. This initially had taken some hard listening from both sets of ears, but many of the words were similar. David was a Yellowknife, a tribe who were long-time enemies of the Tłįchǫ, so they'd both been wary of one another at first. At this school, though, it was easy to see that here they were alike, doing the same work, learning the same kwet'įį things. Eventually, working together to stay out of trouble overrode the learned, old-time fear.

David showed Sascho what to do, and had at first kept him out of trouble with Guy, who was the more likely of the two older men to take the strap to their "new boy."

"Will you go home when they have their— N'asi?"

"Feast? Christmas, you mean? No, I won't go anywhere. It's a pretty long trip to Dettah and that costs money. None of my family can afford to get me, even though Tındeè is frozen. I sure wish they could! If it weren't for Auntie Blanche over there in that kitchen, we'd starve. It'll be summer before I get anything good to eat again."

David was seventeen and still growing—his arms stuck out of his shirts and his legs stuck out of his trousers. He was always hungry, but that didn't make him any different from Sascho or any one else. It was hard to pass through the kitchen sometimes, for here they could see all the good food being prepared, the roasts of pork and whole chickens—all for the Chekaa and the priests and nuns. This was when the misery of his situation struck Sascho hardest. He too was growing, and his belly grumbled all the time.

Occasionally, "Auntie" Blanche would slip them a chunk of pork crackling, chicken skin, or a piece of beef bone they could sneak away and suck the marrow from, so the best time to find a reason to go to the kitchen was while she was taking the staff's food out of the big black stove.

Blanche had to be careful, though, not to be seen by Mrs. Le Pen, who presided over the cook staff, or she'd have to endure a lecture, just as if she was one of the children. "Auntie"

Blanche was not her real name, of course. Her official name was Mrs. Marsh, but she, like many of the servants, had native blood. Her Mamàcho was from Detah like him, David said, in this way claiming kinship to their biggest benefactor. Mrs. Marsh baked meat and bread in the big ovens, coming early and not leaving until the Chekaa had their supper served, even though she had a family of her own to care for in the village nearby.

One afternoon Sascho arrived with an armload of wood for the stove in the bosses' shed. He knocked, received an answering "Come in" and entered quickly. The man who'd opened the door was someone new, a man with dark skin and a long lean face framed by an old wide brimmed hat. He wore his hair gathered into a knot at the nape of his neck. A speckled summer-phase ptarmigan feather was tucked into his hatband, but otherwise he wore trousers, shirt and a blanket wool coat, like a white man.

Sascho thought the man must be another Métis, some friend of Frank's who still worked the river. Occasionally, Frank's old acquaintances came by to visit, often on Saturday afternoon. Usually a bottle of strong spirits would come along too, especially if the man hung around into the evening. Though work at the barn was a respite from the school, Sascho had soon learned that this was a time to stay as far away from his bosses as possible.

This particular man, much to his relief, had brought a pair of nice Uldai along with him instead of booze. Their silver-gray bodies lay upon a newspaper atop the rough table his bosses used for eating and playing cards. There was a stirring of memory, as he studied the man's face. His long head reminded Sascho of some distant relatives he'd met last year when he and Uncle John had traveled to Wha't'i.

"This here's my new boy." Frank sat by the stove, pipe in one permanently grimy hand. "Here now Bernard, you stack those nice and neat for me."

Sascho did not need to be told what to do, but he knew Frank enjoyed bossing him around. Quietly he set the stove-size pieces one atop the other, banking the pile against the cabin wall. At first, the constant stream of English had been maddening, like running headfirst into a tree over and over again, but sometime during the last weeks, he'd begun to understand better.

"Haven't you ever been to school before?" The man seemed to be studying him, too.

"No sir."

No sir! Yes sir! Please and thank-you-sir or ma'am—that was how you addressed them.

"This here is Mr. Zoe, Bernard."

"Hello, Mr. Zoe, sir."

"'Sir' is for them over there." The feather tilted to point toward the peeling white building whose long shadow hung over everything. "Sylvain's my name." The man spoke quietly and put out his hand kwet'ìì style. Sascho hesitated and then shook it.

Sylvain studied him for a long moment and then asked, "Your family keep you out of here till now?" He mimed family, making a circle with his arms.

"Yes, sir, Mr. Sylvain."

"Mounties caught Bernard up in Behchok'o, didn't they? Sent him and a bunch of others down from Yellowknife to get civilized. He ain't happy, but I am. He's a damn good worker. Don't know how much they're gonna teach him, though. He's a pretty big dog to teach new tricks like readin' and writin' too."

"Bernard will learn some English, some French, and after he'll get along good in Canada."

Canada, Sascho had learned, was what the kwet'ı̨ı̨ now called the land. It was a new baptism for the Tłı̨chǫ dèè', just as all the names of the students had been changed, all the traditional names of places like mountains and rivers had been changed too.

"Not Slavey or Dene, is he?" Frank grinned, showed stained teeth clamped onto the pipe stem. "Seems to get along okay with the Yellowknife kid, though he ain't one of them, either."

"Thlingchadinne, maybe."

So good to hear the name of his people spoken! Sascho, who worked hard to never give anything away, felt his eyes light up for a moment before he looked away.

Frank puffed on his pipe; breathed out a blue cloud into the hot, close room. The oil

175

barrel was full of blazing pine slab. It hissed, threatening to burn through the rusty sides.

"You're one of 'em, ain't you, Sylvain? Didn't you once tell me you come from Lac La Martre?"

"Spent time there." Mr. Zoe, his face unmoving, replied. "Lived all over this territory, you know."

"Well, well. Just thought I remembered you said you was born there."

Mr. Zoe, his face blank in a way Sascho wished he could reproduce, began to feel in his pocket for his own pipe. Clearly, he wasn't going to say another word.

"Well, never mind. Sit yourself down and we'll eat these fine jack you've brought. You can give me all the River news."

Sascho finished his task, sweeping bark chips that had fallen to the floor and putting them into the kindling box. He was about to leave, when Frank suddenly issued a new directive.

"Here's a knife, young fella." His boss reached into his pocket and extended the knife bone handle first. "Why don't you cut up them fish for us before you go? You know how?"

When Sascho replied with a "Yessir," Frank said, "You can eat with us tonight, Bernard, instead of that slop they feed you kids."

Sascho did not wait for a second invitation. Taking the proffered blade, he went over to the table and straightaway began what to him was a fairly straightforward task, one he'd learned young. He kept his eyes on both the extremely sharp knife and his fingers, for it was easy to lose track of what you were cutting among the Uldai's many bones. Nevertheless, at the back of his neck, he could feel Mr. Zoe's brown eyes, thoughtfully studying him.

* * *

Sascho had his hand on the latch to the door to Frank and Guy's cabin, when David, who was piling wood against the wall, signed him to stop.

"I wouldn't go in there right now."

"Why? I just brought this hot water from the kitchen. He told me he wanted it right away."

"Never mind. Pour it into the cattle tank. It'll melt the ice and you can get more after the trader leaves. Frank won't want to see you now."

"Why?" Sascho set the steaming pail down. "You know Mrs. Le Pen will be angry if I take more water right away. Supper dishes and all that." There was a big tank over the kitchen stove into which water was regularly hand pumped, but it took time to heat it, and clean up time in the evening required plenty. In fact, they'd just finished stacking wood for the kitchen's needs just an hour ago. This time of year, it was a constant battle against the cold.

David placed the last piece on the pile, and then walked toward Sascho, emerging from the half light at the back of the barn. The place smelled of over-wintering animals, but Sascho had grown to like the smell of the unfamiliar cattle and the horses—even the strong odor that came from the sow's pen. He'd found comfort in their presence, and had grown to know something of their ways as he tended them. These were the only creatures, besides men, on the place. To him, this land was barren.

Sascho understood that all these animals in the barn were dependent upon man, the same way dogs were. Wild animals, the moose or caribou, the beaver or muskrat, didn't need the help of any two-legged creature to get along. All these tame animals that the white man had brought lived inside a great deal, for the wind and chill during winter here—especially on this exposed hill by the river—could easily kill them.

"Yeah, well, Frank will be even angrier than Mrs. Le Pen if you go in there now. He's been drinking and he's selling clothes and stuff like that to the trader."

"Clothes?"

"Oh, the really nice deer skin dresses and moccasins they took off all of you when you came here—the good things, anyway, the stuff with lots of beads. The trader sends them down south somewhere and makes money."

"They sell our clothing?" This gave Sascho pause. Stealing, among Sascho's people, was a terrible crime. He'd also been told that their clothing would be destroyed because it was "heathen"—whatever that meant.

"Yeah, but we're not supposed to know about it."

"What do we go home in then? Our skin?"

The kwet'įį say they think stealing is a sin, but they do it all the time.

"Oh, if you go home, they'll let you wear some of the oldest stuff they can find, but, hell, don't worry about it. I don't think your lot from the north will go home until they're done with you."

That was alarming news, but Sascho was still inwardly raging about what he'd heard.

"Do the priests know they steal from us?"

"I don't think they care. Who knows? Maybe they get a share of what Frank gets."

Sascho didn't know what to say. Learning English and learning about money and numbers, these ideas which were supposed to benefit him—and he even thought it would, especially now that he'd seen so many kwet'įį already living here in the south—did not always seem uppermost at this school.

"Go on and pour that water into the cattle tank. We can hope it won't freeze up overnight. If it does, you know we'll be out here busting ice before breakfast."

Tomorrow, Sascho thought, would probably begin like that anyway. They'd entered the time of long dark. Even at this hour, it was already bitterly cold in the yard. On his way over from the main building, after his class time had ended, the wind had blown straight through the old wool jacket and knit mittens he'd donned and given him an all-over skin-searing nip.

Today, that wind blew straight out of the north, direct from the icy sea that lay beyond the fabled lands of the Inuktitut. Still, the barn, with the animals inside, mostly stayed—except for strips along the windward wall—above freezing. Guy and Frank had actually hauled some of the wood that needed cutting inside this morning so that the boys could chop it there, rather than sending them outside. Both boys had been glad of that bit of kindness from an unusual source.

So Sascho did as David suggested and lugged the bucket across the barn floor to the cattle tank then heaved it in. The red and white cow came to watch what he was doing. Sascho enjoyed the way she gazed into the tank with round eyes while the water, ever so briefly, steamed at the surface.

David wandered back to where the logs were piled. Slowly, he selected and then began to split another piece. He'd been at it for a long time today already and was pretty tired. As his workmate collected the resulting pieces and stacked them, he said, "I heard Frank talking about a really nice knife they'd got from your lot."

"Knife?"

Sascho had lost his own fine fish knife right away in Behchok'o when the Mountie had taken it from him, but he knew that Yaot'l had retained hers, which was smaller.

"Yes, you should have heard him laughing about how the priest and the nuns were all squawking about finding it on the stairs the day you all came in. They were sure one of the boys had tried to smuggle it inside. All of 'em actin' like they were afraid for their lives, or something, I guess, but Frank said it wasn't very big. Still, it was sharp enough to cut through anything, and could have done a fair amount of damage if somebody knew how to use it. The handle is antler and it's got a nice goose carving. Frank figures the trader will pay pretty good."

"A goose?"

"Yeah. Hey, it wasn't yours, was it?" David studied him. His companion wasn't above the occasional cruelty to a newcomer. He grinned, which indicated he thought he'd discovered the knife's original owner.

"Not mine." Sascho was able to answer truthfully. "The Mountie got my good hunting knife when he caught me." He did the best he could to look disinterested, but it was hard, because the object under discussion he knew well. He even knew how Charlie Snow Goose, the carver, had made it for a little sister, the very girl that he, Sascho, loved.

With an ache in his heart, he wondered how Yaot'l was enduring the hardships of this place. He was sad as he thought of the beautiful knife, now stolen and gone forever, but he was thankful, too, she had not been caught with it still in her possession.

And if she had been, he didn't want to even begin to imagine what might have happened.

"At last!" David set the final log on end. "After this piece, I'm done. Come on, Sascho, help me sweep up. Maybe Auntie Blanche is still in the kitchen—'cause if she is—we need to see if she's saved anything for us tonight."

* * *

Kele looked different now, without his fancy white cowboy outfit and his head cropped to the skin. He carried himself differently too. No longer a laughing bold boy, proud of himself and of his family—and of his fine clothing—he was just one of two boys, heads down, dressed in gray trousers, wearing threadbare baggy jackets which didn't fit them.

Kele's sudden appearance was a surprise. As the boys were kept separate by age, Sascho hadn't seen him—only distantly in Church and meals—since they'd come off the boat. Now, it was deep winter. Snow piled against the house; it hissed and slithered across the bare landscape. It was some time after the kwet'ı̨ı̨ had had one of their big festivals, about the birth of their god to a human woman, but all the pomp and prayer hadn't meant much to Sascho, who spent most of his time among the workmen.

Suddenly, all these months later, here stood Kele, whose small self he'd almost forgotten.

He'd been sent with two others to ferry wood to the main building. Sascho nonchalantly picked up another large piece and set it on end, then readied his ax. He had become the complete expert at handling wood, from the familiar splitting of kindling to the less familiar saw. While his English remained scant, he stayed out of trouble by careful observation. As the kwet'ı̨ı̨ lived by routine, it did not take long to understand what was expected of him.

Curiously, he watched as Kele began to pile kindling onto the sledge. Sascho gathered an armload of what he'd just split and made it an excuse to walk over. Hearing his approach, Kele turned and looked straight into Sascho's eyes, but at first he seemed not to recognize him.

"Kele." Sascho dared to speak his now forbidden name.

The boy's eyes brightened, but just for a moment. Almost at once, the light went out. He even flushed, as if ashamed. To Sascho, such a reaction to one's true name made no sense.

"I'm Gregorie now."

"I'm Bernard."

"I have to keep working." Kele's shoulders slumped and he returned his attention to the wood pile.

"That's right, he does. And so do you, Bernard." A balding priest, whom Sascho knew as Brother Corbeau, came through the door accompanied by a swirl of snow. He pounded his leather gloves together vigorously and smiled.

"Hurry up now, you kids. We don't want Father McCarthy's parlor to get any colder, do we? He'll be cross as two sticks." His smile widened as he reached over, took Kele familiarly by his shoulders and gave him a little shake.

Sascho noted how the boy shrank. It was clear, though, that he did not dare to evade that touch. Like a woman accepting the false caress of an unkind husband, Kele allowed the gloved hands to rub his shoulders. When the handling was done, he carried the bundle high on his chest, with his face tilted toward it. Only Sascho saw the tears glinting in his long-lashed eyes.

* * *

"See you down here a lot, Bernard." Sylvain spoke to him in Tłı̨chǫ. The familiar sound was welcome, even if the man did not pronounce his words exactly the same way Sascho did.

"Yes. I like to watch Dehcho." Sascho had never seen such an enormous river. He found it frightening—the expanse of it, and the incredible power it displayed in every season. In winter, mountains of ice grew into elaborate towers, while beneath the surface it continued to flood north. Sometimes these ice mountains would break and then fall with a deafening roar before the whole process would begin once again.

Spring was still a ways off, but he knew the days had lengthened. The sun would stay above the horizon for longer and longer, it would turn hot, and afterward—very soon—heat and the push of the underlying water would break open the ice. In no time, the land beyond would be sweaty and buggy again, but also full of game and fish and berries.

An idea had been forming in Sascho's mind, one about running away and heading home. He'd listened to the men talk, and was beginning to get a sense of what lay around him, although he had never traveled it on foot. He wanted to be ready to escape if an opportunity showed itself, and he didn't plan on going alone.

He'd seen Yaot'l out hanging clothes a few times, but mostly he only saw her in profile, across the aisle at church or at a distance in the big room at supper while they all sat in silence, spooning up whatever gruel Mrs. Marsh had been allowed to concoct for them, while Brother DiSante read aloud from the Holy Book. If he and Yaot'l were so lucky as to look at one another at the same moment, he'd feel the spark she desperately sent. He was punished once for gazing at her for too long, so he'd quickly learned not to be so obvious. He also knew she'd been punished for his offence as well, and he didn't like to think about that.

"Water is always a good guide—water shows a wise man the way. To his home in Behchok'o, maybe?" Sylvain cracked a crooked smile.

Sascho could not help wondering, when Sylvain talked in a confiding manner, whether he was being baited to say or do something that would get him in trouble. After all, the man was friendly with Frank and Guy, and sometimes he even drank with them. Then, as far as Sascho was concerned, none of them were fit to be around.

As if seeing it for the first time, Sascho suddenly noted that stippled feather on his hatband.

Perhaps he has ɪk'o̱o̱. How else can he hear the thoughts circling in my head?

Suddenly, for the very first time, Sascho wondered if Sylvain, like his uncle John, possessed special knowledge. Nothing, though, here in the south, was as it should be. Everyone pretended—like the priests and nuns who talked about a god of love while they beat children with canes and straps.

Although his intuition was usually good, he resolved to test it. After all, Sylvain was on good terms with his bosses. Which means, Sascho thought, I cannot be sure of him.

"I don't like Behchok'o."

"Behchok'o ain't home, then."

Sascho looked down toward the river. The barren willows shuddered in a gust of wind. Deep in the audible register, the river ground with menace, as it shuffled and reshuffled the ice.

"Gam'e't'i's more like it for you. Yes, Gam`e`t`i, I think." When Sascho still refused to speak, Sylvain continued to study him, now with a glint in his eyes, "Maybe I'm wrong. Maybe it's Wekweeti?"

Wekweeti? That was where Sascho's legendary great-great-grandparents had visited, the origin of his stocky build, his high cheeks, and his striking eyes.

"You got a family name, Bernard?"

The last name was not forbidden, but it still stuck in his throat. "I'm Lynx." He admitted, knowing full well from his visit last year with John that there were Lynx family members in Wha't'i. If Sylvain was really from Wha't'i, he would know that.

Sylvain nodded. "Thought so." He looked away, out at the frozen river. "Ever travel the Horn?"

"No." Uncle John had spoken of this river, but they had not used it when they'd been traveling west last year. The southern most part lay, after all, outside traditional Tłįchǫ territory.

"The Horn meets Dehcho some ways northwest of here. You can paddle the Horn north, though there's a strong current where it's wide. It goes all the way to Sahtu, but it's not good paddling, because there are too many rapids and forks. Where another river angles into it, you portage or start walking, and keep on by northwest till you find Tłįchǫ trail. It's a hard walk through bush to Wha't'i, in and out of muskeg, lakes and bogs, but old Wha't'i is hard to miss, even for a Gam`e`t`i boy who don't know the way." Sylvain winked. "If you get to

Wha't'i before łk'àdèè k'è is over, you can borrow a boat and paddle home. Get home before snow flies and then go hunt caribou with your uncles. You'll never have to see this place again."

Sascho straightened and gazed into the man's eyes. He tried not to twitch, to smile, or move any facial muscles. He did not want to give his thoughts away, although his thoughts reeled with excitement.

He's just told me exactly what I must do.

"Now David comes," Sylvain said. His cool hazel eyes subtly shifted to look across Sascho's right shoulder. "You and I—we will talk more. This school is no place for a man."

It warmed Sascho's heart to be called a man, but there was a tickle of apprehension as well. He remembered the days it had taken to get here and he'd now seen the enormous size of Tındeè and the raging power of Dehcho. Gam`e`t`i, he knew, was very far away.

* * *

Guy went out to town to drink on Saturday night. This made Frank angry, because he, the fix-it man, was supposed to always be at the school. On some of these Saturdays, David explained to Sascho, Frank had a woman sneak in to visit him in the shack. They'd have to bring a lot of wood in to him early and carry hot water for one of Frank's infrequent baths in the tin tub.

On most Saturdays, they were sent into the school, for whatever treat had been arranged for them, often a moving picture show. Movies were at first a wonder, but these black and white shadow stories were filled with little but the killing of villainous Indians by brave courageous white men. Sometimes, though, he enjoyed the short intervals where the Indians rode bareback and did tricks, like dropping over the horse's side and shooting from behind, but as one after another of these "injuns" fell into the dirt and died, the sense of amazement did too.

The woman's visits to Frank was one of those things Sascho wasn't supposed to know about—like the night he'd blundered, with an armload of wood, into the wrong upstairs room in the school and come upon rosy-faced Father Corbeau with a small naked boy seated upon his knee. The beating he'd received for this mistake, along with a month of banishment from the warmth and handouts he'd had from the kitchen, let him know the only action he could take was to forget. He felt like a coward and he was ashamed, and this left him angrier than anything else that had yet happened.

Although he never told anyone what he'd seen, not even David—who seemed to have a good notion anyway—he found himself thinking about Kele often, remembering the wooden hopelessness he'd seen when they'd had that chance meeting in the barn. Fury welled inside him whenever he imagined Kele as the one seated on that black knee—a kid, who'd come to school with such confidence and pride.

* * *

"When is break up?"

Sascho stood again by the willow tree, watching the river. His thoughts had been interrupted by the sound of Sylvain's feet crunching toward him over dry snow. Today on the river, the mountains of ice were busy rearranging themselves. They grumbled, shook, and then collapsed.

"Not soon enough for either of us," Sylvain said. He frowned down at the river.

At their last meeting, Sascho had decided to trust him, and more—he'd asked for help. He couldn't see any other way for them to escape and to quickly put some miles between them and the school.

If I escape, it's not going to be like those kids who run away every summer and get caught in a week. When I go, I will not be caught.

"It'll be about the same time the ice breaks up in Gam`e`t`i, but I know the signs. I'll be ready for it. It's my first trading trip of the season and I'm ready to get out of here myself."

He'd seen Mr. Zoe's boat canvassed down on the bank nearby. It was Indian-style, a long

190

boat, one which could hold as many as fourteen paddlers—or just four paddlers and a lot of baggage in the middle. It wasn't something you'd want to take on Decho until the ice was gone and the flow rate had settled. Running a big river like that too early, Mr. Zoe explained, was a recipe for disaster.

Today, he wondered if he should say something about Yaot'l—and how he—somehow—intended to bring her along, too, but he thought it might be too early for that. Besides, he had no idea of how to contact her. He had a feeling she was as isolated as he was.

In a moment of weakness near that big midwinter feast, he'd asked David if he'd heard anything about a tall girl who'd come in this fall. He dared to do it when they'd were working in the barn together, one of the few alone moments they would have during the day. Frank had been hammering away at something, and Guy too was out, chauffeuring Father McCarthy.

David said he had heard of some older girl among the new ones who'd been locked up for "a couple of weeks" in the attic on bread and water.

"She was pretty quiet after she came out."

Was David baiting him? Sascho's heart plummeted, even as he strove to control any outward expression.

What have they done to her?

"What's she to you, then?" David's eyes pried. "Is that the girl who was with you when you was caught? She's your cousin, right?"

Sascho nodded.

"Well, she bit Sister Louise while the old bitch was trying to cut her hair." David pulled off his woolen cap and then reflexively scratched at his own, stripped head. After putting the hat back on, he grinned at Sascho, this time in a far friendlier way, and said, with real feeling, "Wish I'd seen it!"

* * *

The moon had waxed and waned several times since he'd heard the story. As he studied the older man beside him, he thought, odd though it was, that despite his constant hunger, right after the turn of the year, he'd grown. He was able to look Mr. Zoe in the eye.

"If—if I can get someone else out, would you take them too?"

"Depends."

Sascho stiffened his jaw. "On what, Mr. Zoe?"

"On how hard they can paddle."

"Well, they can paddle hard, yes sir." Sascho remembered the leg of their journey to Gam`e`t`i and the loaded canoe. He remembered her, paddling down to Behchok'o with the others for the pow-wow. He and Yaot'l had labored in perfect harmony.

192

"More than one?"

"Um—no. Just one other."

"You said 'they.' Is this one—female?"

Well, here it was, the dreaded question, but Sascho knew it was best to speak truth.

"She—she's my gots'èke—or—or she will be after I've paid the bride price—but I can't do anything right for her—or for me—when I'm stuck in here."

The admission spilled out. Some of what he'd claimed was no sure thing, even if they got home.

Mr. Zoe's eyebrows lifted. For once, his expression gave something away. Surprise—amusement?

"Yaot'l has been raised like me, in the bush. She knows how to travel, how to hunt and fish—and paddle—good as me. Her parents never wanted her to come here."

A long silence fell between them. Mr. Zoe returned to his study of the river. A big boom and splash as one of the ice towers toppled and fell seemed to have all his attention. Somewhere holes were opening in the ice. Water was freeing itself from the grasp of winter—and every day, the sun stayed longer and grew hotter.

The lucky ones, whose parents longed to see them, would soon be going home, some on buses, but most in hired cars. It was another wall for the families to climb, put there to keep them apart from their kids. The priests, it was said, were quick enough to give you a ride to school, but they never, ever, took you home. Your family had to come up with the money for that. He'd seen boys in his class in agony, anticipating the wait—and possible disappointment—if family didn't arrive.

For him, things had come rushing to a point. The river would run free soon, then it would require a week or two to clear and settle down. He knew Mr. Zoe was anxious to leave and that he would do so as soon as he believed he could safely navigate.

"Yaot'l, huh?" Mr. Zoe turned to face Sascho again, and now he smiled. "'Warrior'?"

Sascho, suddenly shy at her name, wanted to look away from those bright hazel eyes, but he didn't.

"Yes."

"How are you going to tell her your plan? I couldn't even talk to my own sister while I was inside that place."

"I will find a way. I have to." Sascho had already been turning that particular problem over in his mind. Almost anything he could come up with involved asking Mrs. Marsh to pass a note, but he was not sure it was wise to do that. Writing, he was learning, had its uses.

"But—Mr. Zoe—you were in—in this school?"

"Five years. Then, one summer, my uncle took me out to hunt caribou and he kept me with him to trap through the winter. My babàcho told the Indian agent they needed me more than the school did and so they went away. Now they've made going to school into a law, getting out is harder."

"Is that when you met Frank?"

"Yes. Before I came here, I'd never heard any English, or talked to Métis, or to any Slavey, neither. Talking to the other Nations now, that's good for us to learn. Indians shouldn't fight each other, not anymore."

Sascho considered. It was true; he never would have known David, or any of the other boys—not Philip, a Cree youth in his dorm who had not forgotten how to laugh and joke, all of them now, just like him, in the same captivity.

"White men are smart. They know that when they put us so young into these schools, we will forget how to be Indians. Already, here in the south, children learn English, instead of the tongue of the gocho."

"This school has taught me one thing— about my enemy."

It was as if someone else, from deep inside, spoke those words. The sound of his own voice, the cold rage he heard, took Sascho by surprise.

Some time passed before Mr. Zoe broke the following silence. "Even brave young men need some gear for a journey. I will help."

* * *

Kele's eyes snapped open. One of Brother Corbeau's boys stood over his cot.

"Get up. He wants you downstairs."

Kele tossed aside his thin blanket and sat on the side of the cot. "Why? Did he say what he wanted?" Kele's voice cracked.

The older boy smirked and shrugged. "You'll find out. Just come with me, and don't make a fuss. If you get him mad, we'll all suffer.

Kele nodded.

"Okay. Come on."

Head down, shoulders slumped, Kele followed the older boy along the row of cots to the end of the sleeping room. With every step he felt the eyes of others burn into his back. No one spoke, but Kele knew the shame that lurked behind all those haunted eyes,

Outside, they headed downstairs, and then walked along the main hallway until they entered an area generally off limits to students. Kele's guide reached in his pocket and took out a large key. After unlocking the final door, he stepped back and turned to Kele.

"There's stairs, just go down. There's a room at the bottom," he said, then reached out and squeezed Kele's shoulder, hard. "Just do what Chekaa wants and don't be a bebì." The older boy stepped back and motioned Kele inside.

The basement was an area reserved for kwejii yatı (white man's prayers) an area forbidden to students unless summoned by one of the priests.

* * *

Kele blinked several times to adjust his eyes to the dim light of a single candle burning on the stand beside a large iron bed. Across the room, waiting like diga stalking prey, Brother Corbeau, wearing a black cloak with a fur ruff around the neck rose from his chair and pointed a long-fingered pale hand towards Kele. "I want you to get out of those dirty clothes and put on this robe."

Reluctantly Kele took what looked like a flimsy nightshirt from the other's hands.

The monster smiled down at the young boy and then pulled open his robe. Kele shuddered and closed his eyes to block the sight of crêpe white skin and blood engorged genitals.

Brother Corbeau laughed and strolled over to the bed. "Come on, get that undershirt on and come join me. It's time you and I got to know each other better."

Fighting tears, and remembering what the older boy had said about not causing all of them to be punished, Kele obeyed.

* * *

Sascho had been stacking wood onto a sledge in the barnyard when he heard David yelling his name. Looking over his shoulder, eyes scanning the yard, Sascho saw his work mate's head sticking out of the door. David

197

gestured wildly, urging Sascho to stop what he was doing and hurry inside.

Dropping his load and running across the yard, Sascho entered the barn, careful to close the door as fast as possible against the cold.

"Get over here and talk to him, will you?" David's voice came from an empty stall at the back of the barn.

"What's going on?" Sascho demanded. He hurried to join David.

A boy shaking off straw was getting to his feet. It took a moment for Sascho to recognize him as Kele. The boy had grown much taller, but it was as if he'd been stretched, like a bite of spruce gum. Now he was gangly and hollow-eyed, his eyes were red; and he had a bruise on one cheek.

"I'll go finish the wood." David said from behind them. "I'll cuss real loud like I hurt myself if I see anyone coming." He turned up his coat collar before he picked up the saw and went out.

As the cold daylight blinked out, Kele said, "I mean to run away. I'd go it alone if it was just me, but Tanis has to come too. We talk through the fence when we can. She says she's afraid, but she wants to come with me."

"You must wait until the ice breaks." Sascho cast an anxious glance over his shoulder, but the only thing he saw was the cow, her jaws working on a wisp of straw. Her red and white head poked over the stall.

"I thought you'd want to escape." It was said with the old Kele flash, but Sascho could see the quiver beneath the dare.

"You have never traveled so far."

"I have gone hunting with my father." Kele growled the words; he looked down and away while he spoke. "And I will run whether you do or not."

"After the ice breaks, there's a way."

"That's too long!" Kele fell to his knees in the straw. His face flamed in an agony of shame.

"Kele; tell me what has happened." Sascho got down beside him, this little brother.

"No. I cannot. "

Sascho could see how hard Kele fought to contain tears, so when they spilled down his cheeks, he knew what these had cost. The pity Sascho felt must have shown on his face, because Kele's expression swiftly changed to anger. He jumped to his feet, kicking at Sascho so forcefully, he had to back away.

"You're just a coward!" Kele yelled, hurling himself at Sascho and pummeling the older boy with his fists. Sascho had to take some punishment before he could get hold of those thin arms and hold Kele still.

"Stop! What if Chekaa comes looking?"

The words fell like stones and Kele froze—but only for an instant. He renewed his attack with a vicious kick to Sascho's shins, forcing him to deliver a blow which knocked Kele backwards and down into the straw again.

"Cut it out, Kele! Don't act crazy. We'll die for sure if we run before ice break. We need a plan, or we'll end up like Jacob Hay."

Jacob Hay's was a story they'd heard almost as soon as they'd got to Fort Providence, one meant to discourage running away. It seemed Jacob and two friends had tried to cross Dehcho in a small boat one summer after no one had arrived to take them home. They'd started out, but were almost at once struck by river debris. When the boat sank, the other two boys had been lucky to make it to shore. Jacob had not. His body was never found.

Standing in the dimly lit barn, Sascho breathed a sigh of relief when Kele sat still, covered his face with his hands, and broke into sobs.

"June is too long. I can't..." Muffled sobs shook his thin body. Angrily, he scrubbed away tears with the sleeves of his shirt.

"Come on, let's talk." Sascho extended his hand and when Kele accepted it, drew him upright. "We are in the camp of the enemy gochı. You must endure and be patient. I promise; we will escape together."

Finally, Kele nodded, although his body drooped with eloquent despair.

"Meet me here later tonight," Sascho said. "I'll mix a medicine that will keep kwejii from coming near you. They'll think you're sick and be afraid. You'll probably be put in the sick room for days, but they won't touch you. Do you want that?"

"Yes, anything." Kele nodded his head violently.

"Hell's bells and bloody damnation!" A resounding shout came from David. Here was the promised warning!

"I'll hide." Kele dropped back into the straw.

"No," Sascho said, quickly pulling him upright again. "Listen! We'll say you came in to get something special for Father McCarthy—I'll help you find the balsam poplar he's always asking for. We cut some yesterday."

* * *

An epidemic of vomiting swept through the school. It spared no one, neither young nor old, neither pupil, servants of house or barn, priests or teachers. In a few days this plague had passed through the building and was done. The exceptions were children whose grasp on life was already precarious—a few of the newly arrived who'd been sick when they reached the school. One of these, a child of eight, an orphan, died.

Yaot'l took her turn, both as one of the afflicted and then as a caregiver. At first, she was so poorly she could hardly drag herself back and forth carrying supplies, while helping to wash up. So many were ill that one entire dormitory room was turned into a sick room.

Death had taken people around her when she'd lived in the bush, so she knew a little of His ways. She'd watched her mother as the older woman tended while Death approached an uncle. The old man had soon passed away, there within the confines of their snow bound shelter.

That had been slow, death as a stalker of the old and the weak. A more terrifying death had been the one of a beautiful cousin. Just a little older than Yaot'l, Tsįą, had died in childbirth. In the anticipation of joy suddenly turned to sorrow, Yaot'l had witnessed the here and gone of life, the effect all the worse for being unexpected.

At last, Yaot'l was well again. At first, she was glad Patricia was still abed because they could sometimes talk and be together. Then, the lack of change in her friend began to worry her. Patricia was ordered back to her dormitory— declared to be "malingering" by Sister Louise. Almost at once she was undeniably sick again, this time, "coming out both ends." So, in a few hours, back into the infirmary she went.

A few deaths that spring, but most recovered—but not Patricia, who complained of an ever-increasing, wandering belly pain. It started as a deep ache in the center and then, as the days passed, it migrated to her lower right side. Patricia said, "Like a stab, like lightening." Of course, she was mocked for saying such "an absurd thing," but when Sister Louise at last took her temperature, it showed one hundred two.

"It will certainly break," Sister Louise declared.

Yaot'l and Clare too, promised to keep working an embroidery they were making for Sister Mary Margaret instead of taking their hour of daily recreation if they could be allowed to sit with Patricia.

"Not both at the same time."

"No, of course not, Sister Louise." The young women hung their heads and studied the floor, inwardly praying for permission. They knew their friend was very ill, for she rarely spoke, just hugged her knees to her belly, groaned and shivered.

"My belly is hot and red." Patricia whispered.

Clare told Yaot'l she'd never seen such a thing before, when the news got around that Sister Louise had finally gone to Father McCarthy and insisted that, after two weeks of pain and a steady temperature of one hundred three, they really must send for a doctor.

The doctor came and then a sleigh came. Everyone disobeyed, and ran to watch the stretcher with Patricia upon it carried out the door. Yaot'l and Clare both wept and prayed for their friend.

They waited for news, but once the infirmary was empty, the daily routine simply went on—the prayers, the school, the tasks, the punishments and fights. No one said anything, and Yaot'l and Clare, began to hope for the best, but did not dare to ask. Finally, Sunday came and that was when they were told Patricia had died.

"Our good doctors operated, but her appendix had burst and Patricia died. Fortunately, because she was baptised. She will go to be judged with Christians. We must all pray for her soul, especially as she is certainly one of those who will wander in purgatory…"

Chapter Nine

Yaot'l was out of doors, in the yard by the wash line, thinking about Patricia and how much she missed her—pretty face, wild, crooked smile, her fists! She and a big kwet'įį woman had been bringing in frozen sheets, tablecloths, and the white wimples the nuns wore, all items which would dry outside even in today's frigid weather.

It was May, by the kwet'įį calendar, where each day had been given a number, exactly like each Indian child inside the school. Nevertheless, winter was not entirely ready to relax her grip. On the hillside where Yaot'l stood, the winds still bit hard. This morning the wind could strip the skin right off your knuckles if you happened to drop a mitten while trying to wrestle frozen clothing away from the line.

And then, all at once, she heard them, coming up from the south. She looked, and what a sight to see! Back home again, free flying— her other-kin—wing tip to wing tip, a great glittering V traveling north-east. Her people told stories round the campfire about the great frozen sea of the white bears, where the seal-hunting Inuktitut lived. There, on rocky plains, the snow geese lived and raised their children. Their re-appearance in a new year and their musical cry brought her joy—but only for an instant, because as the V receded, their purity blending into a milky sky, she was left behind.

Now, a desperate longing surged, one which almost choked her. With all the strength of a still wild heart, she wished—and wished—to follow.

They are surrounded by their tribe, going home. If only I could grow wings, how swiftly I would fly after them!

Yaot'l knew that she would face many dangers if she took goose form. She could be caught by the neck and strangled by a fox or a lynx, or slain by a human hunter, shot on the wing by arrows or bullets, caught in a net. This could happen either in the north or in the summer land to the south. As a mother goose, she would have to fight fearlessly, sometimes to the death, the great birds of prey that came to raid her nest of eggs or precious chicks.

My life would be short, but I'd be with my own kind...

"Hey! Barbara! Stop dawdling and get busy!"

As usual, the time for reflection was brief. The stout kwet'ı̨ı̀ woman, strode up, bawling.

"You stupid Injuns might like to stand out here to gawp at honkers and freeze your ass, but I don't."

Big freckled hands seized the other end of a frozen sheet, the place where Yaot'l had stopped. English was somewhat understandable now, so she caught the gist—the insults, as well as the rage at her inattention.

Slowly, she bent to pick up her mitten and pulled it, all ice, on again, over her reddened wrists. The coverage it offered was minimal, but at this time of year, hands dried into a condition like old leather, she was grateful for anything between her and the wind. It wasn't smart to hurry a task, because all they did was find something else for you to do…

"Come on!" The woman tugged at the sheet, trying to break it free from the line. Whether she was shouting at the sheet or at Yaot'l was unclear. The cloth could have been a board; it was stiff and flat.

Yaot'l picked at her end, using a clothes pin to bend the fold open, so that, between the two of them, they could pull it down. This—*thank heaven!*—was almost the last piece of washing. The cold gnawed at her stiff fingers through the mittens.

She didn't realize it as she pushed her shaking fingers to perform the task, but she was being watched.

"Finish it by yourself, dummy! I'm going in." With a wicker basket jammed against one wide hip, the woman trudged away, big boots already on the track back to the main building.

As Yaot'l bent a linen tablecloth into a square she could carry, someone came up from behind. Yaot'l, her attention engaged, didn't see the shadow fall until the last moment, spun around.

You don't let people sneak up on you in this place.

A young man with a navy wool cap pulled down hard over his ears, seized her woolen mitts in his.

"Yaot'l!"

She couldn't believe she was actually beside him after all this time! Sascho!

His face was winter pale. Beneath his high cheekbones there were hollows—he's hungry too—she thought, but maybe, as she noted the new width of his shoulders beneath the coat, not as hungry as I am.

"I'll help you get this last one down."

His voice, too, came a shade deeper. The two of them were concealed behind that last rigid sheet, one which wobbled rather than flapped in the cold wind. The sound of their shared language was music.

"They'll see us, so we don't have much time." Despite what he'd said about the laundry, he stood where he was, holding her hands and gazing into her eyes as if they were wells from which he could drink.

"The river's going to break up soon. Four weeks from today, after the Night Vigil starts, slip out through the hallway service door and go to the bottom of the yard into the willows. Wait for me there. I'll meet you and if everything works, we'll travel to What'ti on Marten Lake."

"Walk all the way to Wha't'i?"

"We'll canoe down Dehcho and then go inland. I've a friend who has a boat. He will help us with the first part and get us some gear."

She could not help herself. Shivering hard, she leaned against him. When she did, his arms came around her and he hugged her with all his might. How warm he was! Even through those old wool jackets, Yaot'l believed she could feel the drum beat of their hearts.

"We're going to get a whipping if they see us."

"Yes."

He released her and the wind that blew between them seemed even colder than before. Sascho at once went to work on the sheet, dragging it down from the line.

"Don't forget." He forced the sheet into quarters.

"Four weeks, after the river breaks up, Night Vigil—the service door—among the willows." Her heart was in her throat as she repeated his instructions. *What was I just thinking, about the geese?* This journey through the wilderness might take her life, but she'd gladly die beside her sweetheart in the bush, if that's what fate had in store.

* * *

After being beaten for so many small things, it seemed yet another miracle, when she entered lugging that final basket of laundry, to find that no one had seen them. Supper making was underway, here in the kitchen. Mrs. Marsh and a maid were busily banging pots around on the high black stove.

In a long shed-like room adjacent to the kitchen, the door was open. Cold air from the unheated space poured in, although it hardly made a dent in the heat from the stove. The big kwet'ı̨ı̨ woman was just emerging, having hung up some clothes again, this time inside, a place where they'd finish drying.

"Thought you was just gonna stay out there and freeze." The woman pushed past Yaot'l, and then, to signal her continued annoyance, she slammed the door, leaving Yaot'l in the cold again, but this time heaving a sigh of relief. What would happen later was unknowable, so she put any worry about future punishment aside and set to work folding the items that felt damp-dry into a basket for ironing.

Her thoughts were a jumble, tumbling between apprehension and delight. Her heart—from Sascho's embrace, from his news—from his closeness after all these months—still pounded. It is a sign, she decided, that the geese came today. And sure enough, the sign had been followed by pure joy, something she had not felt since that long ago fishing expedition.

The happiness, though always shadowed by fear, refused to be put away. When she came out of the little room, she passed by Mrs. Marsh, who always, no matter how busy she was, had a smile and a treat for school kids.

"Here, Barbara." She turned to Yaot'l, ladle in hand. "Quick!" When Yaot'l looked surprised—the ladle held a stew rich with meat, food that was unmistakeably for the staff. "Hurry, take it! It's not too hot. Eat it while Jenny's gone out."

Yaot'l did not have to be asked again. She took the ladle and gulped the contents, which were hot and absolutely delicious.

"You looked near frozen when you came in."

Yaot'l said a grateful thank-you as she returned the ladle. "I'll start washing the pots."

Yaot'l received a big smile from the cook.

Please Nǫhtsı̨ keep me out of trouble just a few more weeks.

These words Yaot'l prayed silently to herself every day. Meanwhile, it warmed; the river broke up. The ice went north with a sound like rolling thunder.

Then, at last, four weeks to the day were done. She'd seen Sascho's gaze, the look in his eye as the line in which he stood passed her by while she cleaned the supper tables.

As if in answer to all those prayers, chores were done and evening chapel finished with no incidents. Her flour sack pillow case she'd surreptitiously packed with jacket, mitts and scarf, lay beneath her, hidden under the mattress. Late into the night she lay awake listening to the others settling in, and, at last, to the steady hum of sleep.

The hall clock chimed, hours, half hours and quarter hours, till at last the appointed time came. There was the shuffling of feet as the nuns went to their night vigil. Sweat broke out all over her body as she eased herself from the bed, and knelt to ease the pillowcase free. Then, not daring to look around, senses alert for any sound, she slipped out of the dorm and then down the stairs. The corridor by the service door was pitch black, but she kept one hand on the wall and crept along until she reached it. Tonight, as Sascho had said and as she'd hoped and prayed—it was unlocked.

* * *

Brother Corbeau kept his boys close—running errands when he went to town, polishing his shoes, pressing his clothes. There were sweets, apples, and sometimes meat from the priest's table for the chosen ones. There was, of course, always a price to pay—time in his bed. While Kele suffered agonies of guilt, disgust, and shame, a few of the other boys so "favored" did not appear to feel that way. In fact, they were jealous of the other boys Brother Corbeau liked. The "corruption" that the priests were always talking about was what had happened to them, or so Kele believed, but he could not imagine how anyone could wish to do such things.

Kele did learn things about the school, though, as he walked behind Brother Corbeau, carrying books or a cup of coffee, things that were good to know—such as where keys to certain doors were kept, each one marked with a colored tag. Father McCarthy called Corbeau a "night owl" and so he was, the last stalking the halls every night. Of course, this habit of his also made predation easier, for it put him in charge of locking up—the doors into the boys' dormitory—the outer doors, as well—were all in his charge.

To know about the keys was special knowledge, and Kele intended to put what he knew to good use. He prayed that when the night came, Brother Corbeau did not call for him. He had a task to perform, and Sascho was relying on him.

* * *

Tanis lay in the darkness, listening to the chorus of breathing around her. She'd been counting chimes—from the clock in the hall, from the chapel bells. She'd fallen asleep for a time and jerked awake in terror that she'd missed her chance, but the clock in the hall had called out 11, so she knew she wasn't too late. In the end she'd been glad she'd slept, for she was always tired—so very tired—half sick throughout the whole winter. Besides, it had made the wait pass more quickly.

At the quarter hour, she readied herself, curled onto one side. She'd wait until the bell for the Night Vigil had rung and then she'd roll up her blanket, throw a dress and coat on over her nightgown, grab her shoes and socks, and slip along the hallway to the side door where Kele said he'd be. Almost fainting with fear, she'd held her breath while she'd gathered her things, crossed the room, opened the door and slipped out. Sure enough, down the hall a ways, there he'd been, tying his shoe. When he turned at the sound of her approach, his eyes burned against his thin face as if he were feverish. A blanket roll lay on the floor at his feet.

She'd remembered that the service door was locked in the evenings, but before she had a chance to whisper anything, he'd produced a key and opened it. Crossing the yard in twilight had been another terror. They'd both run to the bottom as quickly as possible. There was a hole under that fence Kele knew he could squirm through, but tonight, as they approached it they saw that a ladder had been placed there. They went over it, throwing the blanket roll down on the other side. Then they were in brush, close to the galloping river. Edging along, occasionally stumbling as they made their way between the bushes and rocks, they followed the bank until suddenly, the fence on the upside disappeared. Nearby a host of small boats were drawn up, in various states of readiness.

They'd left school property! Kele turned, grabbed her arm and signaled for silence with a finger to his lips. He pulled her down to the ground and crawled under a boat tarp, signaling for her to follow his lead.

It wasn't long before something happened. A pair of rough leather boots appeared, the round toed workman's kind. The man bent down for a moment, and Kele thought he would soon pull back the tarp, but, after a long pause, he did nothing. Just as he'd heaved a sigh of relief, with Tanis shuddering beside him, he heard others approaching. They stepped softly, but the mud of the still melting earth squelched as they drew close.

"Who are these?" Mr. Zoe lifted the canvas that hung over the fishing boat.

Two hollow little faces peered up. They wore ragged school jackets and had woolen scarves tied around their heads

Yaot'l reached to help Tanis, who looked greatly relieved at the sight of familiar faces.

"They came with us from Yellowknife." Sascho explained as Mr. Zoe shook his head at the sight of them.

"Kids like that will slow you down," said Zoe. For a moment, he looked so dubious that Sascho feared he'd change his mind.

"Yes, they will—but Kele got us out—so he and his sister must come."

Sascho swallowed hard and reached for Yaot'l's hand. It had been one thing to want this, but now the plan was underway, he felt responsibility descend like a great stone. Soon, minutes now, and they would be off. They would be out in the bush with so many dangers—from men, from animals, from the elements.

We, who still have so much more to learn from our goʔǫhdaà.

"You two wait here," Mr. Zoe indicated the growth of thick brush on the edge of the riverbank. "Someone else is on their way."

* * *

"Don't be troubled," Yaot'l reached for Sascho's hand. "I'd brave a thousand dangers to be with you."

Sascho drew her close, but almost at once released her, for his mind—even with her warmth in his arms—still ran to the journey ahead. He knew he'd be the leader, whether he was ready or not. As for Yaot'l, he hadn't a second's doubt about her bush craft.

We will find our families, get married, and disappear.

The thought of that, of her laughter and of her wise, beautiful self ever beside him, strengthened his resolve.

* * *

"No, no, no." Michel Lafferty said when he arrived with Zoe and saw the four children. . "No! I won't cross them up there," He gestured, index finger pointing at the big white building above. "No, Zoe, I'm not paddling this trip. You and those runaways are on your own."

"What do you think those church people are going to do to you, Michael Lafferty? Beat you with a belt and your pants down like they used to?"

"I had some trouble from the RCMP last month thanks to them. I don't want more"

"Okay, Lafferty. Go on, then. Find another way up the Horn, but no hard feelings, okay? Just keep your mouth shut."

Zoe cocked his head toward the youngsters. The two youngest had been following the men's conversation anxiously, heads swiveling back and forth.

"Anyway, I've got all the paddlers I need right here."

Lafferty, after a final dismissive wave, disappeared among the boats. Kele still had his arm around Tanis. His sister looked scared and uncertain. Yaot'l hadn't expected them, and so she too felt anxious about the added responsibility.

They were all going to have to work hard for Mr. Zoe as they moved that loaded boat up the tributary. There would be places where they'd have to paddle instead of, or alongside the putt-putt, and, if Horn was like most of the rivers Sascho knew, there would be portages.

Even the first part of this journey—if we manage to get safely away—will not be easy.

"We will go now," said Mr. Zoe. He moved toward his boat, half in shadow on the shore, half in the gleaming backwash of the river. "Yaot'l, you get behind the load; there's a paddle back there. You, Sascho, you go front and watch the river for me and stay paddle ready. You two little ones, fit in wherever you can and don't you move so much as an inch once we're out on that river."

* * *

That night, while the sun skulked just below the horizon, they ran the river. It was like falling head-first, facing a west that never ceased to glow. In May, when the sun vanished, it would not be out of view for long. The current snarled against the slim sides of the boat as it cut through the water. Dehcho was unimaginably deep and the speed was beyond that of any rapid they'd ever run. Sascho felt as if the boat was an arrow in flight, hurtling downstream. Danger sang in the wind that flew past his ears. Away they went, almost air-borne, atop the glimmering twilight body of the river.

Yaot'l held her paddle in readiness, across her knees, braced upon boat's sides. She too felt the overwhelming might beneath her, as river rushed under her feet and roared on either side. It was difficult not to fear this great water, to hold panic at bay.

218

One wrong move and we and all of Mr. Zoe's stock will be lost, swallowed up in this icy torrent...

She was out-of-doors, her free flesh beneath naked sky. There should have been spirits dancing on the gold trim of the narrow clouds in the west, each gilded by the just-hidden sun, but all Yaot'l could feel was fear.

I am afraid! Even here, as I escape into the ekììka.

She could see the bank rushing by, high humps of dirt, with spruce behind—level and nothing but spruce, spruce, and more spruce.

I'm even more afraid than I was in that school! I don't know this place. It has forgotten me, or I have forgotten it.

No, a voice inside her said. Only say that Dehcho is not your Tłįchǫ dèè...

In a backwash on the near shore, she spied a dead tree topped with an osprey nest. Here a parent sat and gazed down, as if keeping watch over the violent water.

All I have studied at that school is how to be a prisoner...

Just as Yaot'l took some comfort from the idea that this fear she experienced was not her fault—that her Tłįchǫ awareness remained—another doubt assailed her.

Even if I try, I will never again feel safe— not anywhere. Not just the dèè, but everywhere. I've been changed from "Warrior" into Rabbit, one lost in a world overrun by dogs, foxes, and birds of prey with powerful hooked beaks and

talons, with stealthy lynx, their yellow eyes
freeze-gazing into mine while I sit and wait for
the inevitable fangs. Or, worst of all, for a poor
rabbit—men with all their traps, snares, rifles
and shotguns, arrows, slings and all the rest of
their devices of death...

Yaot'l could feel her lips moving; she was speaking aloud! She shook her head, trying to drive all these terrible thoughts away—before something even worse, something attracted by her fear—a boulder, a whirlpool, a rapid—appeared in their path.

Still, they rode safe, though moving at incredible velocity. Sinuous water rolled beneath them, a fat gray snake. Yaot'l was afraid she'd upset the boat because her head was so full of words, words in two languages. The new words, the ones that came after a big dose of terror, full of those cold sharp sounds, each a shield behind which her captors hid...

But no one died; the boat did not tip over. They did not collide with rocks, or the hurrying mats of brush, whole spruce, and slabs of ice. Mr. Zoe deftly piloted them through everything.

She had been half crazy with terror and anticipation all day, her nerves stretched to breaking. At last though, she'd reached her limit. Sinews stretched so tight and for so long, were finally exhausted. Yaot'l felt herself suddenly slump, limp as a reed.

"Hey! All of you! No sleeping!" Mr. Zoe's voice boomed above the roaring water. A stick of some kind prodded Yaot'l between the shoulder blades.

"Don't drop that paddle, girl!"

* * *

At last, they went to shore to sleep, which came after they'd pulled—with great effort—the heavy boat partially on shore. They lit no fire. The night circling sun never quite ~~went~~ disappeared—or at least their ability to see never did. Sascho knelt to whisper to Kele and Tanis, huddled together. Then he moved close to Yaot'l .

"I was scared on that river." An inadvertent shiver gripped her. If she hadn't been so exhausted, she might have been embarrassed.

"I was too!" Tanis, still shivering, spoke from inside her blanket.

"So was I." Sascho smiled, and the girls found comfort in the sight. "I'm sitting first watch."

"I'm going to stay by Tanis," Yaot'l said. The child looked up gratefully, and Yaot'l thought that at the same age, she would have been out of her mind with fear. That big river had scared her more than she'd ever thought possible. No wonder the younger ones had been sleepwalkers since they'd come ashore. Even Kele had had nothing to say.

They all curled up in their blankets. Yaot'l quickly lost consciousness, but in her dreams the river went on carrying her madly toward the midnight horizon, while beneath lay the terrors of that icy deep.

* * *

Sascho had already performed this traveler's task beside his uncles, one all hunters learned young. He too was bone weary, but Mr. Zoe had called him a man, and so he would be one. He sat, paddle upon his knee for a weapon, startling at every unfamiliar sound.

The sun had crawled back across the horizon when Mr. Zoe stretched and sat up, but Sascho felt his chest swell with pride. He would be able to look the elder man in the eye.

"There are all kinds of people up and down this river all the time. Not until we get up the Horn a ways will I feel safe."

"Shall we make a fire?"

"No. No time for that. We'll eat some dried fish like last night and get on. And Yaot'l Snow Goose…" Mr. Zoe began to feel around in an inside pocket of his heavy jacket. "I got something for you, girl."

Imagine her surprise when he held out Charlie's knife! When, after thanking him—and wondering why her tongue felt so thick and why the proper words came so haltingly—took it in her hand and felt the weight of it, she was overjoyed. She'd thought it lost forever!

There was no time to talk or to share escape stories. Soon, after a mouthful of dried fish and some dried berries taken from a leather pouch, they were on the river again, making their way into the current.

Soon the boat was flying down Dehcho once more. When other travelers passed, ones in larger boats traveling farther from shore, Tanis and Kele had to hide. Mr. Zoe did not want them to be seen in case news of the school's runaways was now traveling down river beside them.

He believed that Frank would quickly realize who had helped "Bernard"—"a real good worker"—disappear. He knew that his friend would be angry about it, for he'd often said how much he'd been looking forward to the extra able pair of hands this summer.

* * *

There were days of Dehcho, a turbulent ride west. The second day was not so frightening. They stopped early and fished in a meander where they'd made camp. Mr Zoe had plenty of line and hooks in his pack. Their first attempt yielded lots of fish. After a winter of scant commons, everyone stuffed themselves.

Having such a good meal cheered the little group. It had been months since they had all been so full. The fish blackening on skewers smelled—and later, tasted—like the finest thing they'd ever eaten. Mr. Zoe looked pleased as he watched them gorge.

By the time of the third day's launch, Yaot'l climbed into the boat feeling confident and ready to face the day. She understood that there were rules to riding this wild river, and now believed that Mr. Zoe had mastered them.

Even Tanis became calmer. She and Kele were now in front of the load, closest to Sascho, so they talked with him sometimes. It was good to be speaking one's own language, but even this "good" remained incomplete. There was always a tinge of fear when she spoke, the remembered pain of the strap when, newly arrived, she'd allowed such words to escape her lips.

Yaot'l often found herself gazing straight ahead into the load. The water gushed and threatened on every side, but now she was able to hold back the unnerving "What if..."

Sometimes Mr. Zoe would tell her to use that paddle, left or right, to help him steer. He'd first cautioned Yaot'l and Sascho to hold tight and not dip too deeply until they had tested the current. The power of this water was something none of these young people had ever experienced.

They were all tired, but it was clear there would be no real rest until they entered the Horn.

The voyage down river was made as quickly as possible, with the mad rushing current sending them along. They quickly learned that Tanis and Kele were not as familiar with traveling as they were. The older children had to coach them when they were on shore about the tasks everyone was expected to do.

"I don't want to," Kele had protested. "Finding wood is women's work. I want to fish."

"We are journeying." Sascho spoke quietly, but firmly. "Everyone has to help when the band travels."

When Tanis, looking worried, pulled on his sleeve, Kele, expression cross, had relented and did as he'd been asked.

Mr. Zoe watched the interchange but said nothing. Once it was settled, he returned to checking that his cargo had not shifted and that his boat was secure.

"When you've got enough wood, you can all start fishing."

There was good luck in this backwater, so they made willow skewers and roasted their catch whole. Yaot'l had spotted some mushrooms when she and Sascho had been scouting away from the water.

After such a meal, as they prepared for sleep again that night, the usually silent Mr. Zoe said, "Now you four are Indians again."

Chapter Ten

Horn River

The Horn, where they'd entered it, was extremely wide. At first, there were low sandy sides. Later, rock and earth banks appeared. The current was now against them and descending fast. Mr. Zoe had to use his engine and maneuver carefully. He called upon them for paddling sometimes, and it was weary work. Muscles out of use since last summer had to awaken and lengthen, although Sascho was stronger than he'd ever been.

The opposite shore remained impressively far away. The banks grew steeper. On such steep slopes, drunken spruce followed their roots in a slow motion slide into the water. This river was not like the clear water of Yaot'l's home. It was cloudy, brown and sometimes milky, full of sediment as it hurried along. They'd traveled without much effort down Dehcho. Now, for the first time, they were pushing daily against current.

Mr. Zoe certainly had packed along containers of gas, but these belonged to an upriver customer. The putt-putt would soon run out of its allotted share.

"We'll soon be paddling hard," he'd said. "The mouth here is full of water, but it will be nothing but a maze by August." Mr. Zoe shouted the information back to Sascho.

The next day they passed a beautiful forested island. At first, Tanis thought the trees she saw were on the opposite shore, but Mr. Zoe said it was called Fawn Island. Here they saw herds of deer and moose, too, wading in boggy shallows. This enormous game rich island hedged by the melt-swollen river looked like a good hunting place.

"We could easily take a deer now, but it takes time to prepare one."

"And there's no more room in this boat." Tanis spoke. She had sat on Yaot'l's side of the load today, just for a change.

"No time for hunting," said Mr. Zoe. "And my friends are expecting me—and that gas—soon." Then, unexpectedly he added, "I had a daughter like you, Little Sister, but it was a very long time ago."

Yaot'l looked over her shoulder and saw Tanis gazing trustingly back at him.

Both Stonypoint children were small and fine-boned, but now that they were so thin, there was something ghostly about them. Such pale faces and gaunt cheeks!

Tonight, I will properly comb and re-braid her hair, be a mother to her.

She'd need to start doing these domestic tasks, as well as checking for lice. Yaot'l resolved to find the time to do so for everyone.

* * *

Sometimes she wanted to pinch herself for it did not seem possible that they had so easily escaped. That school had forced them into one box after another, every day a copy of the last with only a few variations—Saturday, Sunday, a strange language battering her ears, more punishments, more fights.

Now the struggle was elsewhere, but here bathed in the sun and wind, labor unremitting and physical, as all around them, daily, the temperature rose. They rolled jackets and put them away, shoving the clothing into the crevices among the other stuff.

Kele and Tanis were weary almost to speechlessness by the time they reached shore each night. The river was rich, though, and fed them well.

They sometimes saw other spring travelers camped along the river, but Mr. Zoe took pains to avoid them. He had friends camping at Mink Lake, he said, that were expecting what he carried. He'd collect their winter stash of furs and head down river to a trading post at Mills Lake. He wouldn't be able to show his face again in Fort Providence for a long time.

"After a whole winter there, I was tired of that place. I might go down Dehcho next winter, to the Jean-Marie."

This was, Sascho thought, another piece of the wide world about which he knew next to nothing. There wasn't a lot of time before sleep in which he could ponder such things and he often wished there was, but every day they paddled. The river, once so wide, withered away.

They arrived at Mink Lake weary days later. Mr. Zoe greeted his kin, some of whom appeared to be Métis. There was his younger brother, Anton Zoe, his wife, Pearl, and their children. There was also a wary young man, George Lafferte, who looked full Tłı̨chǫ, whom Mr. Zoe called "my nephew."

When they first met George, he immediately made a point of saying that he was "older than" Sascho.

There were also two widowed elders and George's parents, a man, his wife, and three children, two of whom were near the age of Kele and Tanis. Mr. Laferte was Pearl Zoe's brother. It was the sort of kin group with which the runaways were familiar, banded together in a small group to hunt and fish.

At the campfire on the first night, as the four fugitives sat quietly, watching and listening, they learned that two older boys, one Laferte, one Zoe, had just left camp. They were now crossing country toward the Yellowknife road, where they hoped to find work. One of these had left a pregnant wife behind. She seemed very young, and the sight of her unsettled Yaot'l . Here was what she herself might have been, had she been married to Jimmy Tailbone.

It was the subject of much conversation that Achille Zoe had not yet found a wife.

"He's not much to look at," Mr. Laferte said, "but that nephew of yours knows how to trap, Zoe. That's for damn sure."

"It's not his fault he fell into the fire when he was little."

"It was his mother's fault," said Pearl, "and that no good man of hers."

The adults agreed and the conversation moved on. Later, Mr. Laferte talked at length about a group of white hunters they'd seen heading north.

* * *

Pearl, Sylvain's half sister, was a fair skinned Métis, with a tinge of red in her hair. Though a handsome woman, she had lived long years in the bush, which hardened and lined her face. After Yaot'l got to know her, she was reminded of her own Aunt Kathy, for she was sometimes cheerful and sometimes bossy. She always, however, liked the sound of her own voice. Pearl spoke English, but she knew Tłįchǫ and Slavey, too.

For the first days, Yaot'l stayed with the Zoes and did women's work. She and Tanis scrubbed everyone's traveling clothes, but after that, they helped with the hides the women were working, with fishing, preparing, and hanging fillets to dry. It was not a rest, but it was a change from the river, a chance to get used to living on the land once again. Besides, she knew they owed Mr. Zoe. Without his help, they'd never have gotten so far so fast.

"You must stay with us for a while. No need to hurry north." Pearl said it not once but many times. She smiled at Yaot'l whenever she repeated it. On the surface it was hospitality, but there was a lot of summer work to do that required women's hands. Daily, Yaot'l and Tanis were kept busy. Yaot'l was used to these tasks; Tanis knew very little. Yaot'l found she had to teach her young companion as well as get through her own share of work.

"You cut fish pretty good." Mamàcho—Mr. Zoe's mother—with the solemn, withered face, soon offered regular praise. Yaot'l smiled but continued her careful fileting, while the old woman, seated nearby, went on with her own work. She was beading bracelets, quite a task for those old eyes and crooked fingers. The sight of the box of trade goods, gaudy beads shining, returned Yaot'l to last year at Gam`e`t`i and her own box of bracelets, the blue and white ones she'd never finished.

Sascho went away with Mr. Zoe and George to set traps. Muskrat fur was always a good trade item. Mr. Laferte stayed behind to keep an eye on things. Yaot'l and the kids missed Sascho. They were also a little anxious too because Mr. Zoe had left them by themselves among folk who were not their kin.

The four of us will make our own family...

As Yaot'l paused to wipe sweat from her brow—she used the back of her arm—it didn't seem possible that almost an entire year had passed. On the other hand, it was also as if ages had gone by, ages spent in that strange, hurtful place. To wake up out of doors, to hear the birds at dawn, and, at night, the cries of fox and owl, the high quivering voice of the loon, brought her shivers of delight.

The runaways made their own shelter out of branches and spare canvas a little removed from the rest. Yaot'l slept between Tanis and Kele, those weary children who were now her new little brother and sister. They, so fearful and uncertain, both stayed close to Yaot'l. They gathered wood and water and helped her in other ways, but neither showed interest in the other children when sometimes, toward evening, a game started, or playing with the puppies. The little band of escapees kept to themselves and did not try to join in.

Kele did whatever Yaot'l asked, and Mr. Laferte often kept him busy with fishing, which seemed to suit both of them. If the band asked them to help with some task, like setting up a dying rack, they did, although the camp's children were sometimes jealous of the newcomers and were quick to tell on Kele or

Tanis if one or the other made some kind of mistake.

Daisy, the young wife, often complained of illness. She was appreciative of Yaot'l's capable hands at work upon the day-to-day tasks. Pearl Zoe seemed sympathetic to her weariness and discomfort—Daisy could be heard puking every morning—but Mrs. Laferte was not. Sometimes, the next thing after the retching would be Mrs. Laferte's nagging voice.

"I was married same age as you, girl, and all alone with my first husband in the bush. I carried my baby all day and then set up camp for my man at night while he sat by the fire. I prepared his game and cooked it too and then, next day, same thing all over again. We never stopped moving. Now, Daisy, no more of this lying around—get up and get us water."

If poor Daisy, still fighting off her nausea, was slow to obey, or if she asked for a moment longer, Mrs. Laferte would add: "Why, my first husband would have beaten you black and blue, you lazy little slug!"

* * *

"You better watch yourself, girl. Sylvain probably wants you for his wife—or, maybe, for that ugly nephew of his."

Yaot'l, who was standing on a ladder hanging a string of fish, startled. She hadn't heard Mrs. Laferte arrive. When Yaot'l didn't immediately reply, but continued checking over her knots, the woman continued.

"Sylvain said he'd come back from Fort Providence this spring with a wife. Maybe he has."

To give herself time to consider, Yaot'l stayed where she was and went on inspecting each knot which secured the precious load.

What Mrs. Laferte had said was disturbing. The "few days" that Sascho was supposed to be away, setting traps with Mr. Zoe and George, had stretched long beyond a week.

Here they were, so far from their own families, way up this unknown river and living among strangers. Anything could happen. After all, these were not her kin, not even Tłįchǫ—but Métis, whose word, her father had always claimed, was suspect.

Yaot'l knew how men behaved when they were hungry for women. Why, hadn't she had Brother Disante sidling up beside her, surreptitiously touching her—whenever he didn't think anyone else was watching—ever since the Easter feast? He'd even tried to put his arms around her one evening when she'd been carrying dishes away from the priests' parlor. It had been all she could do to evade him and not drop the tray.

"I am promised to Sascho. Mr. Sylvain knows that." Yaot'l, from her perch high on the ladder, met the woman's eyes with the most severe expression she could muster.

Mrs. Laferte laughed shortly. "You'd be smart to stay here with us and not go out into the bush by yourselves with those weak kids, who don't know nothin'. It's easy to die out there."

Yaot'l made no reply. She was better able to deal with spite when she stood a head higher. After a few moments of staring, Mrs. Laferte, apparently having said what she'd come to say, went to tend the cries of one of her kids.

She took her time descending the ladder, thoughts racing. After such a—threat—*or was it a warning?*—she was in no mood to rejoin Pearl and Daisy and the rest.

For a time she simply stood on the tongue of sandy Whagweè. Here, where a strong breeze blew down the river, the fillets would quickly dry. For a time, she rested one hand upon the uprights and focused on the rippling water, surrounded by the strong aroma of newly cut fish.

Sascho! How I long to see him!

What if he never returns? What if I've found him only to lose him again?

What if...?

What if they encountered bad white men in the forest...?

What if Mr. Zoe and George had schemed to leave Sascho behind ...?

A hundred notions besieged her, each darker than the last.

* * *

Yaot'l, Kele and Tanis ate around their own small fire that evening. On a diet of fish and berries—now ripening in the bush on every side—they all felt stronger. The day had continued to bring trouble. Later, Kele, for no good reason, had picked a fight with one of the younger Laferte boys. The others had quickly piled on. Now, once again, he had a black eye and a bloody nose. Mrs. Laferte had yelled and beaten him with a stick until Pearl intervened, but she'd told them all to stay by their own fire tonight.

"That little fellow has a bad temper," Pearl said. "You are going to have to keep him away from our kids. They won't forget, and, after today, they won't let up on him, either."

Yaot'l didn't argue. Kele's behavior upset her. To bully someone younger, to provoke a fight for no reason—that was not the Tłįchǫ way.

"When is Sascho coming back so we can get out of this dump?" Kele, sullen-faced, wanted an answer.

"Yes. Wasn't he supposed to be back by now?" Tanis echoed her brother.

What could she do but nod at her new little brother and sister?

But what, Yaot'l wondered, could be wrong with Kele? He was no longer the cheerful confident little boy she'd met in Behchok'o.

"Yes, he was supposed to be here three days ago, but you know how a journey can be longer than you expect. I hope…" Yaot'l began, but stopped herself.

I am oldest! She must not share her fears with them, especially Kele, who was already on edge.

They'd gone to their shelter for sleep, but Yaot'l lay awake, full of worry. When the camp dogs began to bark wildly, she crawled out at once to see what had set them off.

It was Sascho and the others! They carried a load of field dressed game, muskrat skins and a young deer. Mr. Laferte, still by the fire, observed loudly that there would be plenty of work for the camp's women in the morning.

* * *

"What troubles you, Yaot'l ?" Mr. Zoe had noticed how she'd been avoiding him. She was now preparing a muskrat carcass—skinning muskrat was a careful, tedious task. You couldn't really rush at it, or you'd ruin the skin or slice into the gut and defile the flesh.

Mr. Zoe had come to sit nearby, but had not yet spoken. Instead, he appeared to be engaged in an attempt to light his pipe. So far, it had refused to draw. He'd tried knocking it against a stump, but that hadn't served, either.

Squaring her jaw she looked up at him and said, "Mrs. Laferte has said you want to keep me here."

"She told Yaot'l you wanted her for a wife." Sascho, who'd just joined them, filled in what Yaot'l could not quite say. Last night, when she'd told him, he'd been angry.

"Maybe Mrs. Laferte wishes you would stay, as Daisy's so poorly." There was a gleam in his eye. "But I think it is maybe her own George who wants a wife, not a man who travels, like me."

"We don't care what that woman wishes, or what George wants," Sascho said. "Yaot'l goes with me."

"Sounds as if you are ready to leave." Unconcerned, Mr. Zoe scraped the inside of his pipe with a pocket knife. Little lumps of tar and grit fell onto the sandy soil. "No hard feelings, son. I wanted to be sure you kids could make it to Wha't'i, especially with those two tenderfeet in tow." Sylvain tucked the pipe between his teeth, drew, and then spit. "And now," he ended, "after our trapping trip together, I believe you can."

* * *

Yaot'l paddled at the front of the boat, Sascho at the back, Kele in the middle. The Zoe family members had agreed that for the first part of their journey, they could use the old birch bark canoe with the understanding that they cache it up country.

The night before they were to depart, Pearl took Yaot'l aside before she could walk up the hill to their shelter.

"I have something for you, girl. Come over here." Strong woman's hands pulled her back toward the firelight, toward a willow work basket.

"You have already given us much, Mrs. Zoe."

"And you have already done many days work, both you and the little ones. You still have a long hard way to go, but this is something you may need before your journey is over."

She crouched, wide hips flaring her skirt, and began to rummage in a basket. As she got to her feet again, she had a small canvas pouch in hand.

"Here," she said, passing it to Yaot'l . "Inside is for the moon time which will, I think, soon come to a big strong girl like you. You will not have any aunts or grandmothers to help you out in the bush, so you will have to sit by yourself and make do."

"Thank you for your kindness, Mrs. Pearl." Yaot'l received the gift with a flurry of feelings. The embarrassment which had come creeping, she quickly thrust away. Moon time meant shame among the kwet'ìì. They even called it a "curse", and had a story about how all the bad things on earth had come from the first woman's disobedience. Yaot'l's people had no such story, and, as soon as she'd felt embarrassed, she'd quickly reminded herself that she was Tłįchǫ and that kwet'ìì feel-bad stories meant nothing to her.

She'd been taught that when the moon time came, it would be a sign that she was, in all her beauty and strength, a woman. After it came, she would be ready to go with Sascho and be his wife—and there was nothing more that she desired than to live and work beside him.

Mrs. Pearl gave her a quick hug and then turned away, back toward the fire. As Yaot'l, pouch in hand, started back toward her own shelter, she could hear Mr. Zoe's voice. In the darkness along the path, he was speaking to Sascho, words he'd said before, but felt he must say again before they all set out.

"The river gets narrow after a time, and meanders through many pothole lakes and bogs. I know my way through, but it is something you will see for yourself. Once you have left the canoe behind, you'll be traveling through a mix of forest, muskeg, and bush. So, after you begin to walk, follow the stars, watch for trail sign—that's all over—and free running water. You will need to stop and hunt, but before summer's end you will find your way to Tłıchǫ land and to the paths you walked last year with your uncle. You should find plenty to eat."

* * *

They had all felt brave last night by the fire, after they'd packed what they had—more blankets, rope and fishing line, another good knife, a small ax, birch bowls, horn spoons, a sharpening stone for the knives, and a needle and thread, another gift from Pearl. Mr. Zoe had given them a lodestone, too, so they wouldn't be entirely dependent upon a clear night sky.

Now that the encampment was disappearing behind them, the size of the task ahead weighed upon them all. Still, they were Tłįchǫ! Sascho and Yaot'l were young adults, who had already done many seasons of traveling.

They would eventually enter the first of three lakes. This would be the easy part. After that, they'd have to locate the correct feeder to continue further north. When they reached an area of rapids, they'd portage and paddle until they found the place Sylvain had described, a stand of half drowned, dead spruce. Then, a long march onward through the muskeg and forest until Tłįchǫ trail signs appeared.

Sascho had his own worries, that, Yaot'l knew. This morning, he'd been quiet while they'd been getting underway. So much depended upon what Sascho remembered from last year's journey with his Uncle! Yaot'l too certainly knew the stars and Mr. Zoe had shown them both which ones to follow, but stars weren't always visible, and a day or more of journeying in the wrong direction could create hardship—or even tragedy—in the wild. Even the Stonypoint kids understood how risky their journey was to be.

And, Yaot'l thought, if they didn't know it before, the Laferte's warnings over the last few days had made it certain that they do now...

241

Yaot'l shook her head, hoping to drive the Lafertes—and Kele's bad behavior—right out of it. Not only Mr. Zoe, but Pearl had been kind, even after Kele's fight. They had generously given them most of the new items to aid their journey—a small section of canvas, those bowls, a salt supply, and the horn spoons.

Kele, for the first time since the escape, seemed cheerful. He sang while he paddled—in a voice which now and then broke, which made everyone laugh—songs which reminded everyone of happy times. Tanis, in her piping voice, joined in. She looked healthier than she had at the start of the journey, berry brown from being in the sun, and full of a new confidence. They took turns paddling, though Tanis wasn't able to keep at it for long. They were working against the flow still, and Yaot'l and Sascho ended every day weary. They made camp early that first night.

It was important Sascho said, that they not camp in places where there were signs of earlier fires, so as not to attract any unwelcome attention from other regular travelers. Not all folks on the river were Indians, and not all strangers, native or not, were to be trusted.

* * *

It was with heavy hearts that they cached the small canoe in the place of the dead spruce. Sascho, alert to water flow and the subtle trail sign Mr. Zoe had instructed him to follow, had

242

kept them on the correct route even after they'd paddled across the last lake. Finding the way out of that had not been entirely easy, either, as there was a rat's nest of feeders on the north side.

Now they'd feel the weight of gear packed onto their backs! After consulting the lodestone, they'd shouldered their burdens and single-file marched away, Sascho first, Yaot'l walking last. They kept the river in sight for a few days, and then, after entering a bog, which they had to back out of and find a way around, they realized that they'd parted company with the major branch of the friendly Horn.

The supplies of dried fish, meat and berries had run out soon after they left the river, and so a part of each day had to be spent finding food, as well as locating another place to camp. There were plenty of fish in the lakes. Once, by a creek, they'd managed to drive a muskrat from its den on the bank by hitting the earth near the hole with sticks until the creature ran out, only to be dispatched with a blow on the head.

They'd thanked the muskrat where he lay. Then the carcass was skinned and the meat roasted. After the flesh had nourished them, they'd taken the bones down to the water's side and deposited them in a deep pool in the proper way.

"Tell the story of how the muskrat found the earth," Tanis said. "My Mamàcho loved to tell that story." She was sleepily nestled against Yaot'l's side, which made Yaot'l happy. It was

243

such a good feeling, with them all seated by a fire, once more free on their beloved dèè.

She drew a satisfied breath, feeling the warmth of little sister's body beside hers.

"Dotson'sa, great raven, was the first. He made the world and all the creatures. In those long ago days, all the animals were very large, but the world was still nearly empty, so there was room for all of them. They all hunted and fished and ate berries and did the things that were proper to each kind and they all were very happy. Everything was going well until the big rain came. It rained and it rained and it rained, until there was more water than there is even in Tındeè. Finally, all the dèè was covered with water and all the animals sat with Dotson'sa on a big raft in water that spread for as far as any of them could see."

"Kwet'ıì have that story too." Kele, who'd been listening, suddenly looked aghast. "Why?"

"Maybe that means it is a true story," Sascho said, "not needed at least, the part where the rain covers up all the dèè."

"Sister Louise said that the rain drowned everyone and that only one good family was saved." Tanis sat bolt upright as something of the dread she'd felt all winter came creeping back alongside Kele's mention of that much dreaded name.

"There were no people when the big rain came. Dotson'sa had not made people yet." Yaot'l thought she ought to remind them that this was a different story.

"Hush and listen," Sascho added. Yaot'l smiled at him and then continued.

"Dotson'sa knew there was dèè though, way, way down below the water. He knew that this dèè had a powerful magic inside of it and that this could be used to make dry land again. Now, Raven can do many things and he is very wise, though he cannot swim, so he asked the animals if they would try to dive down and bring up some of this magic dèè."

"At first, they were all frightened because there was so much water, deep as they had never before seen. They sat on the edge of the raft and peered down, but no one could see the bottom. First to try to bring up dèè was the Otter, so strong and sleek.

"I can swim fast; I can catch fish in my teeth.

No silver-sided swift fin can escape me,
My white strong teeth.
I am King of the River.
I will swim to the bottom of this deep water
And find magic dèè for Dotson'sa,
So he can make the world again.

So Otter dived down and down and down, but as far as he could swim holding his breath, it was not far enough. With his heart pounding and his chest aching, Otter came back to the surface. When he climbed onto the raft, he shook out his fur and hung his head. He was sorry he'd sung a boasting song now that he had failed.

'I am sorry Dotson'sa. I tried to find dèè, but that water is too deep.'

Next to try was the mink. He said, "I am smaller, but I too can swim fast, I too eat fish. I will try to do what the big otter could not."

I am fast and I am fierce,
I will slip and slide through the water,
And my slender self will succeed where otter could not.

And he too tried. He swam and swam and swam, but he couldn't reach the bottom either. He barely made it back to the raft and climbed up, choking and coughing, his beautiful fur all soaked.

Well, well, said Dotson'sa, let us ask the birds to try.

First to come forward was Grebe, the little round faced bird who keeps his nest so secret among the reeds.

I have marvelous feet, each one webbed,
But I can spread the toes wide so
My feet are like paddles.
I can hold my breath, too,
Yes I can and now I will try to find the magic dèè.

And so saying, in he dived. He swam and swam with his paddle feet and he went down, down, deeper than the others—but he couldn't reach the bottom to find the magic earth. In the end, he popped back up to the surface and climbed back onto the raft quite defeated.

The loon stepped up next. He too sang a song.

Water slides from each feather
And I can swim so fast beneath the water,
Faster than otter, faster than mink,
And faster than Grebe, too,
I am loon who is
Lightning under the water.

So the loon dived down and he swam and swam, holding his breath. Time passed, and still the loon dived down, on and on and on. Dotson'sa and all the other animals thought for sure that loon would be the one to bring back the magic dèè. When he popped to the surface again after the longest time of all, and took a deep, deep breath, everyone was sure he must have done it—but he had not.

I will go—I can find the magic dèè! A little voice cried. Everyone turned to look and there stood muskrat, so small and round. When the creatures saw who had spoken, they all began to laugh. The otter laughed. The mink laughed. The loon and the grebe laughed. The others joined in.

Ha-ha-ha! Puny little Muskrat thinks he can find the magic dèè, when all of us have tried and it was too far. Ha-ha-ha! Foolish unimportant Muskrat!

But Dotson'sa looked at the muskrat and saw that he was sincere. Besides, Dotson'sa knew, though others did not, that the humble muskrat could hold his breath for the longest of any of them. If any creature could reach the magic dèè, it would be him.

Muskrat did not bother to sing a song, though he has one, just as everyone does. Instead, he just dove into the water and began to swim. Down, down, down, down he went, as far as the otter had gone, as far as the mink had gone, as far as the grebe had gone and then, finally, as far as the loon had gone. It was dark and deep and very, very cold here, but he kept on swimming and swimming and holding his breath. Finally, he touched the bottom and here he scooped up a chunk of mud. Holding it to his breast, he kicked like mad until at last, he reached the surface. Puffing and blowing he arrived at the raft where the other animals—that had stopped laughing during his long absence and begun to worry about him—helped him up. At Dotson'sa's feet, he laid down his prize—the magical dèè. Everyone was amazed to see what the little fat fellow had done—how this small animal had brought back exactly what Dotson'sa needed to make a world for them to stand upon again.

And Dotson'sa breathed upon the mud, and it began to grow and grow and make an island. The island continued to grow and grow until at last there was enough dèè for everyone to go and walk about and begin to live in the ways that they had before the coming of the great flood. And that is why people say that muskrat found the dèè and that because he did, in a way, the dèè h belongs to him."

Yaot'l loved to tell this story and had learned it at young age from her own favorite Mamàcho, Josette.

Across the fire, Yaot'l saw Sascho smile.

"We should tell that story to the kwet'įį," he said, "but he wouldn't understand. He thinks everything belongs to him." Sadly, he shook his head.

Across the fire, Kele, too, shivered, as if from some terrible memory. Yaot'l, however, refused to feel anything but the warmth and comfort of the story she'd told.

Someday, she thought, *I'll tell the story of humble can-do muskrat to our children.*

* * *

Trees rose on every side, the species changing with the soil and amount of water beneath their feet. First, they walked through stands of aspen, whose young shoots the beaver loved, and where they could hunt for hares. Sometimes, encountering a riverine bog, they'd pause for a moment to watch as a lordly moose huffed at the sight of them and then turned away, plowing his great body deeper into the water. The large animals seemed to know that no gun was present and rarely abandoned their dignity in flight.

Finding themselves among a grove of k'i, the white birch, they'd stopped for a time, built a small fire and shaped another dish from the bark Sascho carefully peeled from one of the trees. Kele, who'd never seen anyone do this, watched with interest while Sascho demonstrated how to remove the bark without injuring the tree.

It was full summer and some days were very hot, so staying in the forest shade made the journey easier. Just as Mr. Zoe had said, the "tenderfoots" were slowing them down, Tanis in particular. She had a night cough that didn't go away, and one morning she awoke with a fever and an earache. They had to stop for several days while Yaot'l took advantage of a nearby stand of Tamarack, whose needles were good for teas and poultices. Her mother had taught her that tamarack tea was good for colds, earaches, and many other illnesses, so she dosed first Tanis and then everyone else with Tamarack as a preventative, just in case what Tanis suffered from was catching. Later the same day, Kele and Tanis took turns soaking their feet in the brew, to relieve soreness.

They'd settled into a pattern of stopping every day for a time around noon-sun. While Tanis hid "like a fawn" and rested, the others went to scout the area and hunt for supper of some kind. As the days were long, there was always enough light to travel until they were completely worn out.

* * *

For days Yaot'l hadn't felt well. The weight of her pack seemed to grow unbearably heavy by the end of each one.

I hate this ax, Yaot'l thought. This morning, her pack had shifted almost as soon as she'd got it over her shoulders. More, it had been brutally hot as they'd walked in and out of cover. For what seemed an eternity the handle had been banging against her back. She and Sascho took turns every other day of carrying the thing, and although it wasn't full-sized, it was sufficiently bulky to be irritating—and even occasionally painful—if it wasn't tied against the bedroll just right.

As she swung the pack down and then bent to readjust, she had a wild urge to simply throw the ax as far as she could into the brush. Of course, she couldn't do that. The small sharp ax was aggravating to carry constantly, but it was also extremely effective when they needed to apply some real force and a good edge to a piece of wood.

Tonight it was taking forever to find a good spot to camp. Sascho seemed to be more cautious than usual. He'd pause, look around, and even if there was good water nearby, he'd find some other reason to go on. Then Tanis, disappointed and ever-weary, would begin to lag behind, and Yaot'l would have to wait for her, while the load on her own back grew heavier and heavier. It was difficult to be footsore and weary and still keep a careful watch on their surroundings. Sometimes Sascho and Kele would be far ahead. It was frustrating to see their backs recede, knowing that she could keep up, but she didn't want to risk losing Tanis, who was doing her best.

As the sun dropped and they trudged on—and on—she felt herself becoming ever more impatient. Sascho had passed a likely looking pond and then they'd immediately entered an area of bush and brush with no trees or water. Tanis was whimpering softly to herself and Yaot'l's temper on the boil by the time they finally met with water again, probably a feeder of the same cheerful creek they'd left behind two hours ago.

"What's the difference between this place and the last?" Yaot'l grumbled as she shrugged herself out of the pack. The ropes had been digging into her shoulders all afternoon. Tanis, last to stumble in, didn't bother to escape her burden. She simply sank to the ground with a groan, the birch dishes rattling as she collapsed.

Sascho did not reply, just continued to study their surroundings. After she'd helped Tanis disentangle herself from the pack, Yaot'l began to search for the pouch of tamarack bark and needles she'd packed away some days earlier. On the approach to Lac le Martre they'd find more tamarack again for sure. That place, she reasoned, would certainly be wetter, the conditions perfect for more of this not too common, but extremely effective, medicinal.

All of us, she thought, need a dose of tamarack tea—especially me. Maybe I'm catching what Tanis has—and at once she prayed not, for whatever it was afflicting Tanis—or so she'd begun to fear—was the kind of disease which continues to grow.

Like the wasting sickness which struck my father...

She did not want to dwell on such a dark thought, and again resolved to do whatever she could to keep Tanis well enough to reach her kin. Knowing she was the mother of this little band, she at once stopped her busy fingers in their search for the tamarack and instead focused on her surroundings, hoping to calm down. Effective medicine could not be brewed properly in her present state of mind.

"If you want to think clear and stay strong, first you must breathe deep and feel the earth under your feet. Dèè will nourish you." That's what Mamàcho Josette always said, so Yaot'l closed her eyes and took a moment for some deep breaths in and out.

Sure enough, when she looked around again, everything seemed clearer. They had stopped in a beautiful grove of balsam poplar, one of the tallest trees in the dèè. In the gentle breeze the arrow shaped leaves fluttered above her head. Lower down, there was gnawed bark, showing that the beaver sometimes visited. There were also signs of porcupine and hare, for all were creatures who loved to strip and eat young bark and feast upon seedlings.

She would suggest that they stop here for a few days. There was good water and also meat of some kind fit for the pot—perhaps, even one of those porcupines who'd so clearly signaled a presence. They were easy prey and that kind of fat meat was just what everyone needed.

They made fire and cleaned the ptarmigan they'd caught. Sascho had thanked the birds, then plucked them and cut off their wings many hours ago where they were killed, which was the proper way. Tonight, they'd singe them, gut them, and then roast the strong dark red meat. Along with these, they roasted several large spike cap mushrooms they'd gathered earlier in the day.

The first time they had come upon these mushrooms, with their slimy gray look, Kele had thought they were disgusting. Sascho had barely caught him in time to prevent a nice large one from being kicked to bits and wasted. Later, cooked in a bark pot, or skewered and roasted, Kele had learned that these were another wild food that was good to eat.

"Let us rest here for a few days. I see pot herbs in that open area by the creek and there are porcupine and hares around here too. Tanis needs a rest and so do I."

Yaot'l had been in no mood for an argument, so she was relieved when Sascho simply said, "That's a good idea."

Tanis gazed at her in silent gratitude. As he licked his fingers, seated by the fire, Kele outright sighed with relief. Sascho had been pushing them all hard.

* * *

Sascho and Kele had gone to place the ptarmigan bones in the crook of a young tree, a way to give the birds honor for their sacrifice. The moon had begun to rise; Yaot'l could see it through the trees, sailing through the summer sky. For a moment she stood and simply gazed up, noting that once again it was near full. It had been an entire month since they'd left the Zoes' camp!

She could not make out why, as she crouched to pee, her back and stomach ached so. She'd helped prepare food, eaten—although without much of an appetite—and she'd sat by the fire for a little rest. For a moment, she was afraid she might be getting sick, and that was why she felt so unwell, but the real answer to the question, however, came in the hot trickle she felt upon her thighs.

* * *

"Thank-you, Sascho."

He nodded and just stood for a moment, studying her with solemn respect. Yaot'l had returned from the woods and explained that she had become a woman. She'd asked that he help by making a shelter in a place she'd found, while she waited further back in the woods. He knew that the powerful woman's magic had come upon her, and that she now needed to keep

255

her distance from him. Without comment, he'd followed and done as she'd asked.

Now, the cast off antler he'd used to dig still in hand, he turned and disappeared among the saplings, heading back to Kele and their original campfire. Yaot'l and Tanis were now alone together beside a long low shelter made of bent branches. At the back, a pit had been dug. While Sascho had dug the hole and then spliced the branches of their shelter together, she had made use of one of the rag pads she'd taken from the pouch that Pearl had given her. Tanis had been sent to gather dried moss they'd spied deeper among the trees.

Exhausted now, they sat at the shelter. Tanis had gathered her blanket and wordlessly lay down beside her. Yaot'l stroked her hair. "We're going to rest for a few days, little sister. No more walking until my moon time is done."

There was no answer, and from the even breathing, Yaot'l knew she had fallen straight into sleep. As she watched the moon sail into the tree tops, she hoped the boys could find some good meat here before they had to go on. As the sun lowered it grew still. The night would be warm.

It was odd just to rest, but as soon as she'd slept in the shelter once, she awoke feeling much better. With Tanis and herself, things were quiet. Tanis, too, seemed to need a lot of sleep, and while she did, Yaot'l had time to be alone with her self—and with the dèè.

Once, when she'd gone to the creek to wash out the pads, she'd ended just sitting quietly on the bank for a time.

On this warm day, the dèè showed off its splendour. Sunlight danced in and out within the poplar cover and made quavering bracelets of light which slipped first up and then down upon the tree limbs. Kinglets rustled and peeped among the leaves. Green and blue, brown of trees and the smell of moist earth, and overhead the light, the sweet bird song cascade...

For an instant Patricia's laughing face floated before her, and she wished with all her heart that her friend was alive, and traveling with them. Yaot'l imagined it was so, and set Patricia's image beside her, sitting on the bank, enjoying the day.

I will ever remember you, my friend, and in every beautiful place I shall see your spirit! You shall travel with me on every journey for the rest of my life.

After the long imprisonment, the sights and sounds and scents of the place washed over her like a balm, soothing all the old sorrows.

I am a woman now! My feet stand upon the dèè. The strength of ndèonde, of trees, the energy of flowing water, the fiery She Spirit herself, now dwells within me.

* * *

While they fished or gathered food for themselves, Yaot'l told Tanis all the old stories she knew. First she told of the Woman Who Lived Alone, and how she met and married a handsome stranger who wooed her for days with many presents of game.

They lived happily together for a time. One night, while he was away hunting, she heard a disturbance among her dogs, yelping and snarling as if a strange dog, or even a wolf, had come among them. Frightened, she'd crept to the opening of her tent, and, with all her strength, threw her sharpest ax at a shadowy four legged creature, moving among the tethered animals. When silence fell and all the dogs grew quiet, she was afraid no longer, but lay down again to sleep.

When she awoke in the morning and went out, she found the body of her husband. He'd been killed by the ax she'd thrown, so now she was alone again. It was all a sorrowful mystery until some months later she gave birth to five puppies. She understood then that her lost husband must have been one of those who could change his form. She thought she ought to destroy the puppies, but she could not for they were company and all she had left of her good husband.

Now that she had no man, the woman sometimes had to leave her camp and go hunting, leaving her puppies behind. One day, when she came home early, she heard voices and happy cries, like children playing. As she crept through the bushes, she saw that instead of five puppies there were now five children. Their discarded puppy skins lay on the ground near the fire. As soon as they saw their mother, though, they slipped on those skins and changed back again.

"Those who can change shape are devils." Tanis, looking alarmed, interrupted. She used the *kwet'ìì* word "devils."

"That is how *kwet'ìì* thinks." Yaot'l replied sternly. "All great hunters, and many Shamans too, can change their shape at will. If you are part of the dèè', you can learn to do such things."

"So this story means that our ancestor was a dog-man?"

"I haven't yet finished the story. You should not interrupt."

"But that's what it means, though, isn't it?"

"Yes."

Tanis appeared so upset that Yaot'l decided to quickly finish the tale.

"The woman had to try several times before she managed to capture all their dog skins and prevent them from changing back. It is said that from those children the Tłıchǫ People come."

"The *kwet'ìì* call us dogs—and devils, too." Tanis was stricken.

"And what do they know of us and our ways? They could not have lived here without our help, and see how they repay us. As for dogs, well, without them, winter travel would be impossible. Without dogs, everything would have to travel on our backs. A good dog will fight with a wolverine or a wolf to defend his people. Dogs are not as wise as wolves, but they are our truest friends; they hunt with us." Yaot'l slipped an arm around Tanis. "Don't fear what *kwet'įį* calls you. They think they know everything worth knowing, but they don't."

Tanis considered for a time. She appeared to now be more concerned that Yaot'l was angry with her. At last, she said, "I guess it would be nice to have a dog with us now. He could warn us of danger and he could carry a pack, too, just as you say."

* * *

The days had passed, and the moon aged and shrank. Her time of sitting ended, Yaot'l and Tanis returned to the camp, both feeling ready to go on again. The boys were happy to see them, displaying proudly the fish and game they'd taken. The next morning, they set out on their journey again.

Some days later, when they had just entered a sandy, rocky area dappled with Jack Pine, Sascho suddenly signaled them all to be quiet and get down. Yaot'l suddenly realized that all the birds had gone quiet. In the winter, this would be a place where caribou came to browse on lichen. It had seemed empty, with only those strange gray-green clots of life clinging to dead branches and vegetation that straggled upwards from among the low bush blueberries that carpeted the ground.

She startled when up ahead a loud crack rang out—gunfire—and then they heard voices. Kwet'įį̀! They must either be coming toward them, or crossing the trajectory of their path. If Sascho hadn't been paying attention, they might have stumbled right into them. With bullets flying around and with the kwet'įį̀—who sometimes fired at sounds heard, rather than game seen—they didn't want to get any closer.

Yaot'l sent a prayer to the spirits of the place that these men weren't traveling with dogs—and that they weren't coming this way. At her side, Tanis put her fingers in her ears and closed her eyes, as if this would shut out the danger. Kele looked around, his large eyes bulging. A steady crunch-crunch-crunch moved up ahead—boots on the march through the brush.

* * *

"Hurry, crawl inside here," Sascho motioned towards a stand of trees with low lying branches. The undergrowth at the base of the trees grew so thick Yaot'l had to cut away some of the thickest branches with her axe and hold back the smaller ones so that Kele and Tanis could enter.

"What are you going to do?" she turned to Sascho.

"Just scout them out. I won't be seen, I need to find out how many there are, and what they are doing."

"I'll come with you."

"No, there's twice the danger of being heard if there are two of us. Besides you need to stay with the kids. I will not be discovered."

"I trust you." Yaot'l raised her hand to signal acceptance of his decision and then crawled through the small opening to join the youngsters.

* * *

Sascho crept through the woods making no more sound than a small skittering animal. Following the smell of smoke from what was obviously a man-made campfire, he dropped to his knees when he came upon a large clearing. He slipped towards the edge and secreted himself behind an old moss-and-lichen covered log. Three men sat around a smoky campfire eating what smelled like rabbit stew. Sascho eyed the pot that had obviously provided their evening meal and held his breath to still his grumbling stomach.

"Hey Mike. I still don't understand why you wanted us to go traipsing through these woods," A stocky man, dressed in a red plaid shirt and a brown hunting cap spoke in a low pitched nasally voice. "Did you forget your promise to help us bag a grizzly bear?"

"I know what I said." Mike, a weather beaten old timer with long gray hair and a full beard leaned over and pulled a coffee pot out of the embers of the campfire. "I told you. The

Indian Agent we met back at Fort Providence asked me to keep an eye out for four Injun kids that got away from the school. The bounty he's offered for bringing them in would be enough to pay for provisions to take us through a Nunavut winter. We'd be able to do all the hunting you wanted. "

"But what the hell are we going to do with four kids if we do find them?"

"We don't have to do nothing with them. There's an old trappers cabin about fifteen miles north. If we catch the kids, we're supposed to take them there and the agent will be along in five days. He'll pay us enough to last us right through the winter."

"Hey Syd, that don't sound like too bad a deal to me." The third man, younger and with a softer voice, interrupted the two on the edge of an argument. "I'm game if you two are. We can spend a couple days looking for those kids and if we don't find them, nothing lost, we'll still be heading north towards Nunavut."

Syd looked over at his friend then nodded his head. "Okay. If the two of you want to waste a couple of days, I won't object. Just remember, if we don't find those kids by the end of the week, we're heading out and not wasting any more time."

"You've got a deal." Mike nodded his agreement. "Now let's get some sleep tonight and in the morning, we can head back to the creek, follow it for a couple of days and keep a sharp eye out for signs of those youngsters.

They're not from around here, so they're not likely to risk going deep enough into the woods to get around us that way."

* * *

Sascho waited while the men settled into their bed rolls and then, with a rueful look at the stew pot still sitting in the campfire, he backed away from the log and slipped noiselessly into the woods.

Back where Yaot'l and the kids were hidden, Sascho crouched in front of the small entrance, "It's Sascho," he said, alerting them of his return.

Kele and Tanis slept on a bed of spruce boughs that the three of them had fashioned from some of the low hanging branches the tree had provided.

"What did you see?" Yaot'l asked Sascho who had crawled through the narrow entrance and crouched beside her on the ground.

"They're hunters all right, but they're also looking for us."

Yaot'l's eyes widened. "Why would hunters be looking for us?"

"They met up with the kw'ahtıı at Fort Providence. He offered them a bounty if they could find us. They're supposed to follow the creek and meet up with the kw'ahtıı at a kwet'ı̨ı̀ detsı̨kǫ̀ that they say is about fifteen miles north."

"What are we going to do?"

"Stay here. Keep hidden until after they leave their camp. They're not expecting us to go deeper into the forest. They know we're strangers here, and they figure we'll follow the water. They plan on leaving first thing in the morning and heading back that way, then they're going to follow it, searching for our signs."

Yaot'l raised her head and looked into Sascho's eyes. "I'm scared," she said. "I never want to go back to that place. I'd rather die."

"Don't worry. We're not going back. Tonight we'll take turns keeping watch. If they wake up," he nodded towards the sleeping kids, "tell them they have to keep very quiet. We must not be discovered."

"You don't think we should move on into the woods tonight?"

"No. We wouldn't be able to see and it's too easy to fall into danger. We're a lot more likely to make noises that we don't intend and alert the hunters. We'll stay here until they've gone, and then we'll go deep into the woods where no one will be looking for us."

Yaot'l reached up her hand and brushed the hair back on Sascho's forehead. "I trust you my gòichı. You sleep now. I'll take the first watch."

With that she crawled to the entrance of their hiding place and positioned herself so she could see without being seen.

Chapter Eleven

There was light ahead—the first they'd seen since they'd entered the spruce forest, so they pushed toward it. Yaot'l felt as if she walked in a dream. Her stomach was empty and her feet hurt, for the old leather shoes had fallen apart. There was not much left except the soles, around which she'd tied strips of cloth torn from her school apron. At the fireside a few nights back, they'd pulled her broken shoes apart. They'd kept the nails to use as awls.

"We could make moccasins with a nice deer and some camp time." She wasn't sure where the thought had come from, but it was a cheerful one, to imagine such a possibility.

"Big dreams." Kele didn't sound hopeful. He and Tanis huddled together by the fire, both beyond weary. Everyone was hungry. The single rabbit they'd caught a few days back had not made much impression upon their stomachs. This morning, Yaot'l had stripped the inner bark from a young spruce they'd come upon in a clearing where a larger tree had come down.

Small chewy pieces, tasting a little like raw carrot, had been the last food in their mouths.

"We could catch one in a snare. Uncle John taught me how," said Sascho. "I think resting and hunting are good ideas. If we found some deer, we could build a blind and then drive one into it."

"We don't know this land. How will we find deer?"

"Well, first we have to get out of this forest," said Sascho. "When we reach the place where it stops and the light comes in, there will be more food—rabbits, ptarmigans, or muskrats, at least."

"And maybe fish and some bear berries." Tanis sighed and licked her lips at the thought.

Yaot'l stumbled on, lost in a dream. If the boys were fortunate enough to get a deer—she and Tanis could cure the hide. They'd have to make camp for a week to do so, but if they had meat, they could rest and prepare for the remainder of their journey. There would be enough on the hide for more than one pair of moccasins—*at least, on the deer I am imagining...*

At this point, they were all in need of shoes, for they'd been in and out of water since the journey began. Hers, however, were the oldest and so had fallen apart first. Dropping back to walk at her side, Sascho's words broke into her thoughts.

"I dreamed of a deer last night."

"And so did I!"

"I think," Sascho said, taking her hand, "we are feeling like Tłı̨chǫ again."

This made both of them smile.

The light ahead grew brighter. They hadn't realized how deep the shadow of their surroundings until they stepped out through the last trees and found themselves with sky over head and head high brush on every side. She and Sascho walked out a few steps, blinking in the light. The other two hung back.

"Look! Berries!" Yaot'l ran toward a cluster of low bushes. She could see the waxy fruit hanging, and at the mere sight, her mouth watered.

"Yaot'l! Be careful!" When Tanis shouted, she stopped and looked around. She expected to see something – a trap, a snake – something that would elicit such alarm.

"What? Come on—there are bushes full of berries! See?"

"But—Nakan!"

"Where?"

Bushman?

Yaot'l spun around in alarm. For one moment, Patricia's mad fear seized her.

"There could be Nakan here—in this bush."

"Oh," said Sascho. "Could be? Tanis, don't scare us like that." Nevertheless, he studied their surroundings again, this time a little more carefully.

They were all happy to step out of the empty larder of the forest, but the truth was they were also afraid of the Nakan, the wild men, dangerous creatures who were said to dwell in the summer brush. Everyone in every village feared them—male and female alike—and a few people even said they'd seen the evil shaggy creatures.

Kele stepped out into the clearing, as if to distance himself from his sister's fears. "Don't shout 'Nakan' unless you really see one."

Tanis was abashed, but still anxious. After a few hesitant steps, she followed the others as they walked to the patch of low, shrubby bear berries. Very hungry now, especially at the sight of something they knew they could eat, they crawled all over the area locating the bushes and eating as fast as they could. Then, mouths gluey and puckered from the tough-skinned sourness, they searched for water. Fortunately, by standing on a boulder and scanning the area, Sascho discovered it quickly.

The first they found was dark and peaty, a trickling sound beneath the ground which emerged to gather into a pool. Here, they drank and gathered their welcome find. In the wide open lands, water sometimes bubbled up from beneath the surface in the most unexpected places.

An added benefit to the little pond was a cluster of bulrushes—a few long narrow tops still greening. The girls picked the heads. They stored some in the sack, and ate the others, stripping the crunchy green tube of seed heads right from the stalk with their teeth. Plant food helped the ache in the gut some, but what everyone most longed for was meat.

At the outlet, where water spread out and disappeared into the surrounding plain, there was a welcome sight. Tracks in the mud—of foxes, birds—and—best of all—deer!

Unfortunately, there were also swarms of biting flies.

"Ugh! So many insects!" Tanis slapped at her face.

"We can't stay too near here anyway," said Yaot'l. "Our scent will warn the animals. Perhaps we should keep looking and see if we can find moving water. It's still early enough in the year for plenty of that."

"And I'm sure if we keep on northwest, we'll find muskeg again. There is almost always something to eat there."

Sascho went to find the tallest willow in the cluster and then climbed it. Young and soft, it bent under his weight, but it did give him a better view. He turned and twisted until he saw, toward the northwest, a gray line along the horizon, but as much as he stared, he couldn't really make anything out. He noted as many details of the terrain as he could pick out along the sight line. It would be easy, among the brush and sedge-filled lakes for them to lose their way. He spotted a distant rock bald, one that he hoped to find again after his feet were back on the ground. Once he had it firmly etched into his memory, he climbed down.

"I see a scrub line that way, straight out, beyond a big patch of bare rock, but I can't get high enough. Can you try, Kele?"

Kele nodded. He was younger and lighter. Besides, Kele loved to say that the Stonypoint family had "hawk eyes." Ready to prove himself, he scrambled up the quaking tree, far higher than Sascho.

"What do you see?" Yaot'l called to him.

"Look more that way!" Sascho, below him, pointed, aiming straight to the yellowish stones he'd chosen for a marker.

Kele tried to ascend a little higher. Under his weight, the sapling swayed back and forth. He looked like a squirrel clinging to a branch, but as the movement decreased, he raised a hand to shade his face and looked out.

"I see it! There is a creek, I think, with a long line of willows." Kele shouted. "I think I see water shining, too. Yes, Yes! There's a sparkle in between the trees."

"Water is always good to follow. Here it goes north, and that's the way we want to travel." Yaot'l said.

"How far?" Tanis, who looked even thinner and wearier in the clear light, raised her hand against the sun glare.

"We have time to get there before dark, I think."

"If we don't lose our way in the brush." Tanis, gloomy again, heaved a big sigh.

"But we're hungry." Yaot'l had been thinking. "Perhaps we should stay near here, downwind, and set a trap overnight. There is willow and spruce here we can use to make the extra rope we'll need. If we get some meat, we'll walk faster."

"Is that what everyone else thinks?" Sascho asked the question, but the looks on the faces of the others should have been sufficient.

"Yes. Let's try." Kele spoke up in agreement. Tanis only nodded, but it was clear how very tired she was. She looked pale beneath her dark complexion.

Tanis had never made rope before, but was willing to follow Yaot'l's lead. The girls began to look for what they would need, passing the precious knives from hand to hand as they dug stringy roots out of the ground, and peeled willow bark—for that, Yaot'l used her strong teeth. While they worked, Sascho chose a spot by the pond where they could set a foot trap. Again, the troublesome ax was put to frequent use, until they'd cut the stakes that would support the loop of line the girls were making.

Yaot'l removed the cloth around her feet. After plaiting the first strands, she slipped a loop onto one big toe. Her short black hair blew wildly about in a welcome afternoon wind. Although it was dry and hot, blowing up from the south, it was a welcome blessing, for it sent most of the flies away. For a time they were quiet, while, fingers busy, she and Tanis focused on the task.

"Are you sick, gòet'įį?"

"I don't know, maybe. But I am very tired—always. I'm so glad we stopped. I couldn't have walked much longer. I feel dizzy."

"I am tired, too. I think, though, if we get some meat, we will all feel better."

"I wonder if I shall ever see home and my mother and sisters again." Tears sparkled in Tanis' eyes.

Yaot'l had wondered this too, many, many times since she'd been taken from the Snow Geese.

"We're better than half way through. What else can we do but go on? And besides," she added, when Tanis's sad expression didn't change, "we're not in that school with the Chekaa angry all the time, so it's better—even hungry."

"We were hungry there, too, but not this hungry."

"Yes." Yaot'l heaved a sigh and tugged at the line she'd made. The flexible damp roots and willow bark were shaping well.

"But you are right. This is better."

"Yes. Even if we are hungry, we are living like Tłįchǫ." Yaot'l was glad her friend, despite fears and a growling stomach, was able to agree with her. And this last, about living free, was what she told herself every time she felt her spirits fail.

"We should dig bulrush, too, before we leave." Tanis nodded. "Some of it is young and still tender."

There followed much long careful work, but by the time a length of rope was woven, the boys had finished digging the hole for the foothold trap, and cutting and setting the stakes in the ground in a small circle. Then they looped the tough stringy line carefully around the stakes and fastened it to a nearby spruce whose roots were well sunk into the earth. Yaot'l went on with her weaving, just in case what they'd made wouldn't be enough, or would break when it was tested. Tanis pulled up a few young rushes for the bulbs. Still hungry, they began to peel and chew on them at once.

Everyone was glad to leave the pond behind because the insects which returned every time the wind dropped.

"The sooner we leave, the sooner the deer return to drink." Sascho said. "These tracks here are fresh and if they are still in the area, they will certainly come in the evening. We need to move downwind now and wait. I will hide in the brush with Kele and we'll hope for the best."

Yaot'l and Tanis walked off a little further on the downwind side, looking out for a good place to wait. It would be a wearying? while until twilight—the days of high summer were still so very long. Some strips of crunchy green and a little bit of water had not much quieted her stomach. They didn't want to get too far from their trap, although they certainly did not want the deer to smell or sense them.

Everyone was so very tired, though, and just that little bit of water and food, even that

274

tough green, had soothed them. Soon, huddled together in bushy shade, they began to fall asleep. Yaot'l had tried not to, but the one time her eyes opened—just to check—the first thing she saw was Sascho, curled facing her. His eyes were closed. His face was completely relaxed; his breath went evenly in and out.

Already asleep!

She knew that as their leader, he'd carried a heavy responsibility. They'd just passed through a forest of hunger, and even there they'd had to hide a second time as yet another group of white hunters had passed them by. Those men took too much from the land. In their wake, there had been little game.

Somehow, tired as she was, Yaot'l remained awake. If he could not watch, she would. They had come so far! And from now on, the world before them would be more familiar. It was a comforting thought.

* * *

She awoke to the sound of a scream and violent thrashing. Yaot'l and Sascho leapt to their feet and began to run toward the muddy place where the trap was set. At the same time, several deer burst through the thicket and stampeded away, one of them almost knocking Yaot'l over. As the creatures ran, their feet struck the ground with a sound like hammers.

A yearling buck had been caught; the line stretched to the base of that tough little spruce.

At their appearance, he panicked, rushing back and forth. The knots were holding! Yaot'l knew how hard a deer could kick, so she and Sascho approached from opposite sides. Yaot'l made a series of feints to draw his attention. Kele and Tanis, hot on their heels, also added themselves to the ring around the deer, waving their hands. In that instant, Sascho sprang upon the buck's back and used his knife.

* * *

There was blood, some of which they drank from the body. Such a feeling of gratitude and thanks filled Yaot'l's heart as she swallowed it. The deer had given himself to them so generously and in such a time of need!

It is always like this, this joy to eat after you have been so hungry!

She was glad for the power the blood gave her body, for now, there was much to do, but first they must give thanks to this kind other-being who had come to rescue them. As they knelt by the deer, they all placed their hands upon the still warm body and whispered words of thanks.

"Through your sacrifice, we will be able to continue on our journey. Thank-you, White Tail, for your gift to us. Peace to your spirit." Next they set to dressing their kill. Sascho and Yaot'l knew what to do in order to make the most of the animal. There would be food for the journey; there would be hide, too.

The foursome sat around their fire, some distance from the pond. A last strip of meat roasted, though they'd already eaten well. Strips were already cut, strung and hung to dry. They would have to watch again tonight, with such a rich prize in hand. Who knew what animals might appear in the darkness and try to take their food—or attack them? They were glad for fire and food—and freedom.

It was enough, there in the star spangled night that finally came—a pale night, a short night—with the wandering stars and the fixed—showing that they had come through the dark forest on a true path, one that would take them north.

In a half dream, Yaot'l built tomorrow. She and Tanis would cure the hide. Then, with new moccasins, it would be easier to keep traveling.

"When do you think we'll be home?" Tanis's whisper broke in on her thoughts. She, much to everyone's relief, had looked better straight away with red meat inside her.

"It will be a little longer now, because we must cure this good hide."

"No one is sorry we caught the deer." Sascho ate a piece of meat from the spit he held. He had eaten more than anyone, but he was also the largest.

"And, if we hadn't caught the deer—it would have been even harder to keep walking than it was inside the forest," said Kele. "I am glad for the deer, and glad that every part of the trap worked so well."

"I am glad for the deer, that he gave us his life." Tanis spoke with deep feeling.

The flesh and blood of the animal had breathed renewed strength into them all.

"We must honor him once again, for he has given us all his strength."

"I know what to do," Sascho said.

* * *

It was a thing which must be done with bones. Certain pieces, broken with ceremony, set in the crook of a tree—he'd seen the men of his band say the words in the proper way to honor the deer's spirit. Now that he was leader, this was his task.

Yaot'l watched as Sascho collected things he needed for his offering. A sound, like a faint screech, caught her attention and she looked into the bush. Eyes glowed in the shadowy bushes and instinctively she grasped her knife. Then focusing on the eyes, she released her grasp, and called out to Sascho.

"Look there, an owl."

He rested his hand on her shoulder. "It is a good sign. Will you help me prepare the shield?"

"Of course, I've already gathered the willow." She handed him one of the branches and held the other herself. Together they twisted and braided until both willows came together in a circular shield. Sascho used one of the vines they'd gathered to fasten the bones together and

278

then hang them down from the center of the circle.

When they had finished Sascho lifted the shield and moved into the brush towards the glowing eyes. At the base of the tree beneath the owl's perch he took out a long strip of meat he had cut from the ribcage of the deer. Clearing away dead leaves from the spot, he laid the meat in a circle and lifted his voice in the words of a song of thanksgiving to the spirits of the animal kingdom for their gifts. Finished, he laid the shield over top of the meat and lifted his arms, bowing to each of the four directions, giving his thanks and honoring the spirits. Then, after a silent prayer to the gocho to watch over his small group, he returned to the camp.

It was time to get blankets and wrap up. Even in high summer, night could be chilly. Above their heads flat gray clouds had crept in; they were sealed beneath. That was good, for it would not be particularly cold. They'd felt the change in temperature—and welcome it had been—when they'd passed the trees.

Tanis was already asleep now, curled before the fire. Yaot'l roused her sufficiently so she could untie her blanket and then get wrapped up. She was comforted to see that it didn't take very long afterward that the child fell back into the same deep relaxed breathing, knees tucked around her pack. Kele was now on the ground too, arranging himself close to Tanis. They'd worked out the best way to sleep together during chilly nights, with the younger two in the middle.

With enough time—maybe after a day's trek to that creek-line Kele had spied—and if there was water…Yaot'l kept her eyes open, hoping to stave off the very thing she so badly needed. Firelight danced across her body. The nearby bushes seemed to quiver as waves of illumination and shadow passed over them. The glow radiated upward into a gray slate sky.

That was when she noticed the eyes—yes, golden eyes peeping through the long grass! Eyes and pricked ears! And here they all lay, sleeping. She wondered if there were more on the way. Could this evening's kill have attracted them?

The notion of a nearby wolf pack touched her like a finger of ice. She tried to respond, to grasp the knife, still close at hand, but found she could not make either her arm or fingers move.

The eyes came no closer. The expression in them, watchful before, changed to wondering, almost to sadness. A voice in her head seemed to say, "Do you remember who you are?"

"Wake up! Wake up!" Sascho knelt beside her. He gently shook her shoulder.

Yaot'l pulled herself upright, beyond glad to discover she had been dreaming. However, he, too, seemed anxious. Her friend's dark pupils were wide; his hair flared around his head, as if he was on his way to changing into some wild creature himself.

"I dreamed."

"I could see that." He smiled and suddenly didn't look as alarming as he had but a moment before.

"I dreamed of—a wolf."

"A wolf?"

"I thought I was awake and that it was peeking out at me through the long grass over there. Is that a good thing, to dream of a wolf? Or is it a bad thing, saying they are coming? At first I was frightened but then it spoke. It asked me if I remembered who I was."

"Maybe the wolf also wants our thanks because we took that deer from his tribe."

"We've hung our meat as high as we could get it on a creeper, over there by the trees, just in case."

"I hope the wolf in your dream will be content." Sascho rose to his feet, and went into the trees to look around. She leaned on an elbow and watched until he returned, dropped to the ground again and settled down. She could tell he was still worried, but knew he had to be even more tired than she was.

As she relaxed, close to Tanis and with the sound of breathing in her ears, she was glad Sascho had grown—somehow or other—even on the white man's poor food. She'd be even more afraid here in this wild place if he'd remained so boyish. After all, not only bears, but Nakan too, lived in this bush country. She hoped that if either wolves or Nakan was about, they'd think Sascho too big and strong to mess with.

* * *

Throughout the night they slept and waked in turns, always keeping the fire burning, guarding their venison. The next day, Yaot'l's dream stayed with her, even while her hands were busy with the hide. She wondered if she had understood it properly.

Then, while they were scraping, they looked up from their work to find an unexpected visitor.

"Yaot'l! Look!" Tanis retreated to the smoldering fire in case they needed a brand to defend themselves.

Belly crawling out of the brush, wagging his tail hopefully, eyes wide, was a black dog with a few white patches, of the same kind that inhabited every campsite in the north. He had two black ears that stuck up straight and two golden eyes.

Here is the "Wolf" from my dream!

This animal was thin. From his longing expression it was clear that he was hungry.

After the initial surprise, Yaot'l realized that he had come at the right time. She'd just tossed a mass of flesh and silver skin onto the ground nearby. As soon as her eyes met the dog's, they understood one another.

"This dog was in my dream. He's a friend."

Obediently, Tanis crouched by the fire, and awaited the dog's careful approach.

"Here, boy," Yaot'l called. "Good dog—come on." The dog eased closer to where the bits of flesh had accumulated, and then, with a sideways glance, making certain she wasn't going to attack him, he began to snap down flesh and silver skin. When that was gone, he, after casting a few careful glances at her and Tanis, began to cautiously scout the camp, to see if there was anything more.

In the aftermath of butchering, there was. When he'd cleared up everything, Yaot'l called to him again. Uncertain, he studied her face before beginning a slow approach, low to the ground. She extended her hand, palm up. Slick and bloody with the remains of the hide, he was quick to accept this gesture of friendship, licking her hand heartily. While he did, Yaot'l put her other hand upon him. He did not bite, although he was still a little anxious.

"You are a good dog. You can stay, if you want to." She knew that at this time of year he'd been able to survive, hunting for himself, but any creature alone in this place was always in danger. He'd come to them, hoping to join their band for more safety.

She liked the look in his bright eyes, this young and gentle dog. His tail thumped the ground when she bent down to him. He rolled over, and let her touch his belly.

He reminded her of Lucky, now with her family—maybe in Gam`e`t`i, so far away. The fact that he was so tame showed he'd once belonged to someone.

"He doesn't feel too bony."

The dog, ever more sure of his welcome, was on his feet again. Now he thumped his tail against her legs and made little whines of happiness.

Tanis, regaining her courage, returned from the fire, and the dog greeted her too, wagging his tail and bowing. When she too touched him, he gave a yelp of joy and thrust his head wetly against her hand.

"He was lonely."

"I think so. How do you suppose he lost his people?"

"Maybe they weren't kind and he ran away."

"Maybe he was looking for us, and that's why I dreamed."

"We are Dogrib, and so this dog has been sent to help us." Tanis's face brightened, apparently remembering Yaot'l's story. The dog, feeling the circle complete, sat down, close against her leg, tongue lolling. He didn't look frightened anymore.

"Yes, we are Dogrib." Yaot'l spoke to him and crouched to run her own hands over his furry back. "And we are all of us travelers, walking this land like our gocho."

That day, the girls made a collar of rope. When they'd placed it around his neck, he made no objection. When the boys came out of the bush, he leapt up and barked at them.

Kele took a step back and raised the stout stick he carried. Sascho held a wooden spear he'd whittled at the ready.

Yaot'l grabbed the dog's collar.

"No! No! Don't bark! That's Sascho and that's Kele! They are our friends."

The dog stopped as soon as she spoke, but he remained alert. Eyes bright with interest, he first studied her and then Sascho.

"Is this your dream wolf?"

"I think so. He is friendly."

Sascho smiled. He and Kele both knelt so the dog could meet them. By the time they'd begun to clean their catch, this new member of the band was an interested onlooker, waiting for whatever they discarded.

* * *

They stayed at the pond for the time it took to finish the hide. The girls worked it, scraping with hoof bone. Yaot'l made a paste from the animal's brain, using an indentation in a nearby rock ledge as the container.

They decided to move on when the hide was finished, and head toward the distant scrub line. Every day, the boys scouted in the direction they'd chosen, but Sascho didn't want to leave the girls alone for long. Nakan—and other more tangible dangers of bush country, like a bear, or more parties of roaming white hunters like those they'd evaded in the forest— were not to be taken lightly.

285

When they set out again, a part of their kit was now packed onto the back of their new friend, the dog. He seemed to be familiar with exactly what was expected of him. He now had a name: 'Wolf,' given for what Yaot'l had first imagined, certainly not for any ferocity in his nature. Sascho liked him, but joked that "Dìga should be just called Gah (rabbit). That dog is," and here he pointed, "more likely to hide behind us if he's scared."

Yaot'l teased him in return, saying, "He knows he can rely on you, Sascho, to drive away all danger. I say the dog is wise. He knows who is leader."

Tanis, who had been walking beside the dog, also objected.

"Don't make fun of our new friend."

While she patted her companion, Kele also had something to say.

"Wolf helps my sister with her pack, and so I'm glad he is here, whatever his name is."

* * *

For days they walked, following stars or the lodestone when there were clouds. Sometimes they hunted; sometimes they rested and prepared skins so that they'd last until Wha't'i, where such work could be finished. Sometimes they entered muskeg, and here they'd hunt plentiful small game. When they entered an area of bush, there were berries, plants and birds, but bush was also a dangerous place. More than once they had to change or halt the march in order to avoid a bear feeding with her cubs. Anywhere they saw buzzards overhead, they also altered their route. Who knew what large predator was already on the scene?

The walk was sometimes hard, but at night either Yaot'l or Sascho had a story to tell, one about the gocho, and how they had drawn their strength through the soles of their feet, right out of the sacred ground. The gocho had lived beside the animals they hunted, listened for them, looked for their signs, and followed them on their journeys. They'd hunted caribou just as the wolves did, in bands.

Kele, they both knew, sometimes looked upon their talk of staying in right balance as superstitious. His own father had taught him that kwet'ıì took whatever profit they could get from the forest and that the Indian should too. Now, he'd been to school and been taught that mankind was lord over all the other animals. It saddened Yaot'l to think that first Mr. Zoe, and then Sascho, were the first two men Kele had ever met who regularly offered thanks for the food they ate.

Chapter Twelve

It had been a very hot day. They'd been trudging beside the merest ghost of a trail. Sascho believed he recognized the area, and thought they could now not be too far from Wha't'i, maybe a few days, maybe another week. There, they'd certainly find members of their tribe, some of whom would be spending August at the łk'àdèè k'è there. Uncle John's first wife had come from there, and he'd remembered the place and her kin, fondly. So did Sascho, after that visit last summer.

It was comforting to Yaot'l that Sascho had traveled here before. They'd had enough of being lost during the early parts of their escape, and those days of wandering the dark forest— evading kwet'ıı̀ who might have returned them to Fort Providence. Tanis was so weak now that she could not keep up, so they all took turns helping her along. In the afternoons, sometimes Sascho, and sometimes Yaot'l, would carry her on their backs. Kele too did this, though he wasn't big enough for his turn to last very long.

They were carrying some hides now, and were glad to have the dog, familiar as he was with the duties of a pack animal. Obediently, he'd submit to being rope harnessed. Then he'd bravely drag the travois they'd made as long as he was able.

When they stopped for a rest, someone would fish in whatever water they found, or look for berries or young birds, anything for the evening's meal. At their nighttime stop, Sascho made the fire. He'd tried to cheer Tanis by telling stories of the friendly kin he'd been introduced to at last summer's łk'àdèè k'è.

"It won't be long now; we'll find our people. Then, after a rest, you will feel strong again, and one of Uncle John's cousins—or one of yours—will take care of you."

Tanis would always brighten at the idea. Sometimes, though, despite his efforts to cheer her, it would be hard for her to stay awake long enough to eat. Yaot'l would awaken her and encourage her, but their young friend had dwindled to almost nothing but two big black eyes. Pale skin stretched thin over her birds' bones.

One night, when they'd been following a path with a downhill slope, they were stopped by a narrow, high-walled gully. It was late, and Tanis was a heavy burden, so they picked a spot on a ledge to stop. Yaot'l had walked back up the hill to look around. She'd found that if they went higher, they would be exposed, visible from all sides. Besides, there was only meager brush up there to use for fire and shelter.

As she returned to the others, Yaot'l noticed a pile of smoke-stained rocks, so others had used this spot. It had not been too recently, however, for there was still plenty of wood and scrub colonizing the ledge where it ran, just below the lip of the gorge. By following that tomorrow, it would take them easily down to the plain surrounding Marten Lake, the last piece of the journey.

"There are trees on this ledge." Sascho said while they discussed the situation. "That means the water has not come up this far for a very long time."

It was easy to make camp. The dog, also worn out, lay down, panting. For a little, Tanis and Kele whispered to one another. There, by fading firelight—and the smoky aura it cast—they talked over what to do next. They were covering fewer and fewer miles every day. As Tanis became weaker and needed more help, the others grew ever more tired.

"Perhaps we should stop after we get down onto the plain. If there's game, we can hunt."

"It's starting to get cold at night. Every day the light goes earlier. If we delay, the Marten Lake people could leave. Soon it will be time to go for caribou."

Yaot'l knew they'd all despair if they reached the lake only to find everyone gone, already pursuing the migration. They had done well to have gone so far on their own, but summer was running out. They had to find their tribe before winter came.

She knew Sascho was correct. All the signs, the ones she too saw, were present.

"Tanis is very ill, but I think you are right."

Somewhere, to the north, they heard the yip of a fox, perhaps a mother, teaching her children about nighttime hunting. The dog's head shot to attention, angling toward the sound. A long sniff, then he tucked himself up again, apparently unconcerned about the doings of his wild cousins.

"We will travel straight through the bush now until we reach the small lakes which are near Wha't'i. It's either that, or travel due east along the Nàįlįį. We'd meet some Tłįchǫ if we went that way, almost for certain."

"This is almost the same time when Pierre caught us last year."

"I know. And that's why I've kept north and west, even though it's not always easy to keep on straight."

"Well, while we still have food, let us travel on as we have been."

Sascho got to his feet and took a final look at their fire. He added a little more wood, before he lay down close against Kele and wrapped up in his own blanket. Over and above the bodies of their two smaller companions, he reached to link his hand with Yaot'l. It was a thing they did every night now. The warm touch of the other, combined with the in and out breathing of Kele and Tanis, let them be a family.

* * *

291

A flash and then a rumble of thunder sliced open the night. Yaot'l rolled onto her back and crawled to the edge of their lean to, the better to see the sky through the pile of leaves and skins they slept beneath. Over her head, the sky still blazed with stars. The horizon east, however, was even now in the process of disappearing, a tide of blackness quenching the twinkling lights.

A summer storm was nearby, though it might never rain on them.

They'd camped on a ledge about five feet above the dry wash. It was not an ideal location, but it was flat and offered plenty of brush for cover and fuel. Yaot'l lay back down, though all her senses remained alert, as the flashes grew more frequent and brighter. The rumbles turned to booms; around her, the others, all except for Tanis, sat up. With each flash, she had a picture of their dog, sitting, sniffing the air, his ears pricked.

An inrush of blustery, warm wind shook their shelter. Spits of rain fell.

"Father is coming." Sascho quoted the old story about the great storm bird.

"Maybe we should move up higher." Yaot'l studied the flashing darkness.

Sascho got to his feet. "Maybe we should."

"Let's wait and see what happens." Kele shivered and yawned. "Maybe it won't rain here."

"If it's bad, it could still flood, even here."

Sascho went to take a look. Distant lightning strikes illuminated his sturdy form.

"We don't want to lose our furs."

"Or the pots." Yaot'l, remembering how long it had been since she'd seen a good-sized birch tree, knew she didn't want to lose those either.

"I can't get up." Tanis' voice was barely a whisper. "I'm so tired."

"I'll go and watch," Kele said. He crawled out and then got to his feet beside Sascho. The dog, loosed to hunt, came to sit beside them. The three of them, for a time, watched the flashes rip open the night sky.

"I'll stay with you," said Sascho. "If we hear anything—like a rumble or a roar—we can run up the bank." He turned to survey their campsite. "There's a lot of good sized brush in this place, so it can't have flooded this high for several years."

Yaot'l dropped to her knees again and crawled close to Tanis. She touched her friend's brow and felt sickly moisture.

Fever!

She wished she had more of the tamarack, but it was long since gone. With all her heart she hoped they would reach other people soon, maybe some camping at a distance from the lake. Then they could get help for Tanis from elders.

They had made a long journey together and passed through many trials. It was unbearable to imagine that all their hardships and bravery might still end in a death!

She wrapped herself around Tanis' meager body, felt the rattle of her breath. She knew she might catch the sickness by holding her so close, but she would call upon her own strong spirits—white feathers shining, cries that rose to the stars!

No rain came. The wind died, and the storm moved away, sending its water down somewhere else over the dèè. The day passed had been a hard one and there were still more days like that to come, but at last they'd reached a time where the journey neared its end.

Yaot'l fell asleep, taking comfort from the thought that they would not be by themselves for much longer now and also from the thought that it had never rained on them.

* * *

The dog barked and then let out a series of howls, but a grinding roar, closing at great speed, ripped her from sleep.

"Wake up! Run!" Sascho was shouting, pulling on Kele's arm.

She grabbed Tanis by the shoulder, and shook her wildly.

"Get up! Get up! Now!"

Pulling Tanis to her feet, she leapt out of the shelter into starlight. The dry creek below them moved and flowed. It roared like some kwet'įį engine. She had just barely taken this in when water hammered against her ankles. She'd turned up the grade, towing Tanis, when a wall of liquid caught her.

* * *

Yaot'l sat upon a branch, hugging the slim body of a tree. She shivered in the cold air; her muddy legs and chopped hair hung in strings around her face. The half-light of dawn glowed around, while, at the zenith, the bright star clouds still shone.

Below her was a sea of rubble, brush, and mud. Further down, a small creek rattled where yesterday it had been nothing but boulders, low scrub, and dusty cracked ground. A sleepy bird tried a few hesitant notes.

There had been shouts and screams: Sascho, Kele, Tanis...

The girl's narrow hand had ripped away at the first thundering impact. A thin shriek disappeared in the same roar where Yaot'l flailed, using every fiber of her strength. Somehow, she'd kept her head above the muddy flow, thick as jam. There'd been painful breath stopping collisions with bush and deadwood, until she'd struck this tenacious tree and managed to wrap her arms around it.

Remembering, tears plowed down her muddy cheeks.

Above her, a dog barked. She raised her head and looked up.

"Yaot'l! Kele! Tanis!"

A desperate voice—Sascho's—calling. The sound interrupted the buzzing emptiness inside her head.

"Here! I'm here!"

The tree to which she clung leaned toward the wash bottom, but the roots had held. She looked in the direction of the sound and saw him coming through the rubble, climbing over piles of earth, logs, and gravel. He was a man of the same stuff which surrounded them. Only his black eyes stood out, burning.

When he saw her, he began to run. She wanted to jump down to meet him, but she was fairly high up, and shivering hugely. She feared her legs would not hold her, so she waited until he reached the tree and extended his arms. Weeping with joy, she let herself down into them.

They clung to one another, as he too, unashamed, wept with her. They were like the first people in the world, like two lone muskrats, wet and muddy, but alive. She could feel his heart beating against hers.

The moment alone was interrupted by the dog. He raced down to hurl himself at their feet. He too was wet and muddy, but he barked and jumped, clearly delighted to have found his people again.

* * *

They were hungry, thirsty, cold, exhausted. Everything at the camp had gone, except for the knives which she and Sascho always carried. They searched and called for the others, but finding no sign, they at last turned back to follow the storm fed creek. Finally, as the sun rose, barely able to move, they climbed the bank to a place where the flood had never come. It seemed odd to have almost drowned in a world that, away from the wash and the ledge where they'd camped, was completely dry.

Sascho had another treasure—some dried meat in a bag, one they'd hung further up from last night's camp in case they had a visiting bear or wolf.

"It's the single right thing I did." Sascho hung his head and she knew the heartache he felt. It seemed clear that the young ones had not survived. They'd walked along the wash accompanied by the dog, finally climbing down to where it emptied onto a plain of scrub. Here, it spread out into a long foot high tongue of mud and rubble before disappearing.

For a time, they stood, staring. Yaot'l eventually moved to the shade of the nearest stand of useful trees, and began to build a fire with some dry stuff they'd collected. Sascho always kept the fire flints in a little bag at his waist, so that would not be too hard to do. The dog followed. Sascho, after surveying the gravel and deadwood outflow for a time, at last came to join her. He did not sit down, though, only paused to hand down the bag with their remaining scraps of dried meat.

"I do not want to go to Wha't'i."

Startled, she looked at him, at the set of his jaw, at the grief in his dark eyes. Before she could reply, however, he'd added, "but we have to, don't we?"

"Yes. To tell what has happened."

She knew that just as she was, he was in agony. Those younger children had been in their care!

All day they had looked for Tanis and Kele, calling their names, now and then drinking at the ever-clearing pools of water and chewing on the dried meat. The dog, seemingly understanding, had stayed active, sniffing and circling among the debris piles along the way. Now, they faced the inevitability of what had happened, and this, combined with exhaustion and exposure, came crashing in. Yaot'l felt as if all the bones in her body were crumbling.

"We were the oldest."

"And now," Sascho said, "it's just us and Wolf." He reached into the bag and tossed the dog the last of their precious dried meat.

"Our grandparents live in Wha't'i. They will hide us." Tanis had sought Kele's hand while he spoke.

"I too have kin there. Yaot'l and I can find someone going north toward Gam`e`t`i and you two will be safe there."

All those plans they'd made now seemed unreal — and so very long ago.

Chapter Thirteen

The dog's barking woke them. At a little distance an old man stood out upon the rubble, watching. Two fat ptarmigan dangled from his belt.

"We are on a journey." Sascho explained their presence as he scrambled upright. The growling dog crouched low and then whined. Even though he was clearly fearful, he managed to strike a protective pose at their feet.

The man continued to stare. He wore a hat with a single feather tucked into the headband.

"You are young to be alone, but I think you are Tlicho. I am Mr. Drybones."

"Yes, Babàcho. We are on our way to Wha't'i, where our kin fish. I am Sascho Lynx and this is Yaot'l Snow Goose. We have traveled here from the school at Fort Providence."

The old man nodded and then said, "I think you did not want to stay at that school."

"No, the kw'ahtıı caught us while we were visiting in Behchok'o and put us into a truck and then onto a boat. When summer came again, we ran away. We've been following the trail to Wha't'i."

Sascho looked down uncertainly. Perhaps he'd said too much?

"And just last night, the evil spirit in that wash caught you all asleep." The old man spoke the words that Sascho could not.

"We had two young friends with us. We were all caught when the water came down."

"That is a treacherous place. Often it is safe; sometimes it is not."

"All day we have looked and looked, but we can not find our friends."

Moving close, Yaot'l touched Sascho's hands, knotted behind his back.

"But you two are alive. Follow me to my camp, where my wife waits. Tomorrow, you and your woman, Sascho Lynx, will continue your journey together."

They followed him in silence. As old and bent as he was, he seemed to flow through the bush as effortlessly as a marten. They had to struggle to keep pace.

Yaot'l's bones ached. Mud caked her body. At least, she thought, the dirt keeps insects at bay.

"I know a man called John Lynx. Is he your Uncle?"

"Yes, and my teacher. I was to go to Big Bear Lake to learn from him, but instead we were taken away."

* * *

As they walked, the sun rose higher. Yaot'l's head ached with every step while heat poured down. The old man seemed to be leading them in a direction she did not want to go. At last, after a long trek through low scrub, they came to a halt.

Sure enough, they'd arrived at a place she'd seen enough of already. There was a heap of mud and gravel, the last long tongue of the outflow. The walls of the plain from which they'd descended only a day ago rose steeply above them. As they approached, several vultures languidly flew off.

"Why have we come here?" Sascho asked the question on both minds.

"To find one of your friends."

The old man gestured, and there, sure enough, sticking out of a loose heap of debris, a small pale hand, extended toward the sky. As they came closer, it appeared that those birds had already been pecking at the fingers.

Yaot'l's hand flew to her mouth. After a moment's hesitation, Sascho strode forward onto the debris pile. He dropped to one knee when he reached the spot, and began to dig. The dog, who'd been unusually subdued and lagging a good distance behind, came up straightaway to join him. Gathering herself, Yaot'l followed.

Time seemed to hang motionless while all three of them dug, but at last they managed to uncover Tanis. She was now white as a kwet'įį, the tattered dress plastered against her thin, dirty form. Yaot'l thought she'd never seen her young friend so clearly, as when they'd brushed the last of the gravel away. She and Sascho leaned upon one another and unashamedly wept.

The old man did not speak until the first tide of their grief had passed, then he said, "We will carry her back up to the plain, where the water can never reach her and bury her there."

It was a hard climb, up through the rocks, but pain and hunger no longer mattered. It seemed Tanis weighed hardly anything. When they first lifted her, her head fell to one side and water poured from her lips.

"We must bury her far away from the evil spirit," the old man said.

At the top, they dug at the tough ground with their knives. It was more hard work, but Sascho worked like a mad man, Yaot'l beside him. The dog lay at a distance, whining softly. It was as if he did not want to be anywhere near this melancholy scene, and especially he did not want to be anywhere near that strange old man. His humble yellow eyes anxiously followed every movement old Drybones made.

When they had laid Tanis in the narrow groove they'd made, it seemed too terrible to cover her again right away, so the two friends knelt beside the body. The old man began to sing a mourning song. It went on and on, but Yaot'l sat weeping and did not mind. She thought she might never move another step, as exhaustion flowed over her.

At last the old man knelt down alongside them, and, after a long look at the body, he took some things from his pouch, a pebble glinting with quartz and a braided bracelet of hide from which hung a tiny feather and a pierced seed. These, he placed upon her breast. Then, blinded by tears, Yaot'l and Sascho covered their friend, first with earth and gravel, and then with rocks which marked the directions. At this last, the dog joined in with a terrible howl.

Then, steps dragging, they resumed their march again. The sun disc was almost below the horizon when they discovered, set between bear berry bushes and a cluster of windswept stunted spruce, a camp fire. There was no breeze, so only the merest line of white smoke rose into a darkening sky.

Sascho kept trying to get the dog to come, but he hung back. Drybones took something from a bag at his side and threw it to the dog, who, after a little hesitation, gobbled it down.

"Don't worry about him," Drybones said. "He is grieving and hungry. He will follow in his own time."

Yaot'l was so exhausted by grief and racked by hunger now that she could barely stand. The smell of food suddenly permeated the air, which made her feel faint.

An old woman sat on a stool in front of the campfire stirring a black pot with a long-handled wooden spoon. In the other hand she held the pot lid, using a rag in order to shield herself from the heat.

"Good evening, my husband."

"Good evening, my wife."

"What have you brought me for the cookpot now, Drybones?"

"Here are two fine ptarmigan."

As they stepped closer to the fire, the old woman turned her face toward them, and Yaot'l, seeing the milky white of her eyes, knew the old woman was blind. She and Sascho looked at each other in amazement.

How could a blind woman handle fire?

"And who are these two young strangers, my husband?"

The man turned, and, for the first time, showed his many—all still present—teeth. It startled Yaot'l—those young white teeth in an old man's mouth.

"My wife is a woman who sees everything. Speak your names to her."

"I am Sascho Lynx, and Yaot'l Snow Goose travels with me."

A swirl of sparks flew up into the twilight. The old man nodded his head—an affirmation— and said, "They are going home."

"They were locked in a bad place. They were on the river and then walking." The old woman's hair was short, but it stood up like a bush, flaring from her scalp to form a dense halo of spider's web.

"Yes, Mamàcho. The kwet'ı̨ı̨ school was a bad place."

"These youngsters have lost a little sister in the wash."

304

The old man set the ptarmigan close by her feet. After he'd laid them down, his wife reached to gently stroke their feathers.

"We thank you for your lives, little brothers." The woman's words were soft, tender. The manner in which she spoke to the birds brought tears to Yaot'l's eyes, for somehow it caused her remember Tanis, broken and still in the mud.

"We have lost two friends," Sascho said. "The other was called Kele."

"But he is not lost," said Drybones. "He sleeps in our tent." He gestured to what, only a second ago, had appeared as some brush and boulders, just beyond the firelight. Now it was a lodge of boughs covered with hide.

Yaot'l shook her head and then turned to Sascho. He too seemed astonished.

"My husband found a young boy yesterday and brought him here. He will live." The old woman waved her hand over the pot. "Come and have a seat by our fire. Food is ready."

"We must see him! We have looked and looked and could not find him. Where did you find him, Babàcho? "

"Out there." The old man indicated the direction from which they'd just come.

"Please Babàcho, let us see him." Yaot'l asked again. "We have mourned for him, as well as for his sister."

"No, no need to mourn, but you cannot see him now. He must sleep undisturbed in order to come back to himself. Wait until tomorrow. You will be there when he awakens."

Yaot'l wanted to beg, but Drybones spoke in a firm tone.

"My wife has ɪk'ǫ̀. She has done all she that can be done for him."

Yaot'l knew it would be impolite to ask again.

"Sit on the blanket there. Eat and fear nothing. You two will soon find your kin and your young friend will walk beside you."

There was something about all of it, especially those two elders, which made Yaot'l wonder if she was dreaming. She'd had the strangest thought, as the old man walked between her and the fire, that, for, just for an instant, she had seen straight through him to the shelter.

Sascho too must have sensed the otherness, for he took her hand. The feeling that they were of one mind had grown stronger every step of their journey. She could almost hear his voice in her head,

We will talk later.

They sat down side by side, cross-legged upon a worn patchwork blanket. This homely hand sewn item was reassuring and made the situation, once again, seem ordinary. Drybones produced several horn spoons and moved the pot so that it stood on its three black iron legs between them and his wife. The stew within sent up flavor-filled steam.

In the dark, from beyond the circle of fire, they heard the dog whine for attention. He was anxious—for his people and for himself.

"We must feed our dog. He too is hungry."

"He won't come to our fire." The old man stepped just out of the ring of light, where he, speaking to the dog, said: "There are rabbits here—a whole nest. Go sniff them out and eat them. Stay close and nothing will harm you. Come to meet your friends with the sun."

A few beats of silence followed, and then they heard the click of the dog's nails on the stone ledge as he walked away. Yaot'l felt, once more, the prickle at the back of her neck. She squeezed Sascho's hand and was reassured when he squeezed back.

If there is something uncanny here, we will face it together...

"Go ahead. Fill your stomachs," said the old woman. "I know you are hungry."

Once they put the first spoonful to their lips, they could not stop. The old man squatted down and joined them in eating from the pot. The old woman, however, did not share the meal.

"Will you not join us, my wife?"

"I ate before you came." Sitting back on her stool, she felt about until she found the pile of sticks set just behind, and then tossed them one by one unerringly onto the fire. Next, she groped for a bag at her waist and came up with an antler pipe and then a small pouch of leaves from which she filled it.

After she'd placed the pipe between her thin lips, her husband took a stick from the fire and held it to the bowl so that she could draw to light it. Then, glowing pipe in hand, she leaned forward, supporting herself elbows on knees while exhaling a thin stream of smoke. The smell told Yaot'l that this was kinnickkinnick, mixed with a tiny pinch of tobacco.

Each hot mouthful of dried caribou stew entering her mouth was accompanied by the smell of the old time pipe weed scent. *So comforting! Like round the campfire with family.*

How old, Yaot'l wondered, was she? Her round face was cut and crisscrossed by a thousand fine lines; her once full cheeks had sunken till her mouth was only a pucker. Like Yaot'l's Mamàcho Josette, and, unlike her husband, it appeared that most of the old lady's teeth were lost. Her hair was snow white, which was unusual among Tłįchǫ elders. The hair of their old people was iron gray, like the granite slabs that rose from beneath the earth in the north.

At last they both sighed, satiated. Overhead in the clear night sky, a million stars throbbed. Some were white, others, blue, and still others, red. Yaot'l, after eating all her stomach could hold, suddenly wanted nothing more than to fall asleep. Her eyes closed; her head bobbed till her chin touched her chest. Beside her, Sascho was in a like state.

"Look up, young ones."

Their eyes popped open at the urgency in Mr. Drybones' voice.

Over their heads the aurora danced and shed its magical light, this time a dazzling curtain of red, green and yellow. It seemed to blow gently in an unseen wind. It was so quiet here—not a sound, just the faint sighs and crackles of the dying fire. *Spirits are walking.*

"That is your little sister, Tanis. She wants you to see her join the gocho among the stars."

More tears made fresh channels along Yaot'l's salty, muddy cheeks. It hurt to cry again. Her eyes stung and smarted after so much weeping.

"Do not shed tears, young Warrior. Your friend has not been buried by strangers. She was not left where no one of her tribe can find her. We have made her a fine resting place, and set the stones as is proper, right here, on Tłıchǫ dèè."

Yaot'l's shoulders shook as she wept, even though the elder's words brought some comfort. She again sadly remembered Patricia, now buried where no one of her tribe would ever find her. Sascho put his arm around her waist, drew her close.

"We will carry the news of her death to her family."

Overhead the aurora continued to flicker and shudder. Here, by the whispering fire, they were still as stones.

"The gocho have taken her in their arms." The old woman drew deeply upon her pipe and slowly blew a fine stream of scented smoke upwards.

Gradually, the aurora faded, leaving only the piercing stars.

"It is time for these young ones to sleep," said the old man. "Come, Sascho, and help me bring some boughs and hides. You two may sleep by our fire."

Gently, Sascho disengaged his hands from Yaot'l. Then, unsteadily, he got up to join the old man. They bent low as they entered the shadows by the shelter.

Yaot'l thought she would close her eyes, just for a moment. A hand on her shoulder brought her back. It was Sascho, now with an armful of hide for a sleeping pad. It was a luxury they had not had for a long time. How glad her aching body would be! Slowly, she got up and helped him arrange their bedding.

Soon, after a visit to a little spring for a splash to the face and a drink of tooth-ache cold water, they sat and leaned their heads together. A few more handfuls of twigs refreshed the fire.

No more could be said, because they sensed the old pair's eyes were upon them, once again.

"Do you know the way to Wha't'i?"

Sascho peered at the night sky. Try as he might, he could not make sense of the star patterns

"No, and it—it makes me ashamed. I know the stars, but what I see here confuses me."

Beside him, Yaot'l had also looked up. She too could recognize nothing.

"You are tired now," said the old woman. "And this place—" Her cloudy eyes turned upward—"often changes."

Drybones extended a skinny finger to point back toward the shelter. "Just behind that tallest spruce, you will see a flat rock with long scratches. Along that line is the path you must walk. Later, at the bottom of the hill, you will find a lake and a trail marker."

"Yes, Yes. You must be guided by the rock where Father Bird raked his claws, a long time ago, in Gawoo. That points your way."

"The Father Bird?" Yaot'l trembled when she heard the powerful name. The idea that the Father Bird had once been in this place, his immense claws scouring stone—when his storm had just carried away Tanis—brought Yaot'l, once more, near awake.

"He of Thunder. Once, when he was tired, he floated near the earth and his great claws raked the earth on this hill."

"Your kin are closer than you think," the old woman said. "You will soon find them."

"We will watch you sleep and keep you safe," said Drybones. "Tomorrow you will be ready to journey again."

Yaot'l thought that this, his offer to keep the night watch, was the queerest thing yet.

Such old people must certainly be at least as tired as she was!

Still, she was too weary to hold a thought. As she settled down, joining Sascho—once it had seemed so daring—she whispered a final, lingering concern.

"Did you see Kele?"

"He's fast asleep inside the shelter. I saw his chest rise and fall, so he is alive, just as they've said. I wanted to touch him, but Drybones said I must not do that."

"It seems impossible. We searched and searched."

"I know. I don't understand, but I—" Sascho paused, fought to keep tears from his eyes. "I am glad."

Across the fire, Drybones and his wife continued to talk. The words blurred into nonsense by the time they reached Yaot'l's ears.

* * *

Sascho's warm arm came to encircle her. It was wonderful to be alive and be with him, although it would be better when they had their own dwelling, with spruce branches beneath them, soft hides and a trade blanket or two...

Without any noticeable beginning, everything changed.

* * *

They walked among the stars, she and Sascho. They went hand in hand, their feet upon a shining path that led across the night. As one, they gazed downward, and Yaot'l saw all the paths they had walked, all the way from

Dehcho, following the Horn River until it turned west, and then their wandering through the little groves, the bush and the muskeg, where the animals had watched them pass. The beautiful deer lifted his head, leapt across their path and vanished among the stars. He too, was now a soul, wandering the sky. He would travel there until he faded into the body of the Great Spirit, which contained earth and all its creatures, both two-legged and four.

Then, Sascho's hand was gone and she was alone. For a moment, Yaot'l was afraid, but now she was winged, flying. And although his hand was gone, she saw that, there, flashing beside hers was another wing, tipped in black, bravely sculling the heavens! A pure joy welled inside, for she knew that she and her husband were but two among a great flock of others, flying just below the stars, as she and her tribe went soaring toward True North...

* * *

And Sascho too dreamed.

He was a bear, a young brown bear, lying down, hips up and belly flat down on earth, paws extended toward a central fire. Fire—a strange companion for a bear—but in this case it was blue and cool and it barely flickered at all.

Across the fire sat another bear, very large, and back on his haunches. He was bluish in color and his great muzzle was speckled with white. He was big, broad shouldered and old.

"A leader learns from his mistakes. You yourself may die from a mistake you make while you are leading your family. The dèè is a hard teacher."

"Tanis's death is my fault. I will never forget my mistake, Babàcho, but I can no longer help Tanis, only her family."

"To help her family will be a good thing. To grieve long over it, though, does no good. To learn—that's what you must do now."

Sascho looked at the great shaggy creature and felt hope. His step would be lighter if he could put this guilt and shame at his back.

"Your mistake was not that you camped on the edge of the wash. You chose a higher place than the bottom, yes, that you saw, but it was still a part of the wash. The mistake was your belief that you knew bush craft well enough to foresee what would happen in a place you did not really know. Others have camped on that ledge this year and you knew that because you saw the old campfire. The only difference is that when you came, the wind had shifted north and that—a thing known to us here—is when, if it is also raining, the flood comes."

A long silence lay between them. The strange cool fire set the shadows dancing. Sascho wanted to hang his head, but it was soothing to stare into the light. The great bear slowly eased his front legs down until his belly too rested on the ground. Then he curled his paws against his chest and settled with a deep sigh.

"Now you feel the burden of leadership. You and all your friends might have died in that flood. Never forget; as you walk through the dèè, trials of life and death are always waiting."

Another long pause followed. A shower of small glowing objects fell all around him. They reminded Sascho of hail, except for the glitter. They hissed as they landed, and when Sascho reached a curious paw to touch one, it felt cool. As he gazed at it in wonder, the old one spoke again.

"You are a young bear with much to learn, before the gift of ink'on is given. You are fortunate to have found a hard-working, wise mate who will help you."

Ink'on! The old bear had said it would be his—the gift that had come to his Uncle John, the gift which had made him a fortunate hunter, the gift that had given him power to see what others did not, to be a fount of giving to his tribe....

And Yaot'l too—Yaot'l would ever walk beside him! The weight upon his heart lifted.

* * *

Sun struck Yaot'l's face. There was a sound like thunder and her eyes flew open.

Here I am, on Tłıchǫ dèè again!

Nearby was the three-legged pot, standing in the ashy remains of last night's fire. Yaot'l lay on her side and saw Sascho on his knees beside her. She made as if to speak, but he, moving with great care, laid a finger to his lips. Then she heard a sound, one that even deep inside her sleep-filled brain, signaled danger.

Snuffling…huffling!

Some very large animal was nearby, and, from the rank smell, she knew exactly what kind.

A bear!

And not just one, but two! Yaot'l saw their gray muzzles and could almost feel those four, deep-set eyes steadily regarding her. Both animals were enormous. The male was a large blue with a wide head and a gray-white mask. The female was smaller and heavily stippled with white.

Neither she nor Sascho dared to flex so much as a muscle.

Stillness hung in echoing silence. At last, casually, as if they had seen all they cared to see, the great animals turned away. With ponderous dignity, furry pelts rippling over massive shoulders, they withdrew into the brush. Sascho remained frozen where he knelt, while Yaot'l —very, very slowly—sat up.

Both were afraid to breathe, fearing any sound might cause the bears to suddenly return. Everyone knew how unpredictable these large animals were. Bears were not at all afraid of people, puny beings who they sometimes made their prey.

After what seemed a very long time, Sascho got to his feet. He did not speak, but only reached a hand down to help her. As soon as she was up, he touched his lips again, to indicate that she should remain silent. Then, he pointed toward the place where last night there had been a tidy shelter, covered in spruce branches and several large moose hides.

It was now only a pile of dried branches, needles dropping. Yaot'l's hands flew to her mouth.

Kele!

Was he also gone?

They looked at one another, lost in fear and wonder. Sascho's lips formed an unspoken word: Shaman!

A surge of something akin to panic ran through Yaot'l, although, weird as they now knew this place was, the desire to flee almost instantly bled away. Still, not knowing what would happen next, they both carefully looked around them before they dared to take as much as a step.

Rocks, spruce, white saxifrage clinging to rocks, bearberries, the leaves now blushing red...

With the disappearance of their rescuers—and of those bears—the bushes, the stunted windswept spruce—were exactly as they'd observed last night.

Slowly, hand-in-hand—Yaot'l's heart in her throat—they approached the spot among the rocks where the shelter had been.

317

At first, all they could see were the needle-dropping branches, but then they spied their friend. He was curled up like a puppy, his thin body partially wrapped in a deer skin, the one object remaining. One bare muddy foot stuck out.

Yaot'l dropped to her knees beside him.

"Kele!" Yaot'l whispered his name and then laid a hand on his shoulder. "Wake up now. Oh, wake up, please."

She felt a rush of joy that almost burst her chest when he rolled over and looked up at them with his big bright eyes. He was very pale under his film of mud, thinner than ever it seemed, but alive. Yaot'l had never ever expected to see him so again.

Sascho, who had come to kneel beside her, looked as if he might burst into tears.

"Yaot'l ! Sascho!"

Slowly, with their help, Kele sat up, and then, all three were together again, as they had been so many times before. Yaot'l took his hands in hers and chafed them, but they were warm as could be. Somehow, she'd expected him to be cold.

Cold the way Tanis had been...

"Where am I?"

"We're close to Wha't'i." Sascho wanted to say something comforting. He did not know how much to say to someone who looked so pale, someone whose sister had died, someone who had, it seemed, returned from the spirit world.

"Did the flood carry you away too?"

"Yes," Yaot'l said and then nothing more would come. "You remember the flood?"

"Yes—and—and—" Kele shook his head, as if to clear it. "There was an old man and his wife. When I woke up, they were singing a song and holding hands above me inside a shelter. She gave me bitter medicine and said it would heal me." Kele's face went a shade paler. "She said that my sister was dead and that I must be brave, that I must continue my journey. I told her that if my sister was truly dead, I did not want her healing, that I wanted to go back to sleep and never wake up, but the old man said I must not, that I had much yet to do." He paused and looked up at them, his dark eyes full of tears and wonder.

"Tanis is dead, isn't she?"

"Yes, Kele. The old man helped us find her and bury her."

Kele began to weep. He rocked back and forth and shoved his knuckles into his eyes, attempting to stop the tears. Yaot'l, and Sascho too, did their best to comfort him, but he only cried more and said, "My family will not want to see me again. I have lost her and I have done everything wrong."

"If it is anyone's fault that she is dead, it is mine." Sascho's expression turned grim. "But we are happy you are still alive and here with us."

When he'd quieted, Kele said another troubling thing: "Where are those old people?"

Now, as if seeing for the first time, his head swiveled this way and that. "Are they not here?"

"They—they—were gone when we awoke. We do not know where." Yaot'l did not know what else to say. At the same time, she suddenly had the feeling that someone was watching them.

As she looked around, the hair prickled at the back of her neck. Meanwhile, Kele stared forlornly at the branches of spruce among which he'd slept, then back toward the ashes of the campfire.

"Why have they left such a fine big cooking pot behind? Does that mean they are coming back?"

Neither Sascho nor Yaot'l had an answer. This morning there were too many mysteries.

Chapter Fourteen

The three of them sat beside the newly revived fire. Kele, though unsteady, had managed to walk there. Their awe of the place ebbed and flowed, but never entirely disappeared, even after Sascho discovered that the three-legged black pot was, somehow, still full of stew. It seemed that the old couple had intended to provide for them. Besides that, there were two well-tanned deer skins neatly rolled and laid behind a small stack of dry wood.

They squatted and ate. Yaot'l and Sascho hastily, all the time looking over their shoulders. They could not rid themselves of the notion that the bears might suddenly reappear.

When they had emptied the pot, Sascho took Kele upon his back while Yaot'l shouldered the three hides and they set out again, with little else than the remains of their tattered clothing. They all knew it would be hard to finish their journey with bare feet, even tough as theirs were.

"Should we take the pot?" Kele asked.

"No," Sascho replied. "That belongs to the Drybones."

"And to this place, too, I think," Yaot'l added.

As the old man had indicated, directly behind the trees they found a broad flat stone outcrop, the surface of which was heavily grooved in a single direction. Here, too, was another wonder, for upon that stood three pair of moose hide moccasins.

"Look! They fit perfectly!" Kele's face brightened as he put them on. "How kind those old people have been!"

Sascho and Yaot'l, once again, were struck dumb—they did not know how to reply or what to say to one another, although their thoughts were running wild. Instead, they simply stopped, sat down and put on the fine new shoes. To herself, Yaot'l thought that it was a good thing they had behaved in a way worthy of the elders' kindness...*Together, we have walked with spirits.*

Sascho sighted along the stone. As he looked out, he saw a shallow blue pool cupped into the horizon. Was that, after all this time, Marten Lake out there, waiting for them?

Just as he stood considering, he heard a happy bark and their dog came trotting out of the bushes. He greeted them with a few more yelps and bounces while they called to him.

"Good dog! Good dog!" They were all happy to see him. Yaot'l felt bad that she'd forgotten him in the rush of events, but then remembered how the dog had seemed to understand every word that the old man had spoken last night. The dog didn't look the worse for wear today, in fact, his gut was rather distended, as if he'd found many, many small rabbits. They scratched his head and thumped his sides while he made a waggling arc against their legs, his spotted tongue lolling, his wet eyes shining with the pleasure of seeing them again.

* * *

After a time of trudging through the brush, Kele asked to walk. He slowed their passage somewhat as he was not too steady on his feet, but, Sascho, whose will was at its limit, had wearied of carrying him. They found Kele a stick to lean upon, and kept on as well as they could. Kele followed, on his feet now, but clearly as weak Tanis had ever been. Up ahead, Sascho scanned every rock and clump of brush for trail sign.

The strange exhilaration at the beginning of the day when they'd set out, bellies filled with good stew, began to die as the day passed. Every ache and pain drummed inside their bodies.

We are walking ghosts, Yaot'l thought, covered only with mud and rags.

After skirting around over a rocky rise, they made a stop, for there, wonderfully, was a clear spring, squirting right out of the rock. They

323

drank their fill, but nevertheless, they were all feeling tired again. They'd found a few berries here and there along their way, but of a kind they knew they should not eat too many of.

"I believe we are close to the lakes, and to the river, Nàɨlɨɨ, at last."

Sascho dashed forward and then let out a whoop. The pool here had no outlet, but a swamp had formed on the low side, and there was a circle of willow stumps—the cutting clearly done by other travelers. From these, bright new growth gently waved. There were also three small poplars. One of them had a right angle crook in its trunk, a thing that did not happen naturally.

I was here with Uncle John!

Sascho wanted to leap and spin, for his goal was now in sight. Yaot'l, who'd been watching, left Kele where he knelt still splashing his face, and went to join her best friend.

"Look! I've been here, at this very spot, just last year. We are not far from the lake now! It's just two or three days—look! There's the marker."

Looking around, able at last to see something beyond her own feet and his face, Yaot'l spotted the bent poplar. She managed a smile.

"Two days is a long time. I am not hungry at all, but poor Kele is very weak."

"I know what you mean. I'm covered with bruises. Just about everything hurts." Sascho stretched his arms over his head. He felt as stiff as an old man.

"Let's stay by that June berry tree back where the water comes out. We can rest. Then, before the sun goes down, we can travel on a little more."

"I don't know if I can get up again if I go to sleep." Kele slowly lowered himself onto the ground.

"Just rest now," said Yaot'l. "Don't worry about later."

When the boy looked up, eyes full of doubt, Sascho said, "I was here with my Uncle. We'll find Tłįchǫ soon—maybe even tomorrow."

* * *

Barking broke their sleep. Consciousness intruded into their minds like a blunt knife.

"It is past time to make a fire." It was a man's deep voice.

Sascho and Yaot'l sat up as one. Long low rays of sun sent a tongue of light into their bower. Nearby the dog barked and danced, somewhere between fear and acceptance. A spare man squatted nearby, his muscular hands resting upon his knees. On his head was a hat with a short white feather tucked into the headband. On the ground beside him was a bulging leather hunting pack. Before Yaot'l, mind full of sleep, could grasp who, exactly, this was, Sascho leapt to his feet.

"Uncle John! I—I thought you'd be gone after caribou."

"Can't hunt for caribou while I still have family to find." John stood easily. "And here, I have found you and Yaot'l and a young friend—as well as a good dog." He extended his fingers toward the dog and said a few comforting words

Sascho wanted to fling himself into his Uncle's arms, but that would not be manly. He put out his hand, as the kwet'ı̨ı̀ did. John smiled slightly, but took his nephew's hand between both of his.

"How did you know we'd be here?"

John shrugged. "An Indian agent came up to our ɫk'àdèè k'è some weeks back. He asked about you, Yaot'l, and about a brother and sister from Behchok'o. He said you had all run away from their school."

Kele, last to get to his feet, declared stoutly, "I won't ever go back there."

"You must be Kele." John studied the slight boy before him. "You know the government will punish your family if they keep you away. You must speak to your family about what to do."

"I don't care what anyone does to them. I will never go back."

John nodded. It was clear that although he disapproved of the boy's disregard for his family, he also had a fair idea of the desperation that prompted the speech.

"Where is your sister, Kele Stonypoint?"

Kele took the question like a body blow. He staggered, wrapped thin arms around his gut, hung his head. Sascho found the words his friend could not say.

"I camped in a bad place, Uncle. There was rain somewhere. A flood came through our camp and took Tanis." Sascho, filled with grief and guilt, bowed his head. "Mr. Drybones found us and helped us. He led us to where Tanis lay, so we could bury her in the right way."

Yaot'l, remembering slim fingers emerging from the mud, felt a choking grief. Understanding that Sascho could say no more, she said, "Mr. Drybones and his wife fed us and we slept in their camp. They saved Kele."

John's gaze deepened, as he considered the two young people before him. If he had more to say about what had happened, he would not do it now.

"I am glad I found you. Before my friends and I parted this morning, we divided our meat. But before you eat again, Kele Stonypoint, we must build a sweat lodge. I saw an outcrop of Lava Rocks just a little ways back. I think it is a sign that we should do a cleansing ceremony before we travel onward. Yaot'l, if you will do us the honor of preparing the fire."

"Of course, goʔeh. I will gather the wood."

Traditionally the cleansing ceremony was separate for men and women but, there being no others, Yaot'l readily accepted the honor of fire tender.

"I dreamed I'd need to do a ceremony when I found you. We will return to the rocks I saw, find a clear spot and get started. We only need it large enough for three. Three men, three rocks, it is good."

The two boys and Yaot'l followed John as he led them downhill where one small creek made a tinkling joining with another. Just as he'd said, an outcrop of fine-grained lava rock, well fractured, showed along the eroded face abutting the path.

"Here will do well." He stopped in front of a level clearing where a ditch like crevice ran along the ground. "If Yaot'l starts the fire here, Sascho and Kele can dig a small fire pit for the center of our lodge." He walked a few feet away to show them where he wanted the pit. "We'll build the lodge around this spot."

Everyone started their assigned chores. John picked and placed the lava rocks and then, from the creek, refilled the water satchel that he carried with him whenever he traveled.

* * *

"You have done well," he said, when he surveyed the area where the boys had dug out the hole for the fire pit and smoothed the ground.

"Sascho you can get willows for the ribs, strip them down with your knife, and we'll bend them to form the frame. Kele, gather enough leafy bushes to cover the frame and make it tight."

"Shall I start the fire?" Yaot'l asked.

"Yes. The rocks must be glowing hot when we start."

The boys brought the ribs and bushes. John, who had stripped three long slabs from a nearby stand of birch and fastened them into a single panel to cover the entrance, set to work forming the ribs and intertwining the bushes until a tightly covered womblike structure enveloped the pit in the ground and stood ready.

"We will be crowded inside," John said, "but that is good. It is tight inside the womb."

He laid the birch panel against the opening to the structure and turned to Yaot'l. "I will ask you to bring the rocks to me once we are inside. We must remove our clothing to enter grandmother's womb, so you will need to close your eyes."

Yaot'l nodded, and turned back to the fire.

The three removed their clothes and entered the lodge.

"We are ready," John spoke to Yaot'l through the doorway.

Yaot'l picked up the y-shaped stick John had made so that she could safely lift the rocks out of the fire. One by one she brought the rocks, handed the stick through the doorway to John, who took each one, placed it in the fire pit and returned the stick to Yaot'l, repeating the procedure until all of the rocks had been placed in the fire pit.

John then pulled the birch panel across the entrance and closed the sweat. Yaot'l seated herself in front of the opening to await his call to re-open the lodge.

Inside, John began a traditional opening song. His song invited gocho and the nature spirits, the fire spirits and water spirits to join them.

After the song, John poured the first round of water onto the rocks and steam quickly filled the sweat lodge.

John then began a prayer for the women spirits, for Tanis and for Yaot'l and all the female spirits, those just coming to mother earth and those leaving mother earth. When he finished the prayer, he reached for the water satchel and added another round of water.

"This round is for the male spirits," John said. "We will reach inside ourselves with this prayer and bring out any anger and pain we feel. It is time to release all of our rage and despair and allow ourselves to be cleansed."

Kele felt the sweat pouring out of him. In the darkness, his flesh in contact with the men on either side, he remembered what had been done to him. Stew, from the Drybones' never empty black pot, threatened to bubble up and pour from his mouth. He felt as if he would burst.

Silence, broken only by the hissing of steam against the rocks, filled the sweat lodge. John began a rhythmic chant, first slow and then faster and faster. Sascho joined his voice with his uncle and soon Kele began to howl in bursts of anger and grief. John increased the tempo of the chant, faster and faster, and Kele's shrieks of pain shook the leaves of the sweat lodge, until finally, exhausted by what he'd released, he collapsed against Sascho, who held his sobbing little brother in his arms.

"This is good Kele Stonypoint," John said, "for you to let go all of your anger and rage so it will not burden you on your pathway. I will add more water now, to cleanse this pain."

John picked up his satchel and poured more water onto the rocks. Steam filled the space causing them to breathe only in the shortest gasps. John then lifted his voice to the spirits, asking that their little sister Tanis, whose spirit had so recently departed, would be guided by the gocho to join her family in the spirit world.

When he had finished the song, John picked up his satchel. "It is time for our final round," he said, pouring the last of his water onto the rocks.

"This is our warrior round," John signalled the ending of the sweat lodge by raising his voice in the howls and yells of a warrior striding into battle. Sascho and Kele joined him, their voices intensified by the lung-searing heat of the steam rising from the red hot rocks in the pit. Finally, with a long releasing howl, John called out:

"All My Relations, Open the Door."

Yaot'l, summoned by the traditional cry to re-open the sweat lodge, removed the birch panel, and shielding her eyes, opened the doorway for the men to leave grandmother's womb.

* * *

The sun had gone. Two weary young people, a dog, and a man sat facing a small, bright fire. The dog chewed contentedly on a bone held between his paws. Nearby, Kele slept, his slight body curled upon a bed of leaves and spruce branches. The camp of his Grandparents, Uncle John said, was but a few days away beside the Little Marten which lay on their way to Wha't'i. This would easily cut two days from their journey. Very soon, he would be with them.

The rich smell of meat still hung in the air. Preparing the food and eating had been the next order of business; they'd hardly spoken until that was done. Over their heads familiar stars burned in blue black sky.

Yaot'l had wanted to ask a question since they'd sat down, but did not think it her place. Happily, Sascho also had the same question in mind.

"Do you know Mr. Drybones, Goʔeh? He—he said he knew you."

His uncle nodded. "We know one another. I do not know him as well as I could wish, certainly, but there are times when we travel together along the same roads."

"Um—here, by Marten Lake?"

"Here, yes. Sometimes in other places."

Yaot'l and Sascho shared a look. His uncle said no more, but they both still burned with curiosity, wondering what he knew about the mysterious Mr. Drybones and his even more mysterious wife. And were these 'other places' of which he spoke a part of the dreamtime?

John Lynx reached into his pocket and drew out his smoking things, a pipe and a small bag. After he'd lit it, he drew upon the mixture gently.

"You stayed in the Drybones camp overnight?"

His gaze fixed on Yaot'l.

"Yes, Goʔeh Lynx. He found us and his wife fed us from a big black pot."

"I too have eaten from that pot," John replied. "The food that comes from it lasts a very long time."

Yaot'l could only nod. Not knowing exactly what was proper, she continued on. "They had found Kele and were already caring for him when we arrived. Until then we—we thought that he too was dead."

"Kele was asleep in their shelter." Sascho found his voice again. "I—I wanted to speak with him, but Mr. Drybones said I must not—not until morning."

"And in the morning?"

Yaot'l and Sascho gazed at one another, wondering how much they should say—after all, encounters with the ts'ı̨ta were secret, powerful.

"They were both gone," Sascho said.

333

"Yes." Yaot'l nodded. "Two bears were there." She remembered how still she'd lain, how neither of them had moved a muscle, had hardly dared to breathe. She remembered how she'd been afraid—*and,* at once *not afraid.*

"Two bears." The fragrance of John's special blend of bearberries, chokecherries, alder and red osier, filled their nostrils. "And here you are alive and well."

He considered them for a time and then asked, "Did they speak?"

Yaot'l was surprised when Sascho said, "I dreamed of a bear, Uncle John, when I was in their camp. He was old, but he spoke to me. I—I was not afraid because I too was a bear."

"That is good, nephew. We'll speak more of this when our journey is done. There will be plenty of traveling through the winter, I think, in the north."

Yaot'l remembered her own dream. She looked down, feeling the tears, which now came so easily, start into her eyes. Sascho had found his uncle and now he would travel north with him—*but what is to happen to me?*

Her heart began to ache at the thought of losing him, but Sascho's hand enclosed hers.

"I want to go with you, Goʔeh, but I cannot leave Yaot'l behind."

"Neither of you can return to Gam`e`t`i." John said. "The agent will not forget your escape and even now one of those men is in Wha't'i for the children. Yaot'l will travel on with us. We will take her to the winter camp, far

334

beyond Rabesca Lake. Her family will be pleased that my nephew returns to his family and is ready to work for the bride price."

Sascho tucked her hand against his side to be less visible, but he didn't let it go. Yaot'l's heart veered from sorrow to delight at his warm touch.

"Yaot'l, I must tell you that your father died last year, soon after you disappeared. He is buried in Behchok'o."

"My mother and little brother?" The loss of Yaot'l's father was saddening, although she had suspected as much. Tears tugged into her eyes. She had resigned herself during the winter to the idea that her father Rene was dead.

It was yet another loss in a world she thought had been completely rent by the loss of Tanis. That she still had tears amazed her. Rene had been a good provider for all his family. He had not gotten drunk or beaten her mother. He'd worked hard, either at the mine, or out trapping, for much of every year. It was, however, as if she'd just heard of the death of a much looked up to but only occasional visitor. Even so, right this minute, the loss cut to the heart.

"Your brother Charlie is with them now. He is a good son."

"Oh, Charlie! That is good news! I have worried. Before I was taken, we hadn't heard from him in such a long time."

"Everyone is happy that your brother returned."

"And look, Goʔeh Lynx! Thanks to Sylvain Zoe, I still have Charlie's knife." She removed it from the waist pouch that had miraculously stayed with her through everything, culminating in the flood. The bone handle, like everything else, was darkened by mud, but the flying goose was there. The knife now had a long story behind it—about how it had been lost but had come back to her, how it had cut vines, roots, and meat and how it had fleshed hides in the wilderness.

John smiled at the sight of Charlie's handiwork. "That knife could tell us many things—but I think you will tell me more. In winter, there will be time for all our stories. Your brother is a good provider, as was his father, and generous, too. Snow geese clan ate well last winter."

Yaot'l wondered if her mother would marry again, if anyone would ask for her. She was still handsome and skilled, although she was no longer a young woman.

Well, the geese mate for life. Maybe mother feels that way too.

Beside her sat Sascho, attentive to his uncle. As Yaot'l studied his handsome profile, she saw the future she wanted.

* * *

At Little Marten Lake, as John had said, they found the camp of Kele's grandparents as well as a number of other kin. His family took

336

him in and shed tears of joy to have him with them at last. They approved of the burial which Sascho was able to report. They heartily grieved for Tanis, but reassured Kele that his sister lay within the Tłı̨chǫ dèè, so her spirit was at home. When, a few days later, John, Sascho and Yaot'l departed, there were no tears. With those wise people to guide Kele's path, they felt he would be able to find his way to wellbeing again.

* * *

Later, Yaot'l would think of this as the year she and her gòıchı started their life's journey. Paddling sometimes, borrowing canoes, and in company with John, they followed the shining water trail— Nàı̨lı̨ı̨, east, Marian River, north. The leaves of ever smaller and ever more isolated groves of aspen turned gold and then fell. Next, the trees turned to shrubs or simply disappeared. Nights were frigid; the aurora of their gocho shimmered between them and the stars.

East of Gam`e`t`i, they encountered the camp of Yaot'l's mother, of Charlie and others of their family band. Already many had gone further north and east, toward Black Lichen and Rabesca Lake, to trap. Those who were still at camp rejoiced to have these two fine young people restored to them.

When everyone heard the story of their escape and of their travels, it was quickly agreed that it would be best for them to marry at once. They had already journeyed together and shared life's burdens—what unknowns could be left? Both Lynx and Snowgoose families understood the worth of their young people, and knew that such a union would strengthen them both. The women folk, it was decided, would accompany their men deeper into the bush than usual and ready themselves for the winter, somewhere far beyond the ken of kw'ahtıı or ekw'ahtı.

* * *

It was smoky inside the shelter. The huddled forms of sleepers occasionally snuffled, coughed or shifted. This far north, in the dead of winter, it stayed dark much of the time and people slept or woke as it pleased them or as a need arose. John, Charlie and Sascho had returned in the dark, near frozen, from a long circuit of the nearby lakes, carrying skins of marten and fox and the fresh meat, too.

Outside wind sent the dry snow skittering and snaking across a frozen world. Yaot'l had gone outside to the cache to get food for the dogs; each one hunkered down in his own bunker of white. They were happy to see her and roused themselves, shaking off the snow as they each bolted their share of dried fish.

Before returning to the shelter, Yaot'l turned and watched that final shard of sun, her eyes tearing as the long red-gold arms retracted and disappeared beneath a blue glazed horizon. Flying ice stung her high cheeks and froze into her lashes before she finally withdrew her gaze.

When she re-entered, quickly through the canvas flap, she saw that Sascho and John were awake. John leaned on one arm as Sascho turned up the kerosene flame on the camp stove to make tea. Yaot'l removed her fur boots and scuffed on the hide slippers she'd left alongside others at the door.

"Are the dogs all right?"

"Yes. Hungry."

"A lot of work for them, the last few weeks," John said.

Sascho tilted a packet of loose leaves into a tin pot. The scent of mingled sassafras and china tea graced the air.

Later, when everyone else was awake, cups of hot liquid warmed every hand. Yaot'l's mother, Little Brother, John Lynx, Charlie and his wife, Nina, as well as Aunt Dedìi and Uncle Dzemi Lynx shared the shelter. It was crowded, but it was winter, after all.

Uncle John and the others had seen something strange while checking the traps. He'd been pondering this new development for a time and now began to speak of it.

"I have seen a new kwet'ıì machine that runs on gasoline and slides across the snow. It will be another thing of theirs which will change the way we live. Soon, many of these machines will travel everywhere in winter, great distances, and that will lessen the knowledge of our hunters as they speed across the dèè and do not take the time to notice what's around them. Men will be tempted to hunt more than they can eat.

The machines will scare the animals and leave oil on the ground and in the water—worse than any putt-putt."

"Still, to make winter easier, that machine could be a good thing for us, too. If we want to feed our families, we have to find the animals before kwet'ı̨ı̨ does." Charlie, a young man with a new wife, shared his optimistic thoughts on this new development. He too had been pondering long and hard ever since they'd come upon this strange machine, blundering its way through the wilderness.

"You worry too much, John," said Uncle Dzemi. "Gasoline stores are far away and fuel is heavy. I think it will take a long time before such a machine is used by many."

"Well, I shall watch and see what happens among our people. Changes come fast these days. I have spoken as I think," John said, "though I ever hope all will be well."

Everyone sat silently, turning thoughts of the new snow machine over in their minds.

After a time, Sascho got up, put on his mittens and went out. He could feel the heavens calling to him.

A little later, a few last scraps of their meal in hand, Yaot'l followed.

She paused to draw the strings of her fur hood tighter while she emerged through the opening. Above her was the long dark of winter and a sky filled with glory, so she knew her husband had gone out to be a part of it.

Against the hard shine of so many stars, she saw his silhouette illuminated by the glow of a pale yellow-green aurora. It was soft and see-through, tonight lapping gently, like water upon a sandy beach.

At first he continued to look up, but the nearest dog, their mild Dìga, smelled the scraps and let out a little yip, calling to her. When he did, Sascho turned.

Yaot'l tossed the scraps to the dog before she joined her husband. It was something all young couples did during their first winters together, seek ways to be—if only briefly—alone. When they were close, they drew together, hooded face to face, only ice crystal breath moving in and out between them.

"Are you worried by these new snow machines?"

"Yes," Yaot'l whispered. "Everything keeps changing and we can't stop it."

"Perhaps we can learn a right way to use the snow machines, a way where we can also take good care of the dèè. The dèè is our home, our dwelling, so it's important for us to always respect it and respect the animals who give their lives to feed and clothe us. "

She looked sad and doubtful, so, very gently, he kissed her. Before the school, she had never been afraid, but now she often was, though she did her best to hide this and go on as bravely as before.

When the kiss was done, she gazed seriously into his eyes. "But whatever happens, good or ill, from now on, Sascho, wherever we walk will be our home. We will be together while we travel from one end to the other of the dèè, the home that Nǫhtsı̨ has created for us."

"And for that reason," Sascho replied, "We shall always be happy."

End

Novels by Juliet Waldron from BWL Publishing

Alexander Hamilton and Elizabeth Schuyler
Hamilton
A Master Passion

The American Revolution Series
Genesee
Angel's Flight

The Mozart Series
Nightingale
My Mozart
Mozart's Wife

The Magic Series (historical fantasy/adventure)
Red Magic
Black Magic

Pennsylvania Romance
Hand-me-Down Bride
Butterfly Bride

2016 Bestselling Author
Juliet Waldron

"Not all who wander are lost." Juliet Waldron earned a B. A. in English Literature, but has worked at jobs ranging from artist's model and scrub tech to brokerage. Thirty years ago, after the boys left home, she dropped out of 9-5 and began to write, hoping to create a genuine time travel experience for herself as well as for her readers. She loves her grandkids, kitties, and long hikes, bicycles and gardens. She reads mostly non-fiction history and archeology. For over a decade, she's reviewed for The Historical Novel Society as well as presenting writers' workshops at two HNS conventions. When she was eleven, her mother took her to Nevis to see the island where her hero, Alexander Hamilton was born. Now, on 21st Century summer mini-adventures, she rides behind her husband of 50+ years on his "Bucket List" (black, and ridiculously fast) Hayabusa motorcycle

I was taken from my mother at birth and adopted by a white family. I didn't find out until I was in my teens that I was from the north country of British Columbia, descended from the Sekani Nation (which means "mountain people") The Sekani are medicine healers, My Indian name Sus'naqua ootsin' (the Wisdomkeeper) was given to me by a very old lady who looked deep into my eyes and saw into my soul. My journey started on one of the Darkest Days of my life – when I finally decided to put on my red running shoes and follow the magic road.

All My Relations………

Sus' naqua ootsin'

Books by John Wisdomkeeper from BWL Publishing

Gifts from the Grandmothers
The Wisdomkeeper Collection
A Metis Traveler on the Red Road

bookswelove.com

Bibliography

Helm, June. The People of Denendeh, University of Iowa Press, Iowa City, Iowa, 2001

Jarvenpa, Robert. Northern Passage, Waveland Press, State University of New York at Albany, New York, 1998

Legat, Allice. Walking the Land, Feeding the Fire, First People's, New Directions in Indigenous Studies, The University of Arizona Press, Tucson, Arizona, 2012

Tlicho Tribal Links
http://www.tlicho.ca/
https://tlichohistory.ca/maps
https://tlichohistory.com/timeline

The Canadian Encyclopedia
http://www.thecanadianencyclopedia.ca/en/article/tlicho-dogrib/

Bushcraft, material culture

https://vimeo.com/87140307   Birchbark canoes

https://www.goodreads.com/book/show/11
838015-don-t-shoot-from-the-saddle
https://www.goodreads.com/book/show/36
356313-john-wisdomkeeper-s-collection
https://www.goodreads.com/book/show/29
215693-a-knock-on-the-door
Bushcraft,   food
http://northernbushcraft.com/guide.php?ctgy=ed
ible_berries&region=nt

Culture

Testimony of Canadian Residential School
Survivors
https://www.goodreads.com/book/show/16
057250-they-called-me-number-one
https://www.goodreads.com/book/show/94
62473-broken-circleColonization
http://www.explorenorth.com/library/minin
g/nwt-contaminated_sites.html
https://www.youtube.com/watch?v=pohp-
gYL1I0
http://tlichohistory.ca/en/category/stories-
legends
https://www.littlethings.com/native-
american-trees/
1st Nation leader's 1975 speech on pipeline
project which exemplifies
Tlicho wisdom, leadership, diplomacy, and
dignity.
NWT stories:

https://www.nytimes.com/2017/02/07/travel/great-bear-lake-arctic-unesco-biosphere-canada.html

https://tlichohistory.ca/en/stories/lion-people-gave-her-power-heal

http://www.tlicho.ca/sites/default/files/A_Dogrib_Dictionary.pdf